Praise for *Gil*

"*Gilead* is a book that deserves to be and repeatedly. . . . I would like to see copies of it dropped onto pews across our country, where it could sit among the Bibles and hymnals and collection envelopes. It would be a good reminder of what it means to lead a noble and moral life—and, for that matter, what it means to write a truly great novel."

—Ann Patchett, *The Village Voice*

"Good novels about spiritual life are rare. This is one of the best."

—*Newsweek*

"A beautiful work of fiction. . . . A gift."

—*Edmonton Journal*

"Readers with no interest in religion will find pleasure in this hymn to existence. . . . It's a story that captures the splendors and pitfalls of being alive, viewed through the prism of how soon it all ends."

—*The Atlanta Journal-Constitution*

"Quietly powerful [and] moving articles of faith."

—*O* magazine

"*Gilead* . . . should be lingered over and savoured for the precision of its breathtaking prose, the delights of its images and the quiet insistent demands it makes on our conscience."

—*Ottawa Citizen*

"A novel as big as a nation, as quiet as thought, and as moving as prayer. Matchless and towering."

—*Kirkus Reviews* (starred review)

"American culture is enriched by having the whole range of Marilynne Robinson's work."

—*The Boston Globe*

"When I first picked up this book and read a few pages, I [was] overwhelmed by the sheer beauty of the language and the directness with which it spoke to my heart. . . . John Ames says, 'For me writing has always felt like praying,' and we are privileged to overhear this, his prayer."

—*The Roanoke Times*

"This is a morally and emotionally complex novel . . . where every word matters. . . . A classic that should be read, savored, and read again."

—*The Courier-Journal* (Louisville)

"In the sheer beauty of its prose and the fierceness of its passion, *Gilead* is a work of startling power: a seemingly simple artifice that reveals more complex and finer structures the closer we approach it. It is a subtle, gorgeously wrought, and immensely moving novel."

—*The Weekly Standard*

"[*Gilead*] glows with brilliance."

—*The Philadelphia Inquirer*

"At times, in the middle of one quiet passage or another, the reader may sense that the [narrator] has reached out and placed his hand on our head and blessed us with the gift of his humble, noble life."

—*The Miami Herald*

"[*Gilead*] is that rarest of books. The disarmingly simple prose in this novel is filled with profound wisdom."
—*The Wichita Eagle*

"At a time when so many politicians aggressively flaunt religiosity in strategic sound bites, it is refreshing to read an honest account of moral and spiritual quandaries. . . . *Gilead* is remarkable for its sensual evocation of place and keen appreciation for history as well as for its candid, often gripping, examination of conscience."
—*The Women's Review of Books*

"Exceptional in every way . . . *Gilead* is a far more explosive and transgressive work than any other book American culture has had to deal with in years. . . . Whatever level it assays, *Gilead* masters."
—*National Catholic Reporter*

"A quietly breathtaking novel . . . a graceful book, one you will want to keep on your shelf and come back to again and again."
—*The Winston-Salem Journal*

"The wait, gentle readers, was well worth it. . . . One doesn't so much read this novel as take it to heart, live in its little universe, feel blessed by it."
—*The Times-Picayune* (New Orleans)

"Remarkable for its masterly control. . . . Achieves moments of near-Melvillean grandeur and dazzling lucidity."
—*Commentary*

"*Gilead* is gripping. . . . You will hang on every word."
—*Slate*

ALSO BY MARILYNNE ROBINSON

FICTION

Housekeeping

NONFICTION

Mother Country: Britain, the Welfare State and Nuclear Pollution

The Death of Adam: Essays on Modern Thought

George Duncan

Marilynne Robinson is the author of the modern classic *Housekeeping*—winner of the PEN/Hemingway Award—and two books of nonfiction, *Mother Country* and *The Death of Adam*. She teaches at the University of Iowa Writers' Workshop.

Marilynne Robinson

GILEAD

HARPER **PERENNIAL**

My thanks to Ellen Levine,
and to Katharine Stall and Earle McCartney.
—M.R.

Gilead
Copyright © 2004 by Marilynne Robinson.
All rights reserved.

Published by Harper Perennial, an imprint of HarperCollins Publishers Ltd

First published in Canada by HarperCollins Publishers Ltd
in a hardcover edition: 2004
First Harper Perennial trade paperback edition: 2005
This trade paperback edition: 2021

HarperCollins books may be purchased for educational, business,
or sales promotional use through our Special Markets Department.

HarperCollins Publishers Ltd
Bay Adelaide Centre, East Tower
22 Adelaide Street West, 41st Floor
Toronto, Ontario, Canada
M5H 4E3

www.harpercollins.ca

Library and Archives Canada Cataloguing in Publication
information is available upon request

ISBN 978-1-4434-6597-7

Printed and bound in the United States of America
LSC/H 9 8 7 6 5 4 3 2 1

For John and Ellen Summers,
my dear father and mother

I TOLD YOU LAST NIGHT THAT I MIGHT BE GONE sometime, and you said, Where, and I said, To be with the Good Lord, and you said, Why, and I said, Because I'm old, and you said, I don't think you're old. And you put your hand in my hand and you said, You aren't very old, as if that settled it. I told you you might have a very different life from mine, and from the life you've had with me, and that would be a wonderful thing, there are many ways to live a good life. And you said, Mama already told me that. And then you said, Don't laugh! because you thought I was laughing at you. You reached up and put your fingers on my lips and gave me that look I never in my life saw on any other face besides your mother's. It's a kind of furious pride, very passionate and stern. I'm always a little surprised to find my eyebrows unsinged after I've suffered one of those looks. I will miss them.

It seems ridiculous to suppose the dead miss anything. If you're a grown man when you read this—it is my intention for this letter that you will read it then—I'll have been gone a long time. I'll know most of what there is to know about being dead, but I'll probably keep it to myself. That seems to be the way of things.

I don't know how many times people have asked me what death is like, sometimes when they were only an hour or two from finding out for themselves. Even when I was a very young man, people as old as I am now would ask me, hold on to my hands and look into my eyes with their old milky eyes, as if they knew I knew and they were going to *make* me tell them. I used to say it was like going home. We have no home in this world, I used to say, and then I'd walk back up the road to this old place and make myself a pot of coffee and a fried-egg sandwich and listen to the radio, when I got one, in the dark as often as not. Do you remember this house? I think you must, a little. I grew up in parsonages. I've lived in this one most of my life, and I've visited in a good many others, because my father's friends and most of our relatives also lived in parsonages. And when I thought about it in those days, which wasn't too often, I thought this was the worst of them all, the draftiest and the dreariest. Well, that was my state of mind at the time. It's a perfectly good old house, but I was all alone in it then. And that made it seem strange to me. I didn't feel very much at home in the world, that was a fact. Now I do.

And now they say my heart is failing. The doctor used the term "angina pectoris," which has a theological sound, like misericordia. Well, you expect these things at my age. My father died an old man, but his sisters didn't live very long, really. So I can only be grateful. I do regret that I have almost nothing to leave you and your mother. A few old books no one else would want. I never made any money to speak of, and I never paid any attention to the money I had. It was the furthest thing from my mind that I'd be leaving a wife and child, believe me. I'd have been a better father if I'd known. I'd have set something by for you.

That is the main thing I want to tell you, that I regret very deeply the hard times I know you and your mother must have gone through, with no real help from me at all, except my prayers, and I pray all the time. I did while I lived, and I do now, too, if that is how things are in the next life.

I can hear you talking with your mother, you asking, she answering. It's not the words I hear, just the sounds of your voices. You don't like to go to sleep, and every night she has to sort of talk you into it all over again. I never hear her sing except at night, from the next room, when she's coaxing you to sleep. And then I can't make out what song it is she's singing. Her voice is very low. It sounds beautiful to me, but she laughs when I say that.

I really can't tell what's beautiful anymore. I passed two young fellows on the street the other day. I know who they are, they work at the garage. They're not churchgoing, either one of them, just decent rascally young fellows who have to be joking all the time, and there they were, propped against the garage wall in the sunshine, lighting up their cigarettes. They're always so black with grease and so strong with gasoline I don't know why they don't catch fire themselves. They were passing remarks back and forth the way they do and laughing that wicked way they have. And it seemed beautiful to me. It is an amazing thing to watch people laugh, the way it sort of takes them over. Sometimes they really do struggle with it. I see that in church often enough. So I wonder what it is and where it comes from, and I wonder what it expends out of your system, so that you have to do it till you're done, like crying in a way, I suppose, except that laughter is much more easily spent.

When they saw me coming, of course the joking stopped, but I could see they were still laughing to themselves, thinking what the old preacher almost heard them say.

I felt like telling them, I appreciate a joke as much as anybody. There have been many occasions in my life when I have wanted to say that. But it's not a thing people are willing to accept. They want you to be a little bit apart. I felt like saying, I'm a dying man, and I won't have so many more occasions to laugh, in this world at least. But that would just make them serious and polite, I suppose. I'm keeping my condition a secret as long as I can. For a dying man I feel pretty good, and that is a blessing. Of course your mother knows about it. She said if I feel good, maybe the doctor is wrong. But at my age there's a limit to how wrong he can be.

That's the strangest thing about this life, about being in the ministry. People change the subject when they see you coming. And then sometimes those very same people come into your study and tell you the most remarkable things. There's a lot under the surface of life, everyone knows that. A lot of malice and dread and guilt, and so much loneliness, where you wouldn't really expect to find it, either.

My mother's father was a preacher, and my father's father was, too, and his father before him, and before that, nobody knows, but I wouldn't hesitate to guess. That life was second nature to them, just as it is to me. They were fine people, but if there was one thing I should have learned from them and did not learn, it was to control my temper. This is wisdom I should have attained a long time ago. Even now, when a flutter of my pulse makes me think of final things, I find myself losing my temper, because a drawer sticks or because I've misplaced my glasses. I tell you so that you can watch for this in yourself.

A little too much anger, too often or at the wrong time, can destroy more than you would ever imagine. Above all, mind what you say. "Behold how much wood is kindled by how small a fire, and the tongue is a fire"—that's the truth. When my father was old he told me that very thing in a letter he sent me. Which, as it happens, I burned. I dropped it right in the stove. This surprised me a good deal more at the time than it docs in retrospect.

I believe I'll make an experiment with candor here. Now, I say this with all respect. My father was a man who acted from principle, as he said himself. He acted from faithfulness to the truth as he saw it. But something in the way he went about it made him disappointing from time to time, and not just to me. I say this despite all the attention he gave to me bringing me up, for which I am profoundly in his debt, though he himself might dispute that. God rest his soul, I know for a fact I disappointed him. It is a remarkable thing to consider. We meant well by each other, too.

Well, see and see but do not perceive, hear and hear but do not understand, as the Lord says. I can't claim to understand that saying, as many times as I've heard it, and even preached on it. It simply states a deeply mysterious fact. You can know a thing to death and be for all purposes completely ignorant of it. A man can know his father, or his son, and there might still be nothing between them but loyalty and love and mutual incomprehension.

My point in mentioning this is only to say that people who feel any sort of regret where you are concerned will suppose you are angry, and they will see anger in what you do, even if you're just quietly going about a life of your own choosing. They make you doubt yourself, which, depending on cases, can be a severe distraction and a waste of time. This is a thing I wish I had understood much earlier than I did. Just to reflect on it makes me a little irritated. Irritation is a form of anger, I recognize that.

One great benefit of a religious vocation is that it helps you concentrate. It gives you a good basic sense of what is being asked of you and also what you might as well ignore. If I have any wisdom to offer, this is a fair part of it.

You have blessed our house not quite seven years, and fairly lean years, too, so late in my life. There was no way for me to make any changes to provide for the two of you. Still, I think about it and I pray. It is very much in my mind. I want you to know that.

We're having a fine spring, and this is another fine day. You were almost late for school. We stood you on a chair and you ate toast and jam while your mother polished your shoes and I combed your hair. You had a page of sums to do that you should have done last night, and you took forever over them this morning, trying to get all the numbers facing the right way. You're like your mother, so serious about everything. The old men call you Deacon, but that seriousness isn't all from my side of the family. I'd never seen anything like it until I met her. Well, putting aside my grandfather. It seemed to me to be half sadness and half fury, and I wondered what in her life could have put that expression in her eyes. And then when you were about three, just a little fellow, I came into the nursery one morning and there you were down on the floor in the sunlight in your trapdoor pajamas, trying to figure a way to fix a broken crayon. And you looked up at me and it was just that look of hers. I've thought of that moment many times. I'll tell you, sometimes it has seemed to me that you were looking back through life, back through troubles I pray you'll never have, asking me to kindly explain myself.

"You're just like all them old men in the Bible," your mother tells me, and that would be true, if I could manage to live a hundred and twenty years, and maybe have a few cattle and oxen and menservants and maidservants. My father left me a trade, which happened also to be my vocation. But the fact is, it was all second nature to me, I grew up with it. Most likely you will not.

———————

I saw a bubble float past my window, fat and wobbly and ripening toward that dragonfly blue they turn just before they burst. So I looked down at the yard and there you were, you and your mother, blowing bubbles at the cat, such a barrage of them that the poor beast was beside herself at the glut of opportunity. She was actually leaping in the air, our insouciant Soapy! Some of the bubbles drifted up through the branches, even above the trees. You two were too intent on the cat to see the celestial consequences of your worldly endeavors. They were very lovely. Your mother is wearing her blue dress and you are wearing your red shirt and you were kneeling on the ground together with Soapy between and that effulgence of bubbles rising, and so much laughter. Ah, this life, this world.

Your mother told you I'm writing your begats, and you seemed very pleased with the idea. Well, then. What should I record for you? I, John Ames, was born in the Year of Our Lord 1880 in the state of Kansas, the son of John Ames and Martha Turner Ames, grandson of John Ames and Margaret Todd Ames. At this writing I have lived seventy-six years, seventy-four of them here in Gilead, Iowa, excepting study at the college and at seminary.

And what else should I tell you?

When I was twelve years old, my father took me to the grave of my grandfather. At that time my family had been living in Gilead for about ten years, my father serving the church here. His father, who was born in Maine and had come out to Kansas in the 1830s, lived with us for a number of years after his retirement. Then the old man ran off to become a sort of itinerant preacher, or so we believed. He died in Kansas and was buried there, near a town that had pretty well lost its people. A drought had driven most of them away, those who had not already left for towns closer to the railroad. Surely there was only a town in that place to begin with because it was Kansas, and the people who settled it were Free Soilers who weren't really thinking about the long term. I don't often use the expression "godforsaken," but when I think back to that place, that word does come to mind. It took my father months to find where the old man had ended up, lots of letters of inquiry to churches and newspapers and so on. He put a great deal of effort into it. Finally someone wrote back and sent a little package with his watch and a beat-up old Bible and some letters, which I learned later were just a few of my father's letters of inquiry, no doubt given to the old man by people who thought they had induced him to come home.

It grieved my father bitterly that the last words he said to his father were very angry words and there could never be any reconciliation between them in this life. He did truly honor his father, generally speaking, and it was hard for him to accept that things should have ended the way they did.

That was in 1892, so travel was still pretty hard. We went as far as we could by train, and then my father hired a wagon and team. That was more than we needed, but it was all we could find. We took some bad directions and got lost, and we had so much trouble keeping the horses watered that we boarded them at a farmstead and went the rest of the way on foot. The roads were terrible, anyway, swamped in dust where they were traveled and baked into ruts where they were not. My father was carrying some tools in a gunnysack so he could try to put the grave to rights a little, and I was carrying what we had for food, hardtack and jerky and the few little yellow apples we picked up along the road here and there, and our changes of shirts and socks, all by then filthy.

He didn't really have enough money to make the trip at

that time, but it was so much in his thoughts that he couldn't wait until he had saved up for it. I told him I had to go, too, and he respected that, though it did make many things harder. My mother had been reading about how bad the drought was west of us, and she was not at all happy when he said he planned to take me along. He told her it would be educational, and it surely was. My father was set on finding that grave despite any hardship. Never before in my life had I wondered where I would come by my next drink of water, and I number it among my blessings that I have not had occasion to wonder since. There were times when I truly believed we might just wander off and die. Once, when my father was gathering sticks for firewood into my arms, he said we were like Abraham and Isaac on the way to Mount Moriah. I'd thought as much myself.

It was so bad out there we couldn't buy food. We stopped at a farmstead and asked the lady, and she took a little bundle down from a cupboard and showed us some coins and bills and said, "It might as well be Confederate for all the good it does me." The general store had closed, and she couldn't get salt or sugar or flour. We traded her some of our miserable jerky—I've never been able to stand the sight of it since then—for two boiled eggs and two boiled potatoes, which tasted wonderful even without salt.

Then my father asked after his father and she said, Why, yes, he'd been in the neighborhood. She didn't know he had died, but she knew where he was likely to have been buried, and she showed us to what remained of a road that would take us right to the place, not three miles from where we stood. The road was overgrown, but as you walked along you could see the ruts. The brush grew lower in them, because the earth was still packed so hard. We walked past that graveyard twice. The two or three headstones in it had fallen over and it was all grown up with weeds and grass. The third time, my father noticed a fence post, so we walked over to it, and we could see a handful of graves, a row of maybe seven or eight, and below it a half row, swamped with that dead brown grass. I remember that the incompleteness of it seemed sad to me. In the second row we found a marker someone had made by stripping a patch of bark off a log and then driving nails partway in and bending them down flat so they made the letters REV AMES. The R looked like the A and the S was a backward Z, but there was no mistaking it.

It was evening by then, so we walked back to the lady's farm and washed at her cistern and drank from her well and slept in her hayloft. She brought us a supper of cornmeal mush. I loved that woman like a second mother. I loved her to the point of tears. We were up before daylight to milk and cut kindling and draw her a bucket of water, and she met us at the door with a breakfast of fried mush with blackberry preserves melted over it and a spoonful of top milk on it, and we ate standing there at the stoop in the chill and the dark, and it was perfectly wonderful.

Then we went back to the graveyard, which was just a patch of ground with a half-fallen fence around it and a gate on a chain weighted with a cowbell. My father and I fixed up the fence as best we could. He broke up the ground on the grave a little with his jackknife. But then he decided we should go back to the farmhouse again to borrow a couple of hoes and make a better job of it. He said, "We might as well look after these other folks while we're here." This time the lady had a dinner of navy beans waiting for us. I don't remember her name, which seems a pity. She had an index finger that was off at the first knuckle, and she spoke with a lisp. She seemed old to me at the time, but I think she was just a country woman, trying to keep her manners and her sanity, trying to keep alive, weary as could be and all by herself out there. My father said she spoke as if her people might be from Maine, but he didn't ask her. She cried when we said goodbye to her, and wiped her face with her apron. My father asked if there was a letter or a message she would like us to carry back with us and she said no. He asked if she would like to come along, and she thanked us and shook her head and said, "There's the cow." She said, "We'll be just fine when the rain comes."

That graveyard was about the loneliest place you could imagine. If I were to say it was going back to nature, you might get the idea that there was some sort of vitality about the place. But it was parched and sun-stricken. It was hard to imagine the grass had ever been green. Everywhere you stepped, little grasshoppers would fly up by the score, making that snap they do, like striking a match. My father put his hands in his pockets and looked around and shook his head. Then he started cutting the brush back with a hand scythe he had brought, and we set up the markers that had fallen over— most of the graves were just outlined with stones, with no names or dates or anything on them at all. My father said to be careful where I stepped. There were small graves here and there that I hadn't noticed at first, or I hadn't quite realized what they were. I certainly didn't want to walk on them, but until he cut the weeds down I couldn't tell where they were, and then I knew I had stepped on some of them, and I felt sick. Only in childhood have I felt guilt like that, and pity. I still dream about it. My father always said when someone dies the body is just a suit of old clothes the spirit doesn't want any-more. But there we were, half killing ourselves to find a grave, and as cautious as we could be about where we put our feet.

We worked a good while at putting things to rights. It was hot, and there was such a sound of grasshoppers, and of wind rattling that dry grass. Then we scattered seeds around, bee balm and coneflower and sunflower and bachelor's button and sweet pea. They were seeds we always saved out of our own garden. When we finished, my father sat down on the ground beside his father's grave. He stayed there for a good while, plucking at little whiskers of straw that still remained on it, fanning himself with his hat. I think he regretted that there was nothing more for him to do. Finally he got up and brushed himself off, and we stood there together with our miserable clothes all damp and our hands all dirty from the work, and the first crickets rasping and the flies really beginning to bother and the birds crying out the way they do when they're about ready to settle for the night, and my father bowed his head and began to pray, remembering his father to the Lord, and also asking the Lord's pardon, and his father's as well. I missed my grandfather mightily, and I felt the need of pardon, too. But that was a very long prayer.

Every prayer seemed long to me at that age, and I was truly bone tired. I tried to keep my eyes closed, but after a while I had to look around a little. And this is something I remember very well. At first I thought I saw the sun setting in the east; I knew where east was, because the sun was just over the horizon when we got there that morning. Then I realized that what I saw was a full moon rising just as the sun was going down. Each of them was standing on its edge, with the most wonderful light between them. It seemed as if you could touch it, as if there were palpable currents of light passing back and forth, or as if there were great taut skeins of light suspended between them. I wanted my father to see it, but I knew I'd have to startle him out of his prayer, and I wanted to do it the best way, so I took his hand and kissed it. And then I said, "Look at the moon." And he did. We just stood there until the sun was down and the moon was up. They seemed to float on the horizon for quite a long time, I suppose because they were both so bright you couldn't get a clear look at them. And that grave, and my father and I, were exactly between them, which seemed amazing to me at the time, since I hadn't given much thought to the nature of the horizon.

My father said, "I would never have thought this place could be beautiful. I'm glad to know that."

We looked so terrible when we finally got home that my mother just burst into tears at the sight of us. We'd both gotten thin, and our clothes were in bad shape. The whole journey didn't take quite a month, but we'd been sleeping in barns and sheds, and even on the bare ground, during the week or so that we were actually lost. It was a great adventure to look back on, and my father and I used to laugh about some fairly dreadful things. An old man even took a shot at us once. My father was, as he said at the time, intending to glean a few overgrown carrots out of a garden we passed. He'd left a dime on the stoop to pay for whatever we could find to steal, which was always little enough. That was something to see, my father in his shirtsleeves straddling a rickety old garden fence with a hank of carrot tops in his hand and a fellow behind him taking aim. We took off into the brush, and when we decided he wasn't going to follow us, we sat down on the ground and my father scraped the dirt off the carrot with his knife and cut it up into pieces and set them on the crown of his hat, which he'd put between us like a table, and then he commenced to say grace, which he never failed to do. He said, "For all we are about to receive," and then we both started laughing till the tears were pouring down. I realize now that keeping us fed was a desperate concern for him. It actually drove him to something resembling crime. That carrot was so big and old and tough he had to whittle it into chips. It was about like eating a branch, and there was nothing to wash it down with, either.

I really only realized afterward what trouble I'd have been

in if he had gotten shot, even killed, and I was left stranded on my own out there. I still dream about that. I think he felt the sort of shame you feel when you realize what a foolish chance you've taken after you've already taken it. But he was absolutely set on finding that grave.

Once, to make the point that I should study while I was young and learning came easily, my grandfather told me about a man he knew when he first came to Kansas, a preacher newly settled there. He said, "That fellow just was not confident of his Hebrew. He'd walk fifteen miles across open country in the dead of winter to settle a point of interpretation. We'd have to thaw him out before he could tell us what it was he had on his mind." My father laughed and said, "The strange part is, that may even be true." But I remembered the story at the time because it seemed to me we were doing something very similar.

My father gave up gleaning and went back to knocking on doors, which he had been reluctant to do, because when people found out he was a preacher they would sometimes try to give us more than they could spare. That was his belief, at least. And they could tell he was a preacher, rough-looking as we were a few days into our desert wanderings, as he called them. We offered to do some chores in exchange for food at a couple of houses, and the people asked him if he would just open a bit of Scripture or say a prayer. He was interested that they knew, and wondered a good deal what it was that gave him away. It was a matter of pride with him that his hands were hard, and that there was no spare flesh on him to speak of. I have had the same experience many times, and I have wondered about it, too. Well, we spent a good many days on the edge of disaster, and we laughed about it for years. It was always the worst parts that made us laugh. My mother was irked by it all, but she just said, "Don't you ever tell me."

In many ways she was a remarkably careful mother, poor woman. I was in a sense her only child. Before I was born she had bought herself a new home health care book. It was large and expensive, and it was a good deal more particular than Leviticus. On its authority she tried to keep us from making any use of our brains for an hour after supper, or from reading at all when our feet were cold. The idea was to prevent conflicting demands on the circulation of the blood. My grandfather told her once that if you couldn't read with cold feet there wouldn't be a literate soul in the state of Maine, but she was very serious about these things and he only irritated her. She said, "Nobody in Maine gets much of anything to eat, so it all comes out even." When I got home she scrubbed me down and put me to bed and fed me six or seven times a day and forbade me the use of my brain after every single meal. The tedium was considerable.

That journey was a great blessing to me. I realize looking back how young my father was then. He couldn't have been much more than forty-five or -six. He was a fine, vigorous man into his old age. We played catch in the evenings after supper for years, till the sun went down and it was too dark for us to see the ball. I think he just appreciated having a child at home, a son. Well, I was a fine, vigorous old man, too, until recently.

You know, I suppose, that I married a girl when I was young. We had grown up together. We were married during my last year at seminary, and then we came back here so I could take my father's pulpit while he and my mother went south for a few months for the sake of my mother's health. Well, my wife died in childbirth, and the child died with her. Their names were Louisa and Angeline. I saw the baby while she lived, and I held her for a few minutes, and that was a blessing. Boughton baptized her and he gave her the name Angeline, because I was over in Tabor for the day—the child was not expected for another six weeks—and there was no one to tell him what name we had finally decided on. She'd have been Rebecca, but Angeline is a good name.

Last Sunday when we went to Boughton's for supper, I saw you looking at his hands. They are so full of arthritis now that they're all skin and knuckles. You think he's terribly old, and he's younger than I am. He was best man at my first wedding, and he married me and your mother. His daughter Glory is home with him now. Her marriage failed, and that is a sad thing, but it is a blessing for Boughton to have her here. She came by the other day to bring me a magazine. She told me Jack might be coming home, too. It actually took me a minute to think who that was. You probably don't remember much about old Boughton. He is a little cross now from time to time, which is understandable considering his discomfort. It would be a pity if that is what you remembered of him. In his prime he was as fine a preacher as I ever heard.

My father always preached from notes, and I wrote my sermons out word for word. There are boxes of them in the attic, a few recent years of them in stacks in the closet. I've never gone back to them to see if they were worth anything, if I actually said anything. Pretty nearly my whole life's work is in those boxes, which is an amazing thing to reflect on. I could look through them, maybe find a few I would want you to have. I'm a little afraid of them. I believe I may have worked over them as I did just to keep myself occupied. If someone came to the house and found me writing, generally he or she would go away, unless it was something pretty important. I don't know why solitude would be a balm for loneliness, but that is how it always was for me in those days, and people respected me for all those hours I was up here working away in the study, and for the books that used to come in the mail for me—not so many, really, but more than I could afford. That's where some of the money went that I could have put aside.

There was more to it, of course. For me writing has always felt like praying, even when I wasn't writing prayers, as I was often enough. You feel that you are with someone. I feel I am with you now, whatever that can mean, considering that you're only a little fellow now and when you're a man you might find these letters of no interest. Or they might never reach you, for any of a number of reasons. Well, but how deeply I regret any sadness you have suffered and how grateful I am in anticipation of any good you have enjoyed. That is to say, I pray for you. And there's an intimacy in it. That's the truth.

Your mother is respectful of my hours up here in the study. She's proud of my books. She was the one who actually called my attention to the number of boxes I have filled with my sermons and my prayers. Say, fifty sermons a year for forty-five years, not counting funerals and so on, of which there have been a great many. Two thousand two hundred and fifty. If they average thirty pages, that's sixty-seven thousand five hundred pages. Can that be right? I guess it is. I write in a small hand, too, as you know by now. Say three hundred pages make a volume. Then I've written two hundred twenty-five books, which puts me up there with Augustine and Calvin for quantity. That's amazing. I wrote almost all of it in the deepest hope and conviction. Sifting my thoughts and choosing my words. Trying to say what was true. And I'll tell you frankly, that was wonderful. I'm grateful for all those dark years, even though in retrospect they seem like a long, bitter prayer that was answered finally. Your mother walked into church in the middle of the prayer—to get out of the weather, I thought at the time, because it was pouring. And she watched me with eyes so serious I was embarrassed to be preaching to her. As Boughton would say, I felt the poverty of my remarks.

Sometimes I have loved the peacefulness of an ordinary Sunday. It is like standing in a newly planted garden after a warm rain. You can feel the silent and invisible life. All it needs from you is that you take care not to trample on it. And that was such a quiet day, rain on the roof, rain against the windows, and everyone grateful, since it seems we never do have quite enough rain. At times like that I might not care particularly whether people are listening to whatever I have to say, because I know what their thoughts are. Then if some stranger comes in, that very same peace can seem like somnolence and like dull habit, because that is how you're afraid it seems to her.

If Rebecca had lived, she'd be fifty-one, older than your mother is now by ten years. For a long time I used to think how it would be if she walked in that door, what I would not be ashamed, at least, to say in her hearing. Because I always imagined her coming back from a place where everything is known, and hearing my hopes and my speculations the way someone would who has seen the truth face-to-face and would know the full measure of my incomprehension. That was a sort of trick I played on myself, to keep from taking doctrines and controversies too much to heart. I read so many books in those days, and I was always disputing in my mind with one or another of them, but I think I usually knew better than to take too much of that sort of thing into the pulpit. I believe, though, that it was because I wrote those sermons as if Rebecca might sometime walk in the door that I was somewhat prepared when your mother walked in, younger than Rebecca would have been in fact, of course, but not very different from the way I saw her in my mind. It wasn't so much her appearance as it was the way she seemed as if she didn't belong there, and at the same time as if she were the only one of us all who really did belong there.

I say this because there was a seriousness about her that seemed almost like a kind of anger. As though she might say, "I came here from whatever unspeakable distance and from whatever unimaginable otherness just to oblige your prayers. Now say something with a little meaning in it." My sermon was like ashes on my tongue. And it wasn't that I hadn't worked on it, either. I worked on all my sermons. I remember I baptized two infants that day. I could feel how intensely she watched. Both the creatures wept when I touched the water to their heads the first time, and I looked up, and there was just the look of stern amazement in her face that I knew would be there even before I looked up, and I felt like saying quite sincerely, "If you know a better way to do this, I'd appreciate your telling me." Then just six months later I baptized her. And I felt like asking her, "What have I done? What does it mean?" That was a question that came to me often, not because I felt less than certain I had done something that did mean something, but because no matter how much I thought and read and prayed, I felt outside the mystery of it. The tears ran down her face, dear woman. I'll never forget that. Unless I forget everything, as so many of the old people do. It appears I at least won't live long enough to forget much I haven't forgotten already, which is a good deal, I know. I have thought about baptism over the years. Boughton and I have discussed it often.

Now, this might seem a trivial thing to mention, considering the gravity of the subject, but I truly don't feel it is. We were very pious children from pious households in a fairly pious town, and this affected our behavior considerably. Once, we baptized a litter of cats. They were dusty little barn cats just steady on their legs, the kind of waifish creatures that live their anonymous lives keeping the mice down and have no interest in humans at all, except to avoid them. But the animals all seem to start out sociable, so we were always pleased to find new kittens prowling out of whatever cranny their mother had tried to hide them in, as ready to play as we were. It occurred to one of the girls to swaddle them up in a doll's dress—there was only one dress, which was just as well since the cats could hardly tolerate a moment in it and would have to have been unswaddled as soon as they were christened in any case. I myself moistened their brows, repeating the full Trinitarian formula.

Their grim old crooked-tailed mother found us baptizing away by the creek and began carrying her babies off by the napes of their necks, one and then another. We lost track of which was which, but we were fairly sure that some of the creatures had been borne away still in the darkness of paganism, and that worried us a good deal. So finally I asked my father in the most offhand way imaginable what exactly would happen to a cat if one were to, say, baptize it. He replied that the Sacraments must always be treated and regarded with the greatest respect. That wasn't really an answer to my question. We did respect the Sacraments, but we thought the whole world of those cats. I got his meaning, though, and I did no more baptizing until I was ordained.

Two or three of that litter were taken home by the girls and made into fairly respectable house cats. Louisa took a yellow one. She still had it when we were married. The others lived out their feral lives, indistinguishable from their kind, whether pagan or Christian no one could ever tell. She called her cat Sparkle, for the white patch on its forehead. It disappeared finally. I suspect it got caught stealing rabbits, a sin to which it was much given, Christian cat that we knew it to be, stiff-jointed as it was by that time. One of the boys said she should have named it Sprinkle. He was a Baptist, a firm believer in total immersion, which those cats should have been grateful I was not. He told us no effect at all could be achieved by our methods, and we could not prove him wrong. Our Soapy must be a distant relative.

I still remember how those warm little brows felt under the palm of my hand. Everyone has petted a cat, but to touch one like that, with the pure intention of blessing it, is a very different thing. It stays in the mind. For years we would wonder what, from a cosmic viewpoint, we had done to them. It still seems to me to be a real question. There is a reality in blessing, which I take baptism to be, primarily. It doesn't enhance sacredness, but it acknowledges it, and there is a power in that. I have felt it pass through me, so to speak. The sensation is of really knowing a creature, I mean really feeling its mysterious life and your own mysterious life at the same time. I don't wish to be urging the ministry on you, but there are some advantages to it you might not know to take account of if I did not point them out. Not that you have to be a minister to confer blessing. You are simply much more likely to find yourself in that position. It's a thing people expect of you. I don't know why there is so little about this aspect of the calling in the literature.

Ludwig Feuerbach says a wonderful thing about baptism. I have it marked. He says, "Water is the purest, clearest of liquids; in virtue of this its natural character it is the image of the spotless nature of the Divine Spirit. In short, water has a significance in itself, as water; it is on account of its natural quality that it is consecrated and selected as the vehicle of the

Holy Spirit. So far there lies at the foundation of Baptism a beautiful, profound natural significance." Feuerbach is a famous atheist, but he is about as good on the joyful aspects of religion as anybody, and he loves the world. Of course he thinks religion could just stand out of the way and let joy exist pure and undisguised. That is his one error, and it is significant. But he is marvelous on the subject of joy, and also on its religious expressions.

Boughton takes a very dim view of him, because he unsettled the faith of many people, but I take issue as much with those people as with Feuerbach. It seems to me some people just go around looking to get their faith unsettled. That has been the fashion for the last hundred years or so. My brother Edward gave his book to me, *The Essence of Christianity*, thinking to shock me out of my uncritical piety, as I knew at the time. I had to read it in secret, or so I believed. I put it in a biscuit tin and hid it in a tree. You can imagine, reading it in those circumstances gave it a great interest for me. And I was very much in awe of Edward, who had studied at a university in Germany.

I realize I haven't even mentioned Edward, though he has been very important to me. As he is still, God rest his soul. I feel in some ways as if I hardly knew him, and in others as if I have been talking to him my whole life. He thought he would do me a favor, taking a bit of the Middle West out of me. That was the favor Europe had done for him. But here I am, having lived to the end the life he warned me against, and pretty well content with it, too, all in all. Still, I know I am touchy on the subject of parochialism.

Edward studied at Göttingen. He was a remarkable man. He was older than me by almost ten years, so I didn't really know him very well while we were children. There were two sisters and a brother between us, all carried off by diphtheria in less than two months. He knew them and I, of course, did not, so that was another great difference. Though it was rarely spoken of, I was always aware that there had been a crowded, cheerful life the three of them remembered well and I could not really imagine. In any case, Edward left home at sixteen to go to college. He finished at nineteen with a degree in ancient languages and went straight off to Europe. None of us saw him again for years. There weren't even many letters.

Then he came home with a walking stick and a huge mustache. Herr Doktor. He must have been about twenty-seven or twenty-eight. He had published a slender book in German, a monograph of some kind on Feuerbach. He was smart as could be, and my father was a little in awe of him, too, as he had been since Edward was a small boy, I think. My parents told me stories about how he read everything he could put his hands on, memorized a whole book of Longfellow, copied maps of Europe and Asia and learned all the cities and rivers. Of course they thought they were bringing up a little Samuel—so did everyone—so they all kept him supplied with books and paints and a magnifying glass and whatever else came to mind or to hand. My mother sometimes regretted out loud that they hadn't really required him to do much in the way of chores, and she certainly didn't make the same mistake with me. But a child as wonderful as he was is not a thing you see often, and the belief was general that he would be a great preacher. So the congregation took up collections to put him in college and then to send him to Germany. And he came back an atheist. That's what he always claimed to be, at any rate.

He took a position at the state college in Lawrence teaching German literature and philosophy, and stayed there till he died. He married a German girl from Indianapolis and they had six little towheaded children, all of them well into middle age by now. He was a few hundred miles away all those years and I hardly ever saw him. He did send back contributions to the church to repay them for helping him. A check dated January 1 came every year he lived. He was a good man.

He and my father had words when he came back, once at the dinner table that first evening when my father asked him to say grace. Edward cleared his throat and replied, "I am afraid I could not do that in good conscience, sir," and the color drained out of my father's face. I knew there had been letters I was not given to read, and there had been somber words between my parents. So this was the dreaded confirmation of their fears. My father said, "You have lived under this roof. You know the customs of your family. You might show some respect for them." And Edward replied, and this was very wrong of him, "When I was a child, I thought as a child. Now that I am become a man, I have put away childish things." My father left the table, my mother sat still in her chair with tears streaming down her face, and Edward passed me the potatoes. I had no idea what was expected of me, so I took some. Edward passed me the gravy. We ate our unhallowed meal solemnly for a little while, and then we left the house and I walked Edward to the hotel.

And on that walk he said to me, "John, you might as well know now what you're sure to learn sometime. This is a backwater—you must be aware of that already. Leaving here is like waking from a trance." I suppose the neighbors saw us leaving the house just at dinnertime that first day, Edward with one arm bent behind his back, stooped a little to suggest that he had some use for a walking stick, appearing somehow to be plunged in thought of an especially rigorous and distinguished kind, possibly conducted in a foreign language. (Only listen to me!) If they saw him, they'd have known instantly what they had long suspected. They'd have known also that there was rage and weeping in my mother's kitchen and that my father was in the attic or the woodshed, in some hidden, quiet place, down on his knees, wondering to the Lord what it was that was being asked of him. And there I was with Edward, trailing along after him, another grief to my parents, or so they must have thought.

Besides those books I mentioned, Edward also gave me the little painting of a marketplace that hangs by the stairs. I must be sure to tell your mother it belongs to me and not to the parsonage. I doubt it's worth anything to speak of, but she might want it.

I'm going to set aside that Feuerbach with the books I will ask your mother to be sure to save for you. I hope you will read it sometime. There is nothing alarming in it, to my mind. I read it the first time under the covers, and down by the creek, because my mother had forbidden me to have any further contact with Edward, and I knew that would include my reading an atheistical book he had given me. She said, "If you ever spoke to your father that way, it would kill him." In fact, my thought was always to defend my father. I believe I have done that.

There are some notes of mine in the margins of the book which I hope you may find useful.

That mention of Feuerbach and joy reminded me of something I saw early one morning a few years ago, as I was walking up to the church. There was a young couple strolling along half a block ahead of me. The sun had come up brilliantly after a heavy rain, and the trees were glistening and very wet. On some impulse, plain exuberance, I suppose, the fellow jumped up and caught hold of a branch, and a storm of luminous water came pouring down on the two of them, and they laughed and took off running, the girl sweeping water off her hair and her dress as if she were a little bit disgusted, but she wasn't. It was a beautiful thing to see, like something from a myth. I don't know why I thought of that now, except perhaps because it is easy to believe in such moments that water was made primarily for blessing, and only secondarily for growing vegetables or doing the wash. I wish I had paid more attention to it. My list of regrets may seem unusual, but who can know that they are, really. This is an interesting planet. It deserves all the attention you can give it.

In writing this, I notice the care it costs me not to use certain words more than I ought to. I am thinking about the word "just." I almost wish I could have written that the sun just *shone* and the tree just *glistened*, and the water just *poured* out of it and the girl just *laughed*—when it's used that way it does indicate a stress on the word that follows it, and also a particular pitch of the voice. People talk that way when they want to call attention to a thing existing in excess of itself, so to speak, a sort of purity or lavishness, at any rate something ordinary in kind but exceptional in degree. So it seems to me at the moment. There is something real signified by that word "just" that proper language won't acknowledge. It's a little like the German *ge-*. I regret that I must deprive myself of it. It takes half the point out of telling the story.

I am also inclined to overuse the word "old," which actually has less to do with age, as it seems to me, than it does with familiarity. It sets a thing apart as something regarded with a modest, habitual affection. Sometimes it suggests haplessness or vulnerability. I say "old Boughton," I say "this shabby old town," and I mean that they are very near my heart.

I don't write the way I speak. I'm afraid you would think I didn't know any better. I don't write the way I do for the pulpit, either, insofar as I can help it. That would be ridiculous, in the circumstances. I do try to write the way I think. But of course that all changes as soon as I put it into words. And the more it does seem to be my thinking, the more pulpitish it sounds, which I guess is inevitable. I will resist that inflection, nevertheless.

I walked over to Boughton's to see what he was up to. I found him in a terrible state of mind. Tomorrow would have been his fifty-fourth anniversary. He said, "The truth is, I'm just very tired of sitting here alone. That's the truth." Glory is there doing everything she can think of to make him comfortable, but he has his bad days. He said, "When we were young, marriage *meant* something. *Family* meant something. Things weren't at all the way they are today!" Glory rolled her eyes at that and said, "We haven't heard from Jack for a little while and it is making us a bit anxious."

He said, "Glory, why do you always do that? Why do you say *us* when *I'm* the one you're talking about?"

She said, "Papa, as far as I'm concerned, Jack can't get here a minute too soon."

He said, "Well, it's natural to worry and I'm not going to apologize for it."

She said, "I suppose it's natural to take your worrying out on me, too, but I can't pretend I like it."

And so on. So I came back home.

Boughton was always a good-hearted man, but his discomforts weary him, and now and then he says things he really shouldn't. He isn't himself.

I'm sorry you are alone. You are a serious child, with not much occasion to giggle, or to connive. You are shy of other children. I see you standing up on your swing, watching some boys about your age out in the road. One of the bigger ones is trying out a beat-up old bicycle. I suppose you know who they are. You don't speak to them. If they seem to notice you, you'll probably come inside. You are shy like your mother. I see how hard this life is for her that I've brought her into, and I believe you sense it, too. She makes a very unlikely preacher's wife. She says so herself. But she never flinches from any of it. Mary Magdalene probably made an occasional casserole, whatever the ancient equivalent may have been. A mess of pottage, I suppose.

I mean only respect when I say that your mother has always struck me as someone with whom the Lord might have chosen to spend some part of His mortal time. How odd it is to have to say that after all these centuries. There is an earned innocence, I believe, which is as much to be honored as the innocence of children. I have often wanted to preach about that. For all I know, I have preached about it. When the Lord says you must "become as one of these little ones," I take Him to mean you must be stripped of all the accretions of smugness and pretense and triviality. "Naked came I out of my mother's womb," and so on. I think I will preach on that during Advent. I'll make a note. If I can't remember speaking about it before, no one else is likely to remember. I can imagine Jesus befriending my grandfather, too, frying up some breakfast for him, talking things over with him, and in fact the old man did report several experiences of just that kind. I can't say the same for myself. I doubt I'd ever have had the strength for it. This is something that has come to my mind from time to time over the years, and I don't really know what to make of it.

It has pleased me when I have thought your mother felt at home in the world, even momentarily. At peace in it, I should say, because I believe her familiarity with the world may be much deeper than mine. I do truly wish I had the means to spare you the slightest acquaintance with that very poverty the

Lord Himself blessed by word and example. Once when I worried about this out loud, your mother said, "You think I don't know how to be poor? I done it all my life." And still it shames me to think that I will leave you and your mother so naked to the world—dear Lord, I think, spare them that blessing.

I have had a certain acquaintance with a kind of holy poverty. My grandfather never kept anything that was worth giving away, or let us keep it, either, so my mother said. He would take laundry right off the line. She said he was worse than any thief, worse than a house fire. She said she could probably go to any town in the Middle West and see some pair of pants she'd patched walking by in the street. I believe he was a saint of some kind. When someone remarked in his hearing that he had lost an eye in the Civil War, he said, "I prefer to remember that I have kept one." My mother said it was good to know there was anything he could keep. He told me once he was wounded at Wilson's Creek, on the day of the death of General Lyon. "Now *that*," he said, "was a *loss*."

When he left us, we all felt his absence bitterly. But he did make things difficult. It was an innocence in him. He lacked patience for anything but the plainest interpretations of the starkest commandments, "To him who asks, give," in particular.

I wish you could have known my grandfather. I heard a man say once it seemed the one eye he had was somehow ten times an eye. Normally speaking, it seems to me, a gaze, even a stare, is diffused a little when there are two eyes involved. He could make me feel as though he had poked me with a stick, just by looking at me. Not that he meant any harm to speak of. He was just afire with old certainties, and he couldn't bear all the patience that was required of him by the peace and by the aging of his body and by the forgetfulness that had settled over everything. He thought we should all be living at a dead run. I don't say he was wrong. That would be like contradicting John the Baptist.

He really would give anything away. My father would go looking for a saw or a box of nails and it would be gone. My mother used to keep what money she had in the bodice of her dress, tied up in a handkerchief. For a while she was selling stewing hens and eggs because the times were very hard. (In those days we had a little land around this house, a barn and pasture and henhouse and a wood lot and woodshed and a nice little orchard and a grape arbor. But over the years the church has had to sell it all off. I used to expect to hear they were planning to auction off the cellar next, or the roof.) In any case, times were hard and she had the old man to deal with, and he would actually give away the blankets off his bed. He did that several times, and my mother was at a good deal of trouble to replace them. For a while she made me wear my church clothes all the time so he couldn't get at them, and then she never gave me a moment's peace because she was sure I was going to go off and play baseball in them, as of course I did.

I remember once he came into the kitchen while she was doing her ironing. He said, "Daughter, some folks have come to us for help."

"Well," she said, "I hope they can wait a minute. I hope they can wait till this iron is cool." After a few minutes she put the iron on the stove and went into the pantry and came out with a can of baking powder. She delved around in it with a fork until she drew up a quarter. She did this again until she had a quarter and two dimes lying there on the table. She picked them up and polished the powder off with a corner of her apron and held them out to him. Now, forty-five cents represented a good many eggs in those days—she was not an ungenerous woman. He took them, but it was clear enough he knew she had more. (Once when he was in the pantry he found money hidden in an empty can because when he happened to pick it up it rattled, so he took to going into the pantry from time to time just to see what else might rattle. So she took to washing her money and then pushing it into the lard or burying it in the sugar. But from time to time a nickel would show up where she didn't want it to, in the sugar bowl, of course, or in the fried mush.) No doubt she thought she could make him go on believing all her money was hidden in the pantry if she hid part of it there.

But he was never fooled. I believe he may have been a little unbalanced at that time, but he could see through anyone and anything. Except, my mother said, drunkards and ne'er-do-wells. But that wasn't really true either. He just said, "Judge not," and of course that's Scripture and hard to contradict.

But it must be said that my mother took a great deal of pride in looking after her family, which was heavy work in those days and especially hard for her, with her aches and pains. She kept a bottle of whiskey in the pantry for her rheumatism. "The one thing I don't have to hide," she said. But he'd walk off with a jar of her pickled beets without so much as a by-your-leave. That day, though, he stood there with those three coins in his drastic old mummified hand and watched her with that terrible eye, and she crossed her arms right over the handkerchief with the hidden money in it, as he clearly knew, and watched him right back, until he said, "Well, the Lord bless you and keep you," and went out the door.

My mother said, "I stared him down! I stared him down!" She seemed more amazed than anything. As I have said, she had a good deal of respect for him. He always told her she ought not to worry about his generosities, because the Lord would provide. And she used to say that if He weren't put to so much trouble keeping us in shirts and socks, He might have time to provide a cake now and then, or a pie. But she missed him when he was gone, as we all did.

Looking back over what I have written, it seems to me I've described my grandfather in his old age as if he were simply an eccentric, and as if we tolerated him and were respectful of him and loved him and he loved us. And all that is true. But I believe we knew also that his eccentricities were thwarted passion, that he was full of anger, at us not least, and that the tremors of his old age were in some part the tremors of pent grief. And I believe my father on his side was angry, too, at the accusations he knew he could see in his father's unreposefulness, and also in his endless pillaging. In a spirit of Christian forgiveness very becoming to men of the cloth, and to father and son, they had buried their differences. It must be said, however, that they buried them not very deeply, and perhaps more as one would bank a fire than smother it.

They had a particular way of addressing each other when the old bitterness was about to flare up.

"Have I offended you in some way, Reverend?" my father would ask.

And his father would say, "No, Reverend, you have not offended me in any way at all. Not at all."

And my mother would say, "Now, don't you two get started."

My mother took a great deal of pride in her chickens, especially after the old man was gone and her flock was unplundered. Culled judiciously, it throve, yielding eggs at a rate that astonished her. But one afternoon a storm came up and a gust of wind hit the henhouse and lifted the roof right off, and hens came flying out, sucked after it, I suppose, and also just acting like hens. My mother and I saw it happen, because when she smelled the rain coming she called me to help her get the wash off the line.

It was a general disaster. When the roof hit the fence, which was just chicken wire nailed to some posts and might as well have been cobweb, there were chickens taking off toward the pasture and chickens taking off toward the road and chickens with no clear intentions, just being chickens. Then the neighborhood dogs got involved, and our dogs, too, and then the rain really started. We couldn't even call off our own dogs. Their joy took on a tinge of shame, as I remember, but the rest of them didn't even pay us that much attention. They were having the time of their lives.

My mother said, "I don't want to watch this." So I followed her into the kitchen and we sat there listening to the pandemonium and the wind and the rain. Then my mother said, "The wash!" which we had forgotten. She said, "Those sheets must be so heavy that they're dragging in the mud, if they haven't pulled the lines down altogether." That was a day's work lost for her, not to mention the setting hens and the fryers. She closed one eye and looked at me and said, "I know there is a blessing in this somewhere." We did have a habit sometimes of imitating the old man's way of speaking when he wasn't in the room. Still, I was surprised that she would make an outright joke about my grandfather, though he'd been gone a long time by then. She always did like to make me laugh.

When my father found his father at Mount Pleasant after the war ended, he was shocked at first to see how he had been wounded. In fact, he was speechless. So my grandfather's first words to his son were "I am confident that I will find great blessing in it." And that is what he said about everything that happened to him for the rest of his life, all of which tended to be more or less drastic. I remember at least two sprained wrists and a cracked rib. He told me once that being blessed meant being bloodied, and that is true etymologically, in English— but not in Greek or Hebrew. So whatever understanding might be based on that derivation has no scriptural authority behind it. It was unlike him to strain interpretation that way. He did it in order to make an account of himself, I suppose, as most of us do.

In any case, the notion seems to have been important to him. He was always trying to help somebody birth a calf or limb a tree, whether they wanted him to or not. All the regret he ever felt was for his unfortunates, with none left over for himself however he might be injured, until his friends began to die off, as they did one after another in the space of about two years. Then he was terribly lonely, no doubt about it. I think that was a big part of his running off to Kansas. That and the fire at the Negro church. It wasn't a big fire—someone heaped brush against the back wall and put a match to it, and someone else saw the smoke and put the flames out with a shovel. (The Negro church used to be where the soda fountain is now, though I hear that's going out of business. That church sold up some years ago, and what was left of the congregation moved to Chicago. By then it was down to three or four families. The pastor came by with a sack of plants he'd dug up from around the front steps, mainly lilies. He thought I might want them, and they're still there along the front of our church, needing to be thinned. I should tell the deacons where they came from, so they'll know they have some significance and they'll save them when the building comes down. I didn't know the Negro pastor well myself, but he said his father knew my grandfather. He told me they were sorry to leave, because this town had once meant a great deal to them.)

You have begun palling around with a chap you found at school, a freckly little Lutheran named Tobias, a pleasant child. You seem to be spending half your time at his house. We think that is very good for you, but we miss you something terrible. Tonight you are camping out in his backyard, which is just across the street and a few houses down. Supper without you tonight, a melancholy prospect.

You and Tobias came trudging home at dawn and spread your sleeping bags on your bedroom floor and slept till lunchtime. (You had heard growling in the bushes. T. has brothers.) Your mother had fallen asleep in the parlor with a book in her lap. I made you some toasted cheese sandwiches, which I cooked a little too long. So I told you the story you like very much, about how my poor old mother would sleep in her rocker by the kitchen stove while our dinner smoked and sputtered like some unacceptable sacrifice, and you ate your sandwiches, maybe a little more happily for the scorch. And I gave you some of those chocolate cupcakes with the squiggle of white frosting across the top. I buy those for your mother because she loves them and won't buy them for herself. I doubt she slept at all last night. I surprised myself—I slept pretty soundly, and woke out of a harmless sort of dream, an unmemorable conversation with people I did not know. And I was so happy to have you home again.

I was thinking about that henhouse. It stood just across the yard, where the Muellers' house is now. Boughton and I used to sit on the roof of it and look out over the neighbors' gardens and the fields. We used to take sandwiches and eat our dinner up there. I had stilts that Edward had made for himself years before. They were so high I had to stand on the porch railing to get onto them. Boughton (he was Bobby then) got his father to make him a pair, and we pretty well lived on those things for several summers. We had to stay on the paths or where the ground was firm, but we got to be very much at ease on them, and we'd just saunter all over the place, as if it were quite a natural thing. We could sit right down on the branch of a tree. Sometimes wasps were a problem, or mosquitoes. We took a few spills, but mainly it was very nice. Giants in the earth we were, mighty men of valor. We would never have thought that coop could fold up the way it did. The roof was covered in raggedy black tar paper, and it was always warm even when the day was chilly, and sometimes we'd lie back on it to get out of the wind, just lie there and talk. I remember Boughton was already worrying about his vocation. He was afraid it wouldn't come to him, and then he'd have to find another kind of life, and he couldn't really think of one. We'd go through the possibilities we were aware of. There weren't many.

Boughton was slow getting his growth. Then, after a short childhood, he was taller than me for about forty years. Now he's so bent over I don't know how you'd calculate his height. He says his spine has turned into knuckle bones. He says he's been reduced to a heap of joints, and not one of them works. You'd never know what he once was, looking at him now. He was always wonderful at stealing bases, from grade school right through seminary.

I reminded him the other day how he'd said to me, lying there on that roof watching the clouds, "What do you think you would do if you saw an angel? I'll tell you what, I'm scared I'd take off running!" Old Boughton laughed at that and said,

"Well, I still might *want* to." And then he said, "Pretty soon I'll know."

I've always been taller than most, larger than most. It runs in my family. When I was a boy, people took me to be older than I was and often expected more of me—more common sense, usually—than I could come up with at the time. I got pretty good at pretending I understood more than I did, a skill which has served me through life. I say this because I want you to realize that I am not by any means a saint. My life does not compare with my grandfather's. I get much more respect than I deserve. This seems harmless enough in most cases. People want to respect the pastor and I'm not going to interfere with that. But I've developed a great reputation for wisdom by ordering more books than I ever had time to read, and reading more books, by far, than I learned anything useful from, except, of course, that some very tedious gentlemen have written books. This is not a new insight, but the truth of it is something you have to experience to fully grasp.

Thank God for them all, of course, and for that strange interval, which was most of my life, when I read out of loneliness, and when bad company was much better than no company. You can love a bad book for its haplessness or pomposity or gall, if you have that starveling appetite for things human, which I devoutly hope you never will have. "The full soul loatheth an honeycomb; but to the hungry soul every bitter thing is sweet." There are pleasures to be found where you would never look for them. That's a bit of fatherly wisdom, but it's also the Lord's truth, and a thing I know from my own long experience.

Often enough when someone saw the light burning in my study long into the night, it only meant I had fallen asleep in my chair. My reputation is largely the creature of the kindly imaginings of my flock, whom I chose not to disillusion, in part because the truth had the kind of pathos in it that would bring on sympathy in its least bearable forms. Well, my life was known to them all, every significant aspect of it, and they were tactful. I've spent a good share of my life comforting the afflicted, but I could never endure the thought that anyone should try to comfort me, except old Boughton, who always knew better than to talk much. He was such an excellent friend to me in those days, such a help to me. I do wish you could have some idea of what a fine man he was in his prime. His sermons were remarkable, but he never wrote them out. He didn't even keep his notes. So that is all gone. I remember a phrase here and there. I think every day about going through those old sermons of mine to see if there are one or two I might want you to read sometime, but there are so many, and I'm afraid, first of all, that most of them might seem foolish or dull to me. It might be best to burn them, but that would upset your mother, who thinks a great deal more of them than I do—for their sheer mass, I suppose, since she hasn't read them. You will probably remember that the stairs to the attic are a sort of ladder, and that it is terribly hot up there when it is not terribly cold.

It would be worth my life to try to get those big boxes down on my own. It's humiliating to have written as much as Augustine, and then to have to find a way to dispose of it. There is not a word in any of those sermons I didn't mean when I wrote it. If I had the time, I could read my way through fifty years of my innermost life. What a terrible thought. If I don't burn them someone else will sometime, and that's another humiliation. This habit of writing is so deep in me, as you will know well enough if this endless letter is in your hands, if it has not been lost or burned also.

I suppose it's natural to think about those old boxes of sermons upstairs. They are a record of my life, after all, a sort of foretaste of the Last Judgment, really, so how can I not be curious? Here I was a pastor of souls, hundreds and hundreds of them over all those years, and I hope I was speaking to them, not only to myself, as it seems to me sometimes when I look back. I still wake up at night, thinking, *That's* what I should have said! or *That's* what he meant! remembering conversations I had with people years ago, some of them long gone from the world, past any thought of my putting things right with them. And then I do wonder where my attention was. If that is even the question.

One sermon is not up there, one I actually burned the night before I had meant to preach it. People don't talk much now about the Spanish influenza, but that was a terrible thing, and it struck just at the time of the Great War, just when we were getting involved in it. It killed the soldiers by the thousands, healthy men in the prime of life, and then it spread into the rest of the population. It was like a war, it really was. One funeral after another, right here in Iowa. We lost so many of the young people. And we got off pretty lightly. People came to church wearing masks, if they came at all. They'd sit as far from each other as they could. There was talk that the Germans had caused it with some sort of secret weapon, and I think people wanted to believe that, because it saved them from reflecting on what other meaning it might have.

The parents of these young soldiers would come to me and ask me how the Lord could allow such a thing. I felt like asking them what the Lord would have to do to tell us He *didn't* allow something. But instead I would comfort them by saying we would never know what their young men had been spared.

Most of them took me to mean they were spared the trenches and the mustard gas, but what I really meant was that they were spared the act of killing. It was just like a biblical plague, just exactly. I thought of Sennacherib.

It was a strange sickness—I saw it over at Fort Riley. Those boys were drowning in their own blood. They couldn't even speak for the blood in their throats, in their mouths. So many of them died so fast there was noplace to put them, and they just stacked the bodies in the yard. I went over there to help out, and I saw it myself. They drafted all the boys at the college, and influenza swept through there so bad the place had to be closed down and the buildings filled with cots like hospital wards, and there was terrible death, right here in Iowa. Now, if these things were not signs, I don't know what a sign would look like. So I wrote a sermon about it. I said, or I meant to say, that these deaths were rescuing foolish young men from the consequences of their own ignorance and courage, that the Lord was gathering them in before they could go off and commit murder against their brothers. And I said that their deaths were a sign and a warning to the rest of us that the desire for war would bring the consequences of war, because there is no ocean big enough to protect us from the Lord's judgment when we decide to hammer our plowshares into swords and our pruning hooks into spears, in contempt of the will and the grace of God.

It was quite a sermon, I believe. I thought as I wrote it how pleased my father would have been. But my courage failed, because I knew the only people at church would be a few old women who were already about as sad and apprehensive as they could stand to be and no more approving of the war than I was. And they were there even though I might have been contagious. I seemed ridiculous to myself for imagining I could thunder from the pulpit in those circumstances, and I dropped that sermon in the stove and preached on the Parable of the Lost Sheep. I wish I had kept it, because I meant every word. It might have been the only sermon I wouldn't mind answering for in the next world. And I burned it. But Mirabelle Mercer was not Pontius Pilate, and she was not Woodrow Wilson, either.

Now I think how courageous you might have thought I was if you had come across it among my papers and read it. It is hard to understand another time. You would never have imagined that almost empty sanctuary, just a few women there with heavy veils on to try to hide the masks they were wearing, and two or three men. I preached with a scarf around my mouth for more than a year. Everyone smelled like onions, because word went around that flu germs were killed by onions. People rubbed themselves down with tobacco leaves.

In those days there were barrels on the street corners so we could contribute peach pits to the war effort. The army made them into charcoal, they said, for the filters in gas masks. It took hundreds of pits to make just one of them. So we all ate peaches on grounds of patriotism, which actually made them taste a little different. The magazines were full of soldiers wearing gas masks, looking stranger than we did. It was a remarkable time.

Most of the young men seemed to feel that the war was a courageous thing, and maybe new wars have come along since I wrote this that have seemed brave to you. That there have been wars I have no doubt. I believe that plague was a great sign to us, and we refused to see it and take its meaning, and since then we have had war continuously.

I'm not entirely sure I do believe that. Boughton would say, "That's the pulpit speaking." True enough, but what that means I don't know.

My own dark time, as I call it, the time of my loneliness, was most of my life, as I have said, and I can't make any real account of myself without speaking of it. The time passed so strangely, as if every winter were the same winter, and every spring the same spring. And there was baseball. I listened to thousands of baseball games, I suppose. Sometimes I could just make out half a play, and then static, and then a crowd roaring, a flat little sound, almost static itself, like that empty sound in a seashell. It felt good to me to imagine it, like working out some intricate riddle in my mind, planetary motion. If the ball is drifting toward left field and there are runners on first and third, then—moving the runners and the catcher and the shortstop in my mind. I loved to do that, I can't explain why.

And I would think back on conversations I had had in a similar way, really. A great part of my work has been listening to people, in that particular intense privacy of confession, or at least unburdening, and it has been very interesting to me. Not that I thought of these conversations as if they were a contest, I don't mean that. But as you might look at a game more abstractly—where is the strength, what is the strategy? As if you had no interest in it except in seeing how well the two sides bring each other along, how much they can require of each other, how the life that is the real subject of it all is manifest in it. By "life" I mean something like "energy" (as the scientists use the word) or "vitality," and also something very different. When people come to speak to me, whatever they say, I am struck by a kind of incandescence in them, the "I" whose predicate can be "love" or "fear" or "want," and whose object can be "someone" or "nothing" and it won't really matter, because the loveliness is just in that presence, shaped around "I" like a flame on a wick, emanating itself in grief and guilt and joy and whatever else. But quick, and avid, and resourceful. To see this aspect of life is a privilege of the ministry which is seldom mentioned.

A good sermon is one side of a passionate conversation. It has to be heard in that way. There are three parties to it, of course, but so are there even to the most private thought—the self that yields the thought, the self that acknowledges and in some way responds to the thought, and the Lord. That is a remarkable thing to consider.

I am trying to describe what I have never before attempted to put into words. I have made myself a little weary in the struggle.

It was one day as I listened to baseball that it occurred to me how the moon actually moves, in a spiral, because while it orbits the earth it also follows the orbit of the earth around the sun. This is obvious, but the realization pleased me. There was a full moon outside my window, icy white in a blue sky, and the Cubs were playing Cincinnati.

That mention of the sound of a seashell reminds me of a couple of lines of a poem I wrote once:

> Open the scroll of conch and find the text
> That lies behind the priestly susurrus.

There wasn't anything else in it worth remembering. One of Boughton's boys traveled to the Mediterranean for some reason, and he sent back that big shell I have always kept on my desk. I have loved the word "susurrus" for a long time, and I had never found another use for it. Besides, what else did I know in those days but texts and priestliness and static? And what else did I love? There was a book many people read at that time, *The Diary of a Country Priest*. It was by a French writer, Bernanos. I felt a lot of sympathy for the fellow, but Boughton said, "It was the drink." He said, "The Lord simply needed someone more suitable to fill that position." I remember reading that book all night by the radio till every station went off, and still reading when the daylight came.

Once my grandfather took me to Des Moines on the train to see Bud Fowler play. He was with Keokuk for a season or two. The old man fixed me with that eye of his and he told me there was not a man on this round earth who could outrun or outthrow Bud Fowler. I was pretty excited. But nothing happened in that game, or so I thought then. No runs, no hits, no errors. In the fifth inning a thunderstorm that had been lying along the horizon the whole afternoon just sort of sauntered over and put a stop to it all. I remember the groan that went up from the crowd when the heavy rain began. I was only about ten years old, and I was relieved, but it was a terrible frustration to my grandfather. One more terrible frustration for the poor old devil. I say this with all respect. Even my father called him that, and my mother did, too. He had lost that eye in the war, and he was pretty wild-looking generally. But he was a fine preacher in the style of his generation, so my father said.

That day he had brought a little bag of licorice, which really did surprise me. Whenever he put his fingers into it, it rattled with the trembling of his hand, and the sound was just like the sound of fire. I noticed this at the time, and it seemed natural to me. I also more or less assumed that the thunder and the lightning that day were Creation tipping its hat to him, as if to say, Glad to see you here in the stands, Reverend. Or maybe it said, Why, Reverend, what in this grieving world are *you* doing here at a sporting event? My mother said once that he attracted terrible friendship—using "terrible" in the old sense, of course, and meaning only respect. When he was young, he was an acquaintance of John Brown, and of Jim Lane, too. I wish I could tell you more about that. There was a kind of truce in our household that discouraged talk about the old times in Kansas, and about the war. It was not long after the trip to Des Moines that we lost him, or he lost himself. In any case, a few weeks later he took off for Kansas.

I read somewhere that a thing that does not exist in relation to anything else cannot itself be said to exist. I can't quite see the meaning of a statement so purely hypothetical as this, though I may simply lack understanding. But it does remind me of that afternoon when nothing flew through the air, no one slid or drifted or tagged, when there was no waltz at all, so to speak. It seems to me that the storm had to put an end to it, as if it were a fire to be put out, an eruption into this world of an alarming kind of nullity. "There was silence in heaven for about half an hour." It seems a little like that as I remember it, though it went on a good deal longer than half an hour. Null. That word has real power. My grandfather had nowhere to spend his courage, no way to feel it in himself. That was a great pity.

As I write I am aware that my memory has made much of very little. There was that old man my grandfather sitting beside me in his ashy coat, trembling just because he did, sharing out the frugal pleasures of his licorice, maybe with Kansas somehow transforming itself from memory to intention in his mind that very afternoon. (It was Kansas he went back to, not the town where his church used to be. That's why we were so long finding him.) Bud Fowler stood at second base with his glove on his hip and watched the catcher. I know he liked to play bare-handed, but that is what I remember, and it's all I ever could remember about him, so there is no point trying to put the memory right. I followed his career in the newspaper for years, until they started up the Negro Leagues, and then I sort of lost track of him.

I was a fairly decent pitcher in high school and college, and we had a couple of teams up at the seminary. We'd go out on a Saturday to toss the ball around. The diamond was just worn in the grass, so it was anybody's guess where the baselines were. We had some good times. There were remarkable young men studying for the ministry in those days. There are now, too, I'm sure.

When my father and I were walking along the road in the quiet and the moonlight, away from the graveyard where we'd found the old man, my father said, "You know, everybody in Kansas saw the same thing we saw." At the time (remember I was twelve) I took him to mean the entire state was a witness to our miracle. I thought that whole state could vouch for the particular blessing my father had brought down by praying there at his father's grave, or the glory that my grandfather had somehow emanated out of his parched repose. Later I realized my father would have meant that the sun and moon aligned themselves as they did with no special reference to the two of us. He never encouraged any talk about visions or miracles, except the ones in the Bible.

I can't tell you, though, how I felt, walking along beside him that night, along that rutted road, through that empty world—what a sweet strength I felt, in him, and in myself, and all around us. I am glad I didn't understand, because I have rarely felt joy like that, and assurance. It was like one of those dreams where you're filled with some extravagant feeling you might never have in life, it doesn't matter what it is, even guilt or dread, and you learn from it what an amazing instrument you are, so to speak, what a power you have to experience beyond anything you might ever actually need. Who would have thought that the moon could dazzle and flame like that? Despite what he said, I could see that my father was a little shaken. He had to stop and wipe his eyes.

My grandfather told me once about a vision he'd had when he was still living in Maine, not yet sixteen. He had fallen asleep by the fire, worn out from a day helping his father pull stumps. Someone touched him on the shoulder, and when he looked up, there was the Lord, holding out His arms to him, which were bound in chains. My grandfather said, "Those irons had rankled right down to His bones." He told me that as the saddest fact, and eyed me with the one seraph eye he had, the old grief fresh in it. He said he knew then that he had to come to Kansas and make himself useful to the cause of abolition. To be useful was the best thing the old men ever hoped for themselves, and to be aimless was their worst fear. I have a lot of respect for that view. When I spoke to my father about the vision he had described to me, my father just nodded and said, "It was the times." He himself never claimed any such experience, and he seemed to want to assure me I need not fear that the Lord would come to me with His sorrows. And I took comfort in the assurance. That is a remarkable thing to consider.

My grandfather seemed to me stricken and afflicted, and indeed he was, like a man everlastingly struck by lightning, so that there was an ashiness about his clothes and his hair never settled and his eye had a look of tragic alarm when he wasn't actually sleeping. He was the most unreposeful human being I ever knew, except for certain of his friends. All of them could sit on their heels into their old age, and they'd do it by preference, as if they had a grudge against furniture. They had no flesh on them at all. They were like the Hebrew prophets in some unwilling retirement, or like the primitive church still waiting to judge the angels. There was one old fellow whose blessing and baptizing hand had a twist burned into it because he had taken hold of a young Jayhawker's gun by the barrel. "I thought, That child doesn't want to shoot me," he would say. "He was five years shy of a whisker. He should have been home with his mama. So I said, 'Just give me that thing,' and he did, grinning a little as he did it. I couldn't drop the gun—I thought that might be the joke—and I couldn't shift it to the other hand because that arm was in a sling. So I just walked off with it."

They had been to Lane and Oberlin, and they knew their Hebrew and their Greek and their Locke and their Milton. Some of them even set up a nice little college in Tabor. It lasted quite a while. The people who graduated from it, especially the young women, would go by themselves to the other side of the earth as teachers and missionaries and come back decades later to tell us about Turkey and Korea. Still, they were bodacious old men, the lot of them. It was the most natural thing in the world that my grandfather's grave would look like a place where someone had tried to smother a fire.

Just now I was listening to a song on the radio, standing there swaying to it a little, I guess, because your mother saw me from the hallway and she said, "I could show you how to do that." She came and put her arms around me and put her head on my shoulder, and after a while she said, in the gentlest voice you could ever imagine, "Why'd you have to be so damn old?"

I ask myself the same question.

———

A few days ago you and your mother came home with flowers. I knew where you had been. Of course she takes you up there, to get you a little used to the place. And I hear she's made it very pretty, too. She's a thoughtful woman. You had honeysuckle, and you showed me how to suck the nectar out of the blossoms. You would bite the little tip off a flower and then hand it to me, and I pretended I didn't know how to go about it, and I would put the whole flower in my mouth, and pretend to chew it and swallow it, or I'd act as if it were a little whistle and try to blow through it, and you'd laugh and laugh and say, No! no! no!! And then I pretended I had a bee buzzing around in my mouth, and you said, "No, you don't, there wasn't any bee!" and I grabbed you around the shoulders and blew into your ear and you jumped up as though you thought maybe there was a bee after all, and you laughed, and then you got serious and you said, "I want you to do this." And then you put your hand on my cheek and touched the flower to my lips, so gently and carefully, and said, "Now sip." You said, "You have to take your medicine." So I did, and it tasted exactly like honeysuckle, just the way it did when I was your age and it seemed to grow on every fence post and porch railing in creation.

I was struck by the way the light felt that afternoon. I have paid a good deal of attention to light, but no one could begin to do it justice. There was the feeling of a weight of light—pressing the damp out of the grass and pressing the smell of sour old sap out of the boards on the porch floor and burdening even the trees a little as a late snow would do. It was the kind of light that rests on your shoulders the way a cat lies on your lap. So familiar. Old Soapy was lying in the sun, plastered to the sidewalk. You remember Soapy. I don't really know why you should. She is a very unremarkable animal. I'll take a picture of her.

So there we were, sipping honeysuckle till suppertime, and your mother brought out the camera, so maybe you will have some pictures. The film ran out before I could get a shot of her. That's just typical. Sometimes if I try to photograph her she'll hide her face in her hands, or she'll just walk out of the room. She doesn't think she's a pretty woman. I don't know where she got these ideas about herself, and I don't think I ever will know, either. Sometimes I've wondered why she'd marry an old man like me, a fine, vital woman like she is. I'd never have thought to ask her to marry me. I would never have dared to. It was her idea. I remind myself of that often. She reminds me of it, too.

I'd never have believed I'd see a wife of mine doting on a child of mine. It still amazes me every time I think of it. I'm writing this in part to tell you that if you ever wonder what you've done in your life, and everyone does wonder sooner or later, you have been God's grace to me, a miracle, something more than a miracle. You may not remember me very well at all, and it may seem to you to be no great thing to have been the good child of an old man in a shabby little town you will no doubt leave behind. If only I had the words to tell you.

There's a shimmer on a child's hair, in the sunlight. There are rainbow colors in it, tiny, soft beams of just the same colors you can see in the dew sometimes. They're in the petals of flowers, and they're on a child's skin. Your hair is straight and dark, and your skin is very fair. I suppose you're not prettier than most children. You're just a nice-looking boy, a bit slight, well scrubbed and well mannered. All that is fine, but it's your existence I love you for, mainly. Existence seems to me now the most remarkable thing that could ever be imagined. I'm about to put on imperishability. In an instant, in the twinkling of an eye.

The twinkling of an eye. That is the most wonderful expression. I've thought from time to time it was the best thing in life, that little incandescence you see in people when the charm of a thing strikes them, or the humor of it. "The light of the eyes rejoiceth the heart." That's a fact.

While you read this, I am imperishable, somehow more alive than I have ever been, in the strength of my youth, with dear ones beside me. You read the dreams of an anxious, fuddled old man, and I live in a light better than any dream of mine—not waiting for you, though, because I want your dear perishable self to live long and to love this poor perishable world, which I somehow cannot imagine not missing bitterly, even while I do long to see what it will mean to have wife and child restored to me, I mean Louisa and Rebecca. I have wondered about that for many years. Well, this old seed is about to drop into the ground. Then I'll know.

I have a few pictures of Louisa, but I don't think the resemblance is very good. Considering that I haven't seen her in fifty-one years, I guess I can't really judge. When she was nine or ten she used to skip rope like fury, and if you tried to distract her, she would just turn away, still jumping, and never miss a lick. Her braids would bounce and thump on her back. Sometimes I'd try to catch hold of one of them, and then she'd be off down the street, still skipping. She would be trying to make it to a thousand, or to a million, and nothing could distract her. It said in my mother's home health book that a young girl should not be allowed to make that sort of demand on her strength, but when I showed Louisa the very page on which those words were printed, she just told me to mind my own business. She was always running around barefoot with her braids flying and her bonnet askew. I don't know when girls stopped wearing sunbonnets, or why they ever did wear them. If they were supposed to keep off freckles, I can tell you they didn't work.

I've always envied men who could watch their wives grow old. Boughton lost his wife five years ago, and he married before I did. His oldest boy has snow-white hair. His grandchildren are mostly married. And as for me, it is still true that I will never see a child of mine grow up and I will never see a wife of mine grow old. I've shepherded a good many people through their lives, I've baptized babies by the hundred, and all that time I have felt as though a great part of life was closed to me. Your mother says I was like Abraham. But I had no old wife and no promise of a child. I was just getting by on books and baseball and fried-egg sandwiches.

You and the cat have joined me in my study. Soapy is on my lap and you are on your belly on the floor in a square of sunlight, drawing airplanes. Half an hour ago you were on my lap and Soapy was on her belly in the square of sunlight. And while you were on my lap you drew—so you told me—a Messerschmitt 109. That is it in the corner of the page. You know all the names from a book Leon Fitch gave you about a month ago, when my back was turned, as it seems to me, since he could not, surely, have imagined I'd approve. All your drawings look about like that one in the corner, but you give them different names—Spad and Fokker and Zero. You're always trying to get me to read the fine print about how many guns they have and how many bombs they carry. If my father were here, if I were my father, I'd find a way to make you think that the noble and manly thing would be to give the book back to old Fitch. I really should do that. But he means well. Maybe I'll just hide the thing in the pantry. When did you figure out about the pantry? That's where we always put anything we don't want you getting into. Now that I think about it, half the things in that pantry were always there so one or another of us wouldn't get into them.

I could have married again while I was still young. A congregation likes to have a married minister, and I was introduced to every niece and sister-in-law in a hundred miles. In retrospect, I'm very grateful for whatever reluctance it was that kept me alone until your mother came. Now that I look back, it seems to me that in all that deep darkness a miracle was preparing. So I am right to remember it as a blessed time, and myself as waiting in confidence, even if I had no idea what I was waiting for.

Then when your mother did come, when I still hardly knew her, she gave me that look of hers—no twinkle in that eye—and said, very softly and very seriously, "You ought to marry me." That was the first time in my life I ever knew what it was to love another human being. Not that I hadn't loved people before. But I hadn't realized what it *meant* to love them before. Not even my parents. Not even Louisa. I was so startled when she said that to me that for a minute I couldn't find any words to reply. So she walked away, and I had to follow her along the street. I still didn't have the courage to touch her sleeve, but I said, "You're right, I will." And she said, "Then I'll see you tomorrow," and kept on walking. That was the most thrilling thing that ever happened to me in my life. I could wish you such a moment as that one was, though when I think of everything that came before it, for me and for your dear mother, too, I'm not sure I should.

Here I am trying to be wise, the way a father should be, the way an old pastor certainly should be. I don't know what to say except that the worst misfortune isn't only misfortune—and even as I write those words, I have that infant Rebecca in my mind, the way she looked while I held her, which I seem to remember, because every single time I have christened a baby I have thought of her again. That feeling of a baby's brow against the palm of your hand—how I have loved this life. Boughton had christened her, as I said, but I laid my hand on her just to bless her, and I could feel her pulse, her warmth, the damp of her hair. The Lord said, "Their angels in Heaven always see the face of my Father in Heaven" (Matthew 18:10). That's why Boughton named her Angeline. Many, many people have found comfort in that verse.

I have been thinking about existence lately. In fact, I have been so full of admiration for existence that I have hardly been able to enjoy it properly. As I was walking up to the church this morning, I passed that row of big oaks by the war memorial— if you remember them—and I thought of another morning, fall a year or two ago, when they were dropping their acorns thick as hail almost. There was all sorts of thrashing in the leaves and there were acorns hitting the pavement so hard they'd fly past my head. All this in the dark, of course. I remember a slice of moon, no more than that. It was a very clear night, or morning, very still, and then there was such energy in the things transpiring among those trees, like a storm, like travail. I stood there a little out of range, and I thought, It is all still new to me. I have lived my life on the prairie and a line of oak trees can still astonish me.

I feel sometimes as if I were a child who opens its eyes on the world once and sees amazing things it will never know any names for and then has to close its eyes again. I know this is all mere apparition compared to what awaits us, but it is only lovelier for that. There is a human beauty in it. And I can't believe that, when we have all been changed and put on incorruptibility, we will forget our fantastic condition of mortality and impermanence, the great bright dream of procreating and perishing that meant the whole world to us. In eternity this world will be Troy, I believe, and all that has passed here will be the epic of the universe, the ballad they sing in the streets. Because I don't imagine any reality putting this one in the shade entirely, and I think piety forbids me to try.

Lacey Thrush died last night. Isn't that a name? Her mother was a Lacey. They were an old family here, but she was the last of the Laceys, and the Thrushes went on to California. She was a maiden lady. She died promptly and decorously, out of consideration for me, I suspect, since she has been concerned about my health. She was conscious half an hour, unconscious half an hour, and gone. We said the Lord's Prayer and the Twenty-third Psalm, then she wanted to hear "When I Survey the Wondrous Cross" one last time, so I sang and she hummed a little, and then she started nodding off. I am full of admiration for her. She's given me a lot to live up to, so to speak. At any rate, she didn't keep me awake past my bedtime, and the peacefulness of her sleep contributed mightily to the peacefulness of mine. These old saints bless us every chance they get.

Here is a story my grandfather and his friends used to tell, and chuckle over. I can't vouch for it entirely, since, talking among themselves the way they did, I doubt they'd have thought embellishing a story was quite the same thing as departing from the truth.

In any case, in some forgotten little abolitionist settlement around here, as soon as the people had set up a dry-goods store on one side of the road and a livery stable on the other, they set about building a tunnel between them. Tunneling was a popular activity at that time, and a great deal of ingenuity went into devising hiding places and routes of escape. The topsoil in Iowa goes down so deep that more and larger tunnels were possible here than in less favored regions, say in New England. In this part of the state the soil is also very sandy, of course.

Now, these were sensible and well-meaning people. But they became so absorbed in making this tunnel that they lost sight of certain practical considerations. They put so much zeal into it that it became a sort of subterranean civic monument. One of the old men said the only thing missing was a chandelier. Very simply, they made it too large, and too near the surface of the ground, and they couldn't brace it, either, since wood was so scarce on the prairie in those days that the lumber for such buildings as they had was carted in from Minnesota. Even thoughtful people have lapses of judgment from time to time.

When they had just about finished their digging, a stranger on a big black horse came through town. He paused in exactly the wrong spot to ask the name of the place, and he and his horse sank right through the road into that tunnel. When the dust settled, the horse was standing more or less shoulder deep in a hole. The man climbed off him and walked around and around him in a kind of wonderment, not drawing any conclusions at all, try as he might. And when the people came out to ponder this calamity, and took note of his bewilderment, they thought it best to be bewildered, too. So they just stood there with their arms folded, saying, "If that's not the dangedest thing," or words to that effect, and they discussed among themselves the risks that went with owning such a large horse. The poor thing began to struggle, of course, so somebody got a bucket of oats and poured a couple of bottles of whiskey over them, and the horse ate them and pretty soon it nodded off. Then the mood of the stranger became desolate, because the horse was not only standing in a hole but was also unconscious. This latter might not have seemed to crown his afflictions the way it did if he had not himself been a teetotaler. As it was, that snoring horse with its head lying there in the road was a spectacle of gloom for which he truly struggled to find words.

Now, settlements of that kind were the work of people of high religious principle, and they would have taken no pleasure at all in watching this unoffending stranger tear his beard and throw his hat at the ground. Well, of course they took a little pleasure in it. But it did seem best to them to get the fellow out of town as quickly as possible so they could deal with that horse, since any Bushwhacker coming up from Missouri or any slave hunter passing through would be liable to interpret the spectacle by the light of his own grudges and suspicions. So one of them offered to trade his horse for the one in the hole. You might think the fellow would have considered this trade advantageous, but in fact he sat on the stoop of the dry-goods store and weighed it for some time. The horse he was offered was a mare, smallish, which the stranger did allow was an advantage. He tried to look at her teeth and got nipped and cursed the luck that had brought him to that town, and asked to borrow a shovel so he could dig up his horse. So the preacher told him, solemnly, that they had lost all their shovels in a terrible fire. "We've got the blades all right, and you're welcome to the use of them," he said. "It's really just the handles we're missing." That was a lie, of course, but it was compelled by the urgency of the situation.

Finally the stranger agreed to accept the mare and her saddle and bridle and some odds and ends, twine and bootblack, which were meant to restore some part of his faith in cosmic justice, and which he accepted as poor recompense for his trouble, reasonably enough.

Once rid of him, the people of the settlement could begin to consider the problem of that horse. Some of the men went through the tunnel from either end to check the state of its legs, since if one was broken they would have to shoot the creature. Then they could have dismembered it as needed and pulled it underground and filled in the hole in the road so as to conceal it. But the legs were sound.

Excavating around the horse would only open more tunnel, but they decided that they had no other choice than to make a big enough excavation to allow them to walk the horse up out of that hole. In the meantime, there it was, sobering up, nickering and switching its tail. So they decided to lift a shed off what it had for a foundation and set it down over the horse there in the middle of the road. It was a small shed, so it had to be set over the horse at a diagonal, the length of the horse being, in effect, the hypotenuse of two right triangles.

All this seems preposterous. But in fact one lapse of judgment can quickly create a situation in which only foolish choices are possible. Someone noticed that the horse's tail was lying out on the road, so they had to put a child through the shed window to gather it in.

As it happened, there was a young Negro fellow in the settlement at that time, the first fugitive to make his way there.

This made the people feel serious and purposeful, and it also heightened their embarrassment about the matter of the horse. The young man, who stayed in the dry-goods store unless there was some ground for alarm, saw and heard everything. And it was pretty obvious how much he wanted to laugh. He was just lolling and languishing with the effort it cost him not to do it. He avoided their eyes, and he bit his lips almost raw. When the shed had been walked down to the road, and just as it was being set crosswise over the horse, there came from the store one harsh, painful, unwilled whoop of laughter.

It was at that point they bethought themselves of the fact that the fellow might be feeling some justifiable alarm having to do with the question of their good sense. And indeed it was that very night he did escape, so to speak, and headed north on his own, no doubt rightly concluding that so much had happened to make the region suspect that he had best get some distance from it.

When they realized what had happened, a couple of the men rode after him on the two fairly serviceable horses that had not been traded for the horse in the hole (they wanted to be sure the stranger got far enough away not to trouble coming back, so it was their best horse they had given him). In any case, they hoped to overtake the fugitive in order to provide him with some food and clothes and direct him to the next abolitionist settlement, but for two days he eluded them. Then, when they had stopped for the night and were lying down to sleep, he stepped out of the dark and said, "I thank y'all kindly, but I think I best do this on my own." They handed him the bundle they had brought for him and he stepped back into the dark and said, "Y'all get that horse out yet?" and laughed a little, and that was the last they heard of him.

They did dig a sloping trench they could walk the horse up, so that worked out well enough. But then they had to deal with the fact that a tunnel is a hard thing to be rid of. They had taken pains, when they were digging it, to scatter the dirt they removed as widely as possible, to conceal the excavation, and there was of course no way to reverse that process. And while they had made the tunnel secretly and at leisure, they were obliged to unmake it openly and in haste. The edges around the hole kept crumbling, falling in, exposing more of it every day. (They had removed that shed, prudently, since a shed in a hole in the middle of the road would be no easier to account for than a horse.) The quickest solution would have been to collapse the tunnel altogether and fill it in from the top, but then the path it made from the store to the stables would have been visible immediately and indefinitely. So they chose a hill to level and began carting earth into the tunnel day and night, having placed a lookout on the roof of the dry-goods store to signal the approach of strangers. If asked, they would say they were constructing terraces, as in a certain book the preacher had which illustrated the customs of the Orient. I suppose that was the best they could do in the circumstances.

These were hardworking people, but there is simply no way in the world to pack soil from the side, or in any wise to pack it and settle it as firmly as rain and snow and heat have done in the years since the world began. That is to say, with all their hard work to undo all the hard work they had done, with the first good rain the road sagged from one end of that tunnel to the other. Then they began filling it from the top, having no other choice and nothing at all to lose. And still it sagged as often as there was a good rain.

So when the winter finally came and there was a hard freeze and snow, they pried up the few buildings they had and set them on planks and hitched their horses to them and moved the town, such as it was, half a mile down the road. They had to pry up their grave markers to hide where the town had been, and that was a sad thing, though there weren't more than three or four. The tunnel became a kind of creek bed, a freshet in the spring, with nice grassy banks and flowers that had run wild from the old gardens. People who didn't know better would picnic beside it, spreading their blankets and baskets over those poor, forgotten graves, which was, on balance, a pleasant thing.

You and Tobias are hopping around in the sprinkler. The sprinkler is a magnificent invention because it exposes raindrops to sunshine. That does occur in nature, but it is rare. When I was in seminary I used to go sometimes to watch the Baptists down at the river. It was something to see the preacher lifting the one who was being baptized up out of the water and the water pouring off the garments and the hair. It did look like a birth or a resurrection. For us the water just heightens the touch of the pastor's hand on the sweet bones of the head, sort of like making an electrical connection. I've always loved to baptize people, though I have sometimes wished there were more shimmer and splash involved in the way we go about it. Well, but you two are dancing around in your iridescent little downpour, whooping and stomping as sane people ought to do when they encounter a thing so miraculous as water.

During those days after Edward came back from Germany, he was so much on my mind that I kept slipping away to look for him at the hotel. One time I took my baseball and glove and my father's glove and we walked down to a side street and played some catch. At first he was careful of his clothes. He hadn't even seen a baseball in years, he said. But when he got warmed up a little, he was pretty sharp. He threw one that stung my hand, and when I said "Ow!" he laughed with pleasure, because it meant he had his arm back. It wouldn't have stung, though, except that I didn't expect it to be coming hard and I wasn't ready. So then we really started firing. I threw one high and he jumped for it, a lovely catch. By then he was in shirtsleeves with his collar open and his suspenders hanging down at his sides. Some people stood around watching us. It was a dusty little street and a hot day and we were throwing flies and grounders. Edward asked a girl for a glass of water. She brought us each one. I drank mine, but he poured his right over his head, and it spilled off that big mustache of his like rain off a roof.

I thought after that day we would sometime be able to talk. That did not prove to be the case. All the same, after that day I did feel pretty much at ease about the state of his soul. Though of course I am not competent to judge.

Here is what he said, standing there with his hair all plastered to his head and his mustache dripping.

Behold, how good and how pleasant it is,
For brethren to dwell together in unity!
It is like the precious oil upon the head,
That ran down upon the beard;
Even Aaron's beard;
That came down upon the skirt of his garments
Like the dew of Hermon,
That cometh down upon the mountains of Zion.

That is from Psalm 133. It meant he knew everything I knew, every single word. Perhaps he was telling me that he knew everything I knew and he was not persuaded by it. Still, I have often thought what a splendid thing that was for him to do. I wished my father had been there, because I knew it would have made him laugh. He still had a decent arm for a man his age. I, being very young at the time, believed they would never reconcile, and I was surprised that Edward could take the whole situation as calmly as he seemed to. I told him I had begun reading Feuerbach, and he wiggled his big eyebrows at me and said, "Don't you let your mama catch you doing that!"

When I say that my reputation for piety and probity and so on may be a bit exaggerated, I would not wish you to believe therefore that I have taken my vocation lightly. It has been my whole life. I even kept up my Greek and Hebrew pretty well. Boughton and I used to go through the texts we were going to preach on, word by word. He'd come here, to my house, because his house was full of children. He'd bring a nice warm supper in a basket that his wife or his daughters would fix for us. I used to dread walking into his house, because it made mine seem so empty. And Boughton could tell that, he knew it.

Four girls and four boys he had, robustious little heathens, every one of them, as he said himself. But good fortune is not only good fortune, and over the years things happened in that family that caused some terrible regret. Still, for years it all seemed to me to be blindingly beautiful. And it was.

We had some very pleasant evenings here in my kitchen. Boughton is a staunch Presbyterian—as if there were another kind. So we have had our disagreements, though never grave enough to do any harm.

I don't think it was resentment I felt then. It was some sort of loyalty to my own life, as if I wanted to say, I have a wife, too, I have a child, too. It was as if the price of having them was losing them, and I couldn't bear the implication that even that price could be too high. They say an infant can't see when it is as young as your sister was, but she opened her eyes, and she looked at me. She was such a little bit of a thing. But while I was holding her, she opened her eyes. I know she didn't really study my face. Memory can make a thing seem to have been much more than it was. But I know she did look right into my eyes. That is something. And I'm glad I knew it at the time, because now, in my present situation, now that I am about to leave this world, I realize there is nothing more astonishing than a human face. Boughton and I have talked about that, too. It has something to do with incarnation. You feel your obligation to a child when you have seen it and held it. Any human face is a claim on you, because you can't help but understand the singularity of it, the courage and loneliness of it. But this is truest of the face of an infant. I consider that to be one kind of vision, as mystical as any. Boughton agrees.

I was so frightened of you when you were a little baby. I would sit in the rocking chair and your mother would put you in my arms and I would just rock and pray until she finished whatever it was she had to do. I used to sing, too, "Go to Dark Gethsemane," until she asked me if I didn't know a happier song. I wasn't even aware of what I was singing.

This morning I have been trying to think about heaven, but without much success. I don't know why I should expect to have any idea of heaven. I could never have imagined this world if I hadn't spent almost eight decades walking around in it. People talk about how wonderful the world seems to children, and that's true enough. But children think they will grow into it and understand it, and I know very well that I will not, and would not if I had a dozen lives. That's clearer to me every day. Each morning I'm like Adam waking up in Eden, amazed at the cleverness of my hands and at the brilliance pouring into my mind through my eyes—old hands, old eyes, old mind, a very diminished Adam altogether, and still it is just remarkable. What of me will I still have? Well, this old body has been a pretty good companion. Like Balaam's ass, it's seen the angel I haven't seen yet, and it's lying down in the path.

And I must say, too, that my mind, with all its deficiencies, has certainly kept me interested. There's quite a bit of poetry in it that I learned over the years, and a pretty decent vocabulary, much of it unused. And Scripture. I never knew it the way my father did, or his father. But I know it pretty well. I certainly should. When I was younger than you are now, my father would give me a penny every time I learned five verses so that I could repeat them without a mistake. And then he'd make a game of saying a verse, and I had to say the next one. We could go on and on like that, sometimes till we came to a genealogy, or we just got tired. Sometimes we'd take roles: he'd be Moses and I'd be Pharaoh, he'd be the Pharisees and I'd be the Lord. That's how he was brought up, too, and it was a great help to me when I went to seminary. And through the whole of my life.

You know the Lord's Prayer and the Twenty-third Psalm and Psalm 100. And I heard your mother teaching you the Beatitudes last night. She seems to want me to know that she will bring you up in the faith, and that's a wonderful effort for her to make, because frankly, I never knew anyone in my life with a smaller acquaintance with religion than she had when I first knew her. An excellent woman, but unschooled in Scripture, and in just about everything else, according to her, and that may be true. I say this with all respect.

And yet there always was that wonderful seriousness about her. When she first came to church she would sit in the corner at the back of the sanctuary, and still I would feel as if she were the only real listener. I had a dream once that I was preaching to Jesus Himself, saying any foolish thing I could think of, and He was sitting there in His white, white robe looking patient and sad and amazed. That's what it felt like. Afterward I would think, That did it, she'll never come back, and then the next Sunday there she'd be. And once again, the sermon I'd spent the week on would be ashes in my mouth. That happened before I even knew her name.

I had an interesting talk this morning with Mr. Schmidt, T.'s father. It seems he overheard some inappropriate language. I'd overheard it, too, in fact, since it has been the favorite joke between the two of you for the last week. I'll admit I didn't see the need to object. We said the same thing when we were children and emerged unscathed, I believe. One of you asks, in a naïve and fluting voice, AB, CD goldfish? And the other replies in the deepest voice he can muster, a voice full of worldliness and scorn, L, MNO goldfish! And then outrageous and extravagant laughter. (It is the L, need I say, that has disturbed Mr. Schmidt.) That young man was very earnest, and I had a terrible time keeping a straight face. I said gravely that, in my experience, it is better not to attempt too strict an isolation of children, that prohibition loses its force if it is invoked too generally. He finally deferred to my white hair and my vocation, though he did ask me twice if I was Unitarian.

I told Boughton about this, and he said, "I have ong fet that etter ought to be excuded from the aphabet." Then he laughed, tickled with himself. He has been in high spirits since he heard from Jack. "He'll be *home* soon!" he said. When I asked him where he was coming from, Boughton said, "Well, the postmark on his letter said St. Louis."

I won't tell your mother about my talk with Mr. Schmidt.

She wants very much for you to keep your friend. She suffered when you didn't have one. She suffers for your sake much more than she should. She always imagines the fault is with her, even where it appears to me there is no fault at all.

She told me the other day she wants to read those old sermons that are up in the attic, and I believe she will do that, I really do. Not all of them—that would take years. Well, perhaps I can get a box of them down here somehow and do a little sorting. It would put my mind at ease to feel I was leaving a better impression. So often I have known, right there in the pulpit, even as I read the words, how far they fell short of any hopes I had for them. And they were the major work of my life, from a certain point of view. I have to wonder how I have lived with that.

Today was Lord's Supper, and I preached on Mark 14:22, "And as they were eating, he took bread, and when he had blessed, he brake it, and gave to them, and said, Take ye: this is my body." Normally I would not preach on the Words of Institution themselves when the Sacrament is the most beautiful illumination of them there could be. But I have been thinking a great deal about the body these last weeks. Blessed and broken. I used Genesis 32:23–32 as the Old Testament text, Jacob wrestling with the Angel. I wanted to talk about the gift of physical particularity and how blessing and sacrament are mediated through it. I have been thinking lately how I have loved my physical life.

In any case, and you may remember this, when almost everyone had left and the elements were still on the table and the candles still burning, your mother brought you up the aisle to me and said, "You ought to give him some of that." You're too young, of course, but she was completely right. Body of

Christ, broken for you. Blood of Christ, shed for you. Your solemn and beautiful child face lifted up to receive these mysteries at my hands. They are the most wonderful mystery, body and blood.

It was an experience I might have missed. Now I only fear I will not have time enough to fully enjoy the thought of it.

The light in the room was beautiful this morning, as it often is. It's a plain old church and it could use a coat of paint. But in the dark times I used to walk over before sunrise just to sit there and watch the light come into that room. I don't know how beautiful it might seem to anyone else. I felt much at peace those mornings, praying over very dreadful things sometimes—the Depression, the wars. That was a lot of misery for people around here, decades of it. But prayer brings peace, as I trust you know.

In those days, as I have said, I might spend most of a night reading. Then, if I woke up still in my armchair, and if the clock said four or five, I'd think how pleasant it was to walk through the streets in the dark and let myself into the church and watch dawn come in the sanctuary. I loved the sound of the latch lifting. The building has settled into itself so that when you walk down the aisle, you can hear it yielding to the burden of your weight. It's a pleasanter sound than an echo would be, an obliging, accommodating sound. You have to be there alone to hear it. Maybe it can't feel the weight of a child. But if it is still standing when you read this, and if you are not half a world away, sometime you might go there alone, just to see what I mean. After a while I did begin to wonder if I liked the church better with no people in it.

I know they're planning to pull it down. They're waiting me out, which is kind of them.

———

People are always up in the night, with their colicky babies and their sick children, or fighting or worrying or full of guilt. And, of course, the milkmen and all the people on early shifts and late shifts. Sometimes when I walked past the house of one of my own families and saw lights on, I'd think maybe I should stop and see if there was a problem I could help with, but then I'd decide it might be an intrusion and I'd go on. Past the Boughtons' house, too. It was years before I really knew what was troubling them, close as we had always been. It was on the nights I didn't sleep at all and I didn't feel like reading that I'd walk through town at one or two o'clock. In the old days I could walk down every single street, past every house, in about an hour. I'd try to remember the people who lived in each one, and whatever I knew about them, which was often quite a lot, since many of the ones who weren't mine were Boughton's. And I'd pray for them. And I'd imagine peace they didn't expect and couldn't account for descending on their illness or their quarreling or their dreams. Then I'd go into the church and pray some more and wait for daylight. I've often been sorry to see a night end, even while I have loved seeing the dawn come.

Trees sound different at night, and they smell different, too.

If you remember me at all, you may find me explained a little by what I am telling you. If you could see me not as a child but as a grown man, it is surely true that you would observe a certain crepuscular quality in me. As you read this, I hope you will understand that when I speak of the long night that preceded these days of my happiness, I do not remember grief and loneliness so much as I do peace and comfort—grief, but never without comfort; loneliness, but never without peace. Almost never.

———

Once when Boughton and I had spent an evening going through our texts together and we were done talking them over, I walked him out to the porch, and there were more fireflies out there than I had ever seen in my life, thousands of them everywhere, just drifting up out of the grass, extinguishing themselves in midair. We sat on the steps a good while in the dark and the silence, watching them. Finally Boughton said, "Man is born to trouble as the sparks fly upward." And really, it was that night as if the earth were smoldering. Well, it was, and it is. An old fire will make a dark husk for itself and settle in on its core, as in the case of this planet. I believe the same metaphor may describe the human individual, as well. Perhaps Gilead. Perhaps civilization. Prod a little and the sparks will fly. I don't know whether the verse put a blessing on the fireflies or the fireflies put a blessing on the verse, or if both of them together put a blessing on trouble, but I have loved them both a good deal ever since.

There has been a telephone call from Jack Boughton, that is, from John Ames Boughton, my namesake. He is still in St. Louis, and still planning to come home. Glory came to tell me about it, excited and also anxious. She said, "Papa was just so thrilled to hear his voice." I suppose he'll appear sooner or later. I don't know how one boy could have caused so much disappointment without ever giving anyone any grounds for hope. Man, I should say, since he's well into his thirties. No, he must be forty by now. He is not the eldest or the youngest or the best or the bravest, only the most beloved. I suppose I might tell you a story about him, too, or as much of it as behooves me. Another time. I must reflect on it first. When I've had a little opportunity to talk with him, I might decide all that trouble is well forgotten and write nothing about it.

Old Boughton is so eager to see him. Perhaps anxious as well as eager. He has some fine children, yet it always seemed this was the one on whom he truly set his heart. The lost sheep, the lost coin. The prodigal son, not to put too fine a point on it. I have said at least once a week my whole adult life that there is an absolute disjunction between our Father's love and our deserving. Still, when I see this same disjunction between human parents and children, it always irritates me a little. (I know you will be and I hope you are an excellent man, and I will love you absolutely if you are not.)

This morning I did a foolish thing. I woke up in the dark, and that put me in mind to walk over to the church the way I used to. I did leave a note, and your mother found it, so it wasn't as bad as it might have been, I suppose. (The note was an afterthought, I admit.) She seemed to think I'd gone off by myself to breathe my last—which would not be a bad idea, to my way of thinking. I have worried some about those last hours. This is another thing you know and I don't—how this ends. That is to say, how my life will seem to you to have ended. That's a matter of great concern to your mother, as it is to me, of course. But I have trouble remembering that I can't trust my body not to fail me suddenly. I don't feel bad most of the time. The pains are infrequent enough that I forget now and then.

The doctor told me I had to be careful getting up from a chair. He also told me not to climb stairs, which would mean giving up my study, a thing I can't yet bring myself to do. He also told me to take a shot of brandy every day, which I do, in the morning, standing in the pantry with the curtain drawn for your sake. Your mother thinks that's very funny. She says, "It'd do you a lot more good if you enjoyed it a little," but that's how my mother did her drinking, and I'm a traditionalist. The last time she took you to the doctor, he said you might be more robust if you had your tonsils out. She came home so sick at the thought he could find any fault with you that I gave her a dose of my medicinal brandy.

She wants to move my books down to the parlor and set me up there, and I may agree to that, just to spare her worry. I told her I could not add a moment to my span of life, and she said, "Well, I don't want you to go subtracting one from it, either." A year ago she would have said "neither." I've always loved the way she talks, but she thinks she has to improve for your sake.

I walked up to the church in the dark, as I said. There was a very bright moon. It's strange how you never quite get used to the world at night. I have seen moonlight strong enough to cast shadows any number of times. And the wind is the same wind, rustling the same leaves, night or day. When I was a young boy I used to get up before every dawn of the world to fetch water and firewood. It was a very different life then. I remember walking out into the dark and feeling as if the dark were a great, cool sea and the houses and the sheds and the woods were all adrift in it, just about to ease off their moorings. I always felt like an intruder then, and I still do, as if the darkness had a claim on everything, one that I violated just by stepping out my door. This morning the world by moonlight seemed to be an immemorial acquaintance I had always meant to befriend. If there was ever a chance, it has passed. Strange to say, I feel a little that way about myself.

In any case, it felt so necessary to me to walk up the road to the church and let myself in and sit there in the dark waiting for the dawn to come that I forgot all about the worry I might be causing your mother. It is actually hard for me to remember how mortal I am these days. There are pains, as I said, but not so frequent or even so severe when they come that I am as alarmed by them as I should be.

I must try to be more mindful of my condition. I started to lift you up into my arms the other day, the way I used to when you weren't quite so big and I wasn't quite so old. Then I saw your mother watching me with pure apprehension and I realized what a foolish thing to do that was. I just always loved the feeling of how strongly you held on, as if you were a monkey up in a tree. Boy skinniness and boy strength.

But I have strayed a little from my subject, that is to say, from your begats. And there is a good deal more to tell you. My grandfather was in the Union Army, as I think I have said. He thought he should go as a regular soldier, but they told him he was too old. They told him Iowa had a graybeard regiment he could join, for old fellows, which wouldn't go into combat but would guard supplies and rail lines and so on. That idea didn't please him at all. He finally talked them into letting him go as a chaplain. He hadn't brought along any sort of credentials, but my father said he just showed them his Greek New Testament and that was good enough. I still have that somewhere, what remains of it. It fell into a river, as I was told, and never got dried out properly till it was fairly ruined. As I remember the story, he was caught up in a disorderly retreat, in a rout, in fact. That is the same Bible that was sent to my father from Kansas, before we set out to find the old man's grave.

My father was born in Kansas, as I was, because the old man had come there from Maine just to help Free Soilers establish the right to vote, because the constitution was going to be voted on that would decide whether Kansas entered the Union slave or free. Quite a few people went out there at that time for that reason. And, of course, so did people from Missouri who wanted Kansas for the South. So things were badly out of hand for a while. All best forgotten, my father used to say. He didn't like mention of those times, and that did cause some hard feelings between him and his father. I've read up on those events considerably, and I've decided my father was right. And that's just as well, because people have forgotten. Remarkable things went on, certainly, but there has been so much trouble in the world since then it's hard to find time to think about Kansas.

We came to this house when I was still a small boy. We had no electricity for years, just kerosene lamps. No radio. I was remembering how my mother used to love her kitchen. Of course it was very different then, with an icebox and a pump sink and a pie safe and a woodstove. That old table is about all that is the same, and the pantry. She had her rocker so close to the stove that she could open the oven door without getting up. She said it was to keep things from burning. She said we couldn't afford the waste, which was true. She burned things often enough anyway, more often as the years passed, and we ate them anyway, so at least there wasn't any waste. She loved the warmth of that stove, but it put her to sleep, especially if she'd been doing the wash or putting up preserves. Well, bless her heart, she had lumbago, and she had rheumatism, too, and she did take a little whiskey for it. She never slept well during the nights. I suppose I got that from her. She'd wake up if the cat sneezed, she said, but then she'd sleep through the immolation of an entire Sunday dinner two feet away from her. That would be on a Saturday, because our family was pretty strict on Sabbath-keeping. So we'd know for an entire day beforehand what we had to look forward to, burned peas and scorched applesauce I remember particularly.

Your mother was startled the first time I mentioned to her that she might as well not do the ironing on a Sunday evening. It's such hard work for her to stop working that I don't know what I have accomplished by speaking to her about the day of rest. She wants to know the customs, though, and she takes them to heart, the Good Lord knows. It was such a relief to her to find out that studying didn't count as work. I never thought it did, anyway. So now she sits at the dinner table and copies out poems and phrases she likes, and facts of one sort and another. This is mainly for you. It is because I'll be gone and she'll have to be the one to set an example. She said, "You'd better show me what books I got to read." So I pulled down old John Donne, who has in fact meant a lot to me all these years. "One short sleepe past, wee wake eternally, / And death shall be no more; death, thou shalt die." There are some very fine lines in Donne. I hope you will read him, if you have not read him yet. Your mother's trying to like him. I do wish, though, that I could afford to own some new books. I have mostly theology, and some old travel books from before the wars. I'm pretty sure a lot of the treasures and monuments I like to read about now and then don't even exist anymore.

Your mother goes to the public library, which has been down on its luck for a long time, like most things around here. Last time she brought back a copy of *The Trail of the Lonesome Pine* that was worn ragged, all held together with tape. She just sank into it, though, she just melted into it. And I made scrambled eggs and toasted cheese sandwiches for our supper so she wouldn't have to put the book down. I read it years ago when everyone else did. I don't remember enjoying it particularly.

When I was a boy I knew of a murder out in the country where the weapon, a bowie knife, was said to have been thrown into the river. All the children talked about it. An old farmer was attacked from behind in his barn while he was milking. The main suspect was known to have had a bowie knife, because he was proud of it, always showing it around. So they came near hanging him, I guess, since he couldn't produce that knife and nobody else could find it. They thought he must have thrown it in the river. But his lawyer pointed out that someone, maybe a stranger, could have stolen it from him and done the crime and thrown the knife in the river, or just walked off with it, which seemed reasonable enough. Besides, he was certainly not the only man in the world with a knife of that kind. And no one could come up with any sort of motive. So they let him go, finally.

Then nobody knew whom to be scared of, which was terrible. The man who had owned the knife just drifted away. There were rumors from time to time that he was in the area, and he may well have been, poor devil, since he had a sister there and not another soul in the world. The rumors usually circulated right around Christmas.

I worried about all this a great deal, because once my father took me with him to throw a gun into the river. My grandfather had a pistol he'd picked up in Kansas before the war. When he took off west, he left an old army blanket at my father's house, a bundle rolled up and tied with twine. When we learned he'd died out there, we opened it. There were some old shirts that had been white once and a few dozen sermons and some other papers wrapped with twine, and the pistol. Of course it was the pistol that interested me most. And I was a good deal older than you are now. But my father was disgusted. These things my grandfather had left were just an offense to him. So he buried them.

The hole he dug must have been four feet deep. I was impressed at the work he put into it. Then he dropped that bundle into the hole and started filling it in. I asked him why he was burying the sermons, too—at the time I naturally thought anything with handwriting on it was probably a sermon, and this did turn out to be the case. There were some letters, too. I know because not an hour after he'd put it in the ground my father went out and dug it all up again. He put the shirts and the papers aside and buried that gun again. Then a month or so later he dug it up and threw it in the river. If he had left it in the ground, it would be just about under the back fence, maybe a foot or two beyond it.

He didn't say anything to me. Well, he said, "You leave that be," when he dropped that big old gun back into the hole. Then he gave me the sermons to hold while he shook out those shirts and folded them up. He told me to carry the papers into the house, which I did, and he filled in the hole again. He stamped it down and stamped it down. Then about a month later he dug the pistol up again and set it on a stump and broke it up the best he could with a maul he had borrowed and he tied it up in a piece of burlap, and he and I walked to the river, a good way downstream from where we usually went to fish, and he flung the pieces of it as far as he could into the water. I got the impression he wished they didn't exist at all, that he wouldn't really have been content to drop them in the ocean, that he'd have set about to retrieve them again from any depth at all if he'd thought of a way to make them vanish entirely. It was a big old pistol, as I have said, with ornaments on the handle sort of like you see on cast-iron radiators. It seems I can remember the cold of it and the weight of it and the smell of iron it would have left on my hands. But I know my father never did let me touch it. I suppose it would have been nickel, anyway. Frankly, I thought there must have been some terrible crime involved in all this, because my father had never really told me the substance of his quarrel with his father.

He rinsed out those two old shirts at the pump and hung them up by their tails on my mother's clothesline, preparing to burn them, I was sure. They were stained and yellow, miserable-looking things, with the wind dragging their sleeves back and forth. They looked beaten and humiliated, hanging there head down, so to speak, the way you'd hang up a deer to dress it. My mother came out and took them right back down. In those days there was a lot of pride involved in the way a woman's wash looked, especially the white things. It was difficult work. My mother couldn't have dreamed of an electrical wringer or an agitator. She'd rub the laundry clean on a washboard. Then it would all be so beautiful and white. It really was remarkable. And all the women did it, every Monday of the world. When the electricity first came in, they ran it before dawn and at suppertime, to help with the chores, and a few hours extra on Mondays, to help with the wash.

Well, my mother couldn't tolerate the state those pitiful shirts were in. She had a strong sense that the population at large judged her character by what appeared on her clothesline, and I can't say she was wrong. But there was more in her mind than that. My father had a favorite verse of Scripture: "For all the armor of the armed man in the tumult, and the garments rolled in blood, shall be for burning, for fuel of fire." That is Isaiah 9:5. My mother must have felt she knew what he meant to do and felt there was disrespect in it. In any case, she took those shirts and scrubbed them and soaked them overnight and bleached them and rinsed them in bluing till they looked all right except for a few black stains she said were India ink and the brown stains which were blood. She hung them under the grape arbor, where no one would see them. Then she brought them in and ironed them with enormous care, singing while she did it, and when she was done they looked as respectable as their stains and their wounds would allow. Then she folded them—they were so white and polished they looked like marble busts—and she slipped them into a flour sack, and she buried them out by the fence, under the roses. My parents were not always of one mind.

I should dig around a little and see if anything is left of those shirts. It would be a pity if they were sometime just cast out like refuse, after all her hard work. I myself think it would have been the decent thing to burn them.

I got up the courage to ask my father once if my grandfather had done something wrong and he said, "The Good Lord will judge what he did," which left me believing there had been some kind of crime for sure. There is one photograph of my grandfather around the house somewhere, taken in his old age, that might help you understand why I thought this way. It is a good likeness. It shows a wild-haired, one-eyed, scrawny old fellow with a crooked beard, like a paintbrush left to dry with lacquer in it, staring down the camera as if it had accused him of something terrible very suddenly, and he is still thinking how to reply and keeping the question at bay with the sheer ferocity of that stare. Of course there is guilt enough in the best life to account for a look like that.

So I was predisposed to believe that my grandfather had done something pretty terrible and my father was concealing the evidence and I was in on the secret, too—implicated without knowing what I was implicated in. Well, that's the human condition, I suppose. I believe I was implicated, and am, and would have been if I had never seen that pistol. It has been my experience that guilt can burst through the smallest breach and cover the landscape, and abide in it in pools and danknesses, just as native as water. I believe my father was trying to cover up for Cain, more or less. The things that happened in Kansas lay behind it all, as I knew at the time.

After that farmer was killed, all the kids I knew were scared to do the milking. They'd do it with the cow between them and the door if the cow would oblige, but they're particular about that sort of thing and often would not. Little sisters and brothers and dogs would be stationed outside the barn in the dark to watch for strangers. That went on for years, with the story passing down to the younger children, till whoever it was that did the murder would have been an old man. My father had to take over the milking because my brother was in too big a hurry to strip the udder, so the cow stopped giving the way she did before. Then the story went around that someone had been hiding in a henhouse, so all the kids were afraid to gather eggs, and overlooked them or cracked them because they were trying to hurry. Then someone was seen hiding in a woodshed and a root cellar and an attic. It was remarkable what a change came over that place, and how it persisted among the children, especially the younger ones, who didn't remember the time before the murder and thought all that fear was just natural. Chores really mattered in those days, and if every farm in three or four counties lost a pint of milk and a few eggs every day or two for twenty years, it would have added up. I do not know but what the children may still be hearing some version of that old story, and still be dreading their chores, still draining away the local prosperity.

Every one of us had bolted out of a barn or a woodshed when a shadow moved or there was a thump of some kind, so there were always more stories to tell. I remember once Louisa said we ought to pray for the man's conversion. Her thought was that it would be better to go to the source of the problem than to keep praying for divine intervention on behalf of each one of us in every situation of possible danger. She said it would also protect people who had never heard of him and would not think to pray before they did their milking. This struck us as wise and parent-like, and we did, indeed, pray for him concertedly, to what effect only the Lord knows. But if you or Tobias happen to hear this story, I can promise you that the villain is probably about one hundred by this time, and no longer a threat to anyone.

I did know a little about the shirts and the gun because of a quarrel my father and grandfather had had. My grandfather, who of course went to church with us, had stood up and walked out about five minutes into my father's sermon. The text, I remember, was "Consider the lilies, how they grow." My mother sent me to look for him. I saw him walking down the road and I ran to catch up with him, but he turned that eye on me and said, "Get back where you belong!" So I did.

He appeared at the house after dinner. He walked into the kitchen where my mother and I were clearing things away and cut himself a piece of bread and was about to leave again without a single word to us. But my father came up the porch steps just then and stood in the doorway, watching him.

"Reverend," my grandfather said when he saw him.

My father said, "Reverend."

My mother said, "It's Sunday. It's the Lord's Day. It's the Sabbath."

My father said, "We are all well aware of that." But he didn't step out of the doorway. So she said to my grandfather, "Sit down and I'll fix a plate for you. You can't get by on a piece of bread."

And he did sit down. So my father came in and sat down across from him. They were silent for some time.

Then my father said, "Did my sermon offend you in some way? Those few words you heard of it?"

The old man shrugged. "Nothing in it to offend. I just wanted to hear some *preach*ing. So I went over to the Negro church."

After a minute my father asked, "Well, did you hear some preaching?"

My grandfather shrugged. "The text was 'Love your enemies.' "

"That seems to me to be an excellent text in the circumstances," my father said. This was just after somebody set that fire behind the church that I mentioned earlier.

The old man said, "Very Christian."

My father said, "You sound disappointed, Reverend."

My grandfather put his head in his hands. He said, "Reverend, no words could be bitter enough, no day could be long enough. There is just no end to it. Disappointment. I eat and drink it. I wake and sleep it."

My father's lips were white. He said, "Well, Reverend, I know you placed great hope in that war. My hopes are in peace, and I am not disappointed. Because peace is its own reward. Peace is its own justification."

My grandfather said, "And that's just what kills my heart, Reverend. That the Lord never came to you. That the seraphim never touched a coal to your lips—"

My father stood up from his chair. He said, "I remember when you walked to the pulpit in that shot-up, bloody shirt with that pistol in your belt. And I had a thought as powerful and clear as any revelation. And it was, This has *nothing* to do with Jesus. Nothing. Nothing. And I was, and I am, as certain of that as anyone could ever be of any so-called vision. I defer to no one in this. Not to you, not to Paul the Apostle, not to John the Divine. Reverend."

My grandfather said, "So-called vision. The Lord, standing there beside me, had one hundred times the reality for me that you have standing here now!"

After a minute my father said, "No one would doubt that, Reverend."

And that was when a chasm truly opened. Not long afterward my grandfather was gone. He left a note lying on the kitchen table which said:

No good has come, no evil is ended.
That is your peace.
Without vision the people perish.
The Lord bless you and keep you.

I still have that note. I saved it in my Bible.

But I would watch my father preaching about Abel's blood crying out from the ground, and I'd wonder how he could speak about that the way he did. I had so much respect for my father. I felt certain that he should hide the guilt of his father, and that I should also hide the guilt of mine. I loved him with the strangest, most miserable passion when he stood there preaching about how the Lord hates falsehood and how in the end all our works will be exposed in the naked light of truth.

In course of time I learned that my grandfather was involved pretty deeply in the violence in Kansas before the war.

And as I've said, it was a source of contention between the two of them, to the point that they had agreed never to speak of Kansas anymore at all. So I believe my father was disgusted to find that those souvenirs, so to speak, had been left in his house. That was before we went to Kansas to find the old man's grave. I think that fierce anger against him was one of the things my father felt he truly had to repent of.

But my father did hate war. He nearly died in 1914, from pneumonia, the doctors said, but I have no doubt it was mainly from rage and exasperation. There were big celebrations all over Europe at the start of the war, as if the most wonderful thing were about to happen. And there were big celebrations here when we got involved. Parades and marching bands. And we already knew what a miserable thing it was we were sending our troops off to. I didn't read a newspaper for four years without pitying my father. He saw that trouble in Kansas, and then his father went off to the army. He did, too, finally, just before it ended. He had four sisters and a brother younger than he was, and his mother wasn't well. She died young, in her forties, and left all those children to care for themselves and to be cared for by their father and my father and the neighbors and the kindlier souls in his congregation, or what remained of it. His brother, my uncle Edwards, ran off, or so they hoped. At least he disappeared, and in the confusion of the times they never found him. He was named after the theologian Jonathan Edwards, who was much revered in my grandfather's generation. And Edward was named after my uncle, with the final *s*, but he never liked it, and he dropped it when he left for college.

Glory has come to tell me Jack Boughton is home. He is having supper in his father's house this very night. He will come by to pay his respects, she said, in the next day or two. I am grateful for the warning. I will use the time to prepare myself. Boughton named him for me because he thought he might not have another son and I most likely would not have any child at all. It was very kind of him. As it happened, in fourteen months he was blessed with another boy, Theodore Dwight Weld Boughton, who has a medical degree and a doctorate in theology and runs a hospital for the destitute somewhere in Mississippi. He is a great credit to the family. Jack said once he was glad not to be the only one of them who ever got his name in the newspaper. That was a pretty bitter joke, considering how hard his parents took the embarrassments he exposed them to. And it was harder for them because of that way they have of printing the entire name. It was always John Ames Boughton.

While we two were wandering around lost in Kansas, my father told me a great many things, partly to pass the time, I suppose, and partly to explain as he could why he thought his father had come back there, and partly to explain why we needed to find him, that is to say his grave. My father said that in those days after he came back from the war, he used to go off and sit with the Quakers on the Sabbath. He said his father's church was half empty, and most of the people there were widows and orphans and mothers who had lost their sons. Some of the men brought sickness home from the camps— "camp fever," they called it—and their families went down with it. Some of the men had been in Andersonville and came back almost beyond saving. He said half the graves in the churchyard were new. And there was his father, preaching every Sunday on the divine righteousness manifested in it all. That would set the old women to weeping, he said, and then the children would start in. He couldn't bear it.

Now, I've tried to imagine myself in my grandfather's place. I don't know what else he could have said, what else he could have taken to be true. He did preach those young men into the war. And his church was hit terribly hard. They joined up first thing and stayed till it was over, so the Confederates got off a good many shots at them. He went with them, too, even though he'd have been well into his forties. And he lost that eye, and came back finally with it as healed as it was going to be. He was already so used to the loss of it that he seemed to have forgotten to send word to his family about it. It was commonplace, though, to have an injury or a scar of some kind after that war. So many amputations. When I was a boy, there were lots of old fellows around who were missing arms or legs. At least they seemed old to me then.

It was an honorable thing that my grandfather came back to his congregation and stayed with it, to look after those widows and orphans. The Methodists were gathering a church; they'd bought a piece of land just down the road, so his flock need not have stayed with him. And some did leave. I know this from one of those sermons my father buried and took out of the ground again. It remarked on the great attractiveness of Methodist preaching, and the youthfulness of the new minister, who had seen brief but honorable service in the Union cause. I've read that sermon a good many times. The ink ran on most of the others.

The new people and the young people were turning to the Methodists, who were holding outdoor meetings by the river, hundreds of them from all over the countryside, fishing and cooking and washing out their clothes and visiting with one another until about evening. Then there'd be torchlight and preaching and hymn singing into the night. My grandfather went down there, too, and he enjoyed it all very much. On Sundays he would open the doors and windows so that his people could hear the singing that came up from the river. He respected the Methodists because they had borne a great part of the burden of the war. He didn't believe they were the kind of people who would consent to put up with bishops for very much longer.

I suspect he knew he couldn't preach life back into a church that had lost as much as his had. He was hiring himself out as a sort of man of all work, repairing roofs and stoops, tutoring children, butchering hogs—everything you can think of, because what was left of his congregation couldn't pay him anything. Most people couldn't pay him more than a stewing hen or a few potatoes for the choring he did, either. Most of the time he did work just because it needed doing. He'd be splitting kindling at one house, chopping weeds at the next, "relieving the fatherless and widow," my father said (that's Psalm 146). And he wrote any number of letters to the War Department, trying to get the veterans and the widows their bounties and pensions, which came never or slowly. There was an irony in this, because, my father said, he and his sisters were, in a manner of speaking, left fatherless during this time, which was a great hardship because it was clear that their mother would not live long.

He was a grown man by then, in his early twenties, and two of his sisters would have been nearly grown. They would have managed well enough if it hadn't been for their mother's poor health and her considerable suffering. I believe she must have had cancer of some kind. They'd had a doctor in that town, but he went off with the army and never came back. Whether he was killed or not no one knew, though there was a story told around that he caught a shell fragment at the side of his head and was never right afterward. In any case, doctors in those days weren't good for much. It was poultices and cod liver oil and mustard plaster or splints or stitches. Or brandy.

The neighbor women dosed his mother with tea of red clover blossoms, which probably didn't do her any harm, my father said. They also cut off her hair, because they thought it was draining away her strength. She cried when they showed it to her, and she said it was the one thing in her life she was ever proud of. My father said she was weary with the pain and she wasn't herself, but those words lingered with him, and with his sisters, too. In those days, and even when I was a child, women kept their hair long because they felt the Bible said they should (I Corinthians 11:15). But it would be cut off if they were sickly, and that was always a sad thing, a kind of shame for them, along with everything else they had to go through. So it hit her very hard. When my father spoke to his father about how low her spirits were, his father said, "You came back and I came back and we both have our health and the use of our limbs." My father took this to mean that since her grief was not in excess of the average in that region, he could not take any special time for it.

I believe the old reverend's errors were mainly the consequence of a sort of strenuousness in ethical matters that was to be admired finally. He did have many visions over the years, all very demanding of him, so he was less inclined than others to slack off. He lost his Greek Testament in a frantic retreat across a river, as I have said. I always felt there was a metaphor in that. The waters never parted for him, not once in his life, so far as I know. There was just no end to difficulty, and no mitigation of it. Then again, he always sought it out.

The Testament was mailed to him years afterward, from Alabama. Apparently some Confederate had gone to the bother of retrieving it and then finding out which company of which regiment they'd been chasing that day, and who the chaplain of it was. There might have been a bit of a taunt in the gesture, but it was appreciated anyway. The book was pretty well ruined. I hope you have it. It's the sort of thing that might appear to have no value at all.

I believe that the old man did indeed have far too narrow an idea of what a vision might be. He may, so to speak, have been too dazzled by the great light of his experience to realize that an impressive sun shines on us all. Perhaps that is the one thing I wish to tell you. Sometimes the visionary aspect of any particular day comes to you in the memory of it, or it opens to you over time. For example, whenever I take a child into my arms to be baptized, I am, so to speak, comprehended in the experience more fully, having seen more of life, knowing better what it means to affirm the sacredness of the human creature. I believe there are visions that come to us only in memory, in retrospect. That's the pulpit speaking, but it's telling the truth.

Today John Ames Boughton paid a call. I was sitting on the porch with the newspaper and your mother was tending her flowers and he just came walking through the gate and up the steps with his hand held out and a smile on his face. He said, "How are you doing, Papa?"—a name he called me in his childhood, because his parents encouraged it, I believe. I have preferred to think so. He had a precocious charm, if that is the word, and it would not have been beyond him to come up with it himself. I have never felt he was fond of me.

It did shock me how much he takes after his father, though of course in everything that matters they're like night and day. When he introduced himself to your mother as John Ames Boughton, she was visibly surprised, and he laughed. He looked at me and said, "I gather bygones are not bygones yet,

Reverend." What a thing to say! It was an oversight, though, not to have told her such a creature existed, that is, a namesake, a godson, more or less. You were out in the bushes somewhere looking for Soapy, who packs her bags every so often and takes off for parts unknown and worries the life out of you and your mother. You just happened to come around the house then, holding that old cat under the armpits. Her ears were flattened back and her eyes were patiently furious and her tail was twitching. It's so long you might have stepped on it otherwise. It was clear enough she would bolt if you put her down, but you did and she did and you didn't seem to notice because you were about to shake hands with John Ames Boughton. "So good to meet you, little brother!" he said, and you were very pleased with that.

I had no idea you and your mother would be so fascinated by his having my name. I'd have warned you otherwise.

He came up the steps, hat in hand, smiling as if there were some old joke between us. "You're looking wonderful, Papa!" he said, and I thought, after so many years, the first words out of his mouth would have to be prevarication, but I was sort of struggling out of the porch swing at the time, which would be no great problem except of course there's nothing steady about a porch swing to grab on to, and standing up from a seated position is a considerable strain on my heart, the doctor says, and I know from experience how true that is. I thought it best not to die or collapse just there with you two watching, leaving old Boughton to ponder the inevitability of it all, the poor codger. So there was Jack Boughton with that look on his face, lifting me onto my feet by my elbow. And I swear it was as if I had stepped right into a hole, he was so much taller than I than he'd ever been before. Of course I knew I'd been losing some height, but this was downright ridiculous.

It is so strange. One moment I'm a respectable citizen reading up on the political views of Estes Kefauver while his lovely young wife tends her zinnias in the mild morning light and his fine young son comes fondly mishandling that perpetually lost sheep of a cat, Soapy, once more back from perdition for the time being, to what would have been general rejoicing. The flies were bothering a little, but the light was ripe and pure and there was much of interest in the newspaper. Granted I was in my bedroom slippers on account of a little arthritis in my toe. It was pretty nearly a perfect morning.

Then here comes Jack Boughton, who really is the spitting image of his father in terms of physical likeness, with that same black hair and the same high color. He's just about your mother's age. I remember when she lifted her dear face to me to be baptized—lifted it into winter morning light, new-snow light—and I thought, She is neither old nor young, and I was somehow amazed by her, and I could hardly bring myself to touch the water to her brow because she looked a good deal more than beautiful. Sadness was a great part of it, it was. So she has grown younger over the years, and that was because of you. But I have never seen her look so young as she did this morning.

Well, the light was fine, and she was in her garden and you were chasing around in your bare feet with your shirt off and freckles all over your shoulders. Your mother had put a piece of hot dog on a string and tied it to a stick for you to use in luring Soapy. She called it your catting pole, which is just the kind of silliness you love, and so you had spent the morning catting in the bushes and around the house while I read up on the election campaign. One of the pleasures of these days is that I notice them all, minute by minute, and this was a fine one, until I found myself being hoisted to my feet by that Jack Boughton. Then I caught a look on your mother's face and on yours, too, which I know could not have been because of the contrast we made. You didn't wait till this morning to realize that I am old. I don't know what it was I saw, and I'm not going to think about it anymore. It didn't set well with me.

He couldn't stay for coffee. Things went well enough. Then he was off.

If I live, I'll vote for Eisenhower.

How I wish you could have known me in my strength.

I was speaking of visions. I remember once when I was a young child my father helped to pull down a church that had burned. Lightning struck the steeple, and then the steeple fell into the building. It rained the day we came to pull it down. The pulpit was left intact, standing there in the rain, but the pews were mostly kindling. There was a lot of praising the Lord that it happened at midnight on a Tuesday. It was a warm day, a warm rain, and there was no real shelter, so everybody ignored it, more or less. All kinds of people came to help. It was like a camp meeting and a picnic. They unhitched the horses, and we younger children lay on an old quilt under the wagon out of the way and talked and played marbles, and watched the older boys and the men clamber over the ruins, searching out Bibles and hymnals. They would sing, we would all sing, "Blessed Jesus" and "The Old Rugged Cross," and the wind would blow the rain in gusts and the spray would reach us where we were. It was cooler than the rain was. The rain falling on the wagon bed sounded the way it does in an attic eave. It never rains, but I remember that day. And when they had gathered up all the books that were ruined, they made two graves for them, and put the Bibles in one and the hymnals in the other, and then the minister whose church it was—a Baptist, as I recall—said a prayer over them. I was always amazed, watching grownups, at the way they seemed to know what was to be done in any situation, to know what was the decent thing.

The women put the pies and cakes they had brought and the books that could still be used into our wagon and then covered the bed with planks and tarps and lap robes. The food was all pretty damp. No one seems to have thought there might be rain. And harvest was coming, so they'd have been too busy to come back again for a good while. They put that pulpit under a tree and covered it with a horse blanket, and they salvaged whatever they could, which amounted mainly to shingles and nails, and then they pulled down everything that was still standing, to make a bonfire when it all dried out. The ashes turned liquid in the rain and the men who were working in the ruins got entirely black and filthy, till you would hardly know one from another. My father brought me some biscuit that had soot on it from his hands. "Never mind," he said, "there's nothing cleaner than ash." But it affected the taste of that biscuit, which I thought might resemble the bread of affliction, which was often mentioned in those days, though it's rather forgotten now.

"Strange are the uses of adversity." That's a fact. When I'm up here in my study with the radio on and some old book in my hands and it's nighttime and the wind blows and the house creaks, I forget where I am, and it's as though I'm back in hard times for a minute or two, and there's a sweetness in the experience which I don't understand. But that only enhances the value of it. My point here is that you never do know the actual nature even of your own experience. Or perhaps it has no fixed and certain nature. I remember my father down on his heels in the rain, water dripping from his hat, feeding me biscuit from his scorched hand, with that old blackened wreck of a church behind him and steam rising where the rain fell on embers, the rain falling in gusts and the women singing "The Old

Rugged Cross" while they saw to things, moving so gently, as if they were dancing to the hymn, almost. In those days no grown woman ever let herself be seen with her hair undone, but that day even the grand old women had their hair falling down their backs like schoolgirls. It was so joyful and sad. I mention it again because it seems to me much of my life was comprehended in that moment. Grief itself has often returned me to that morning, when I took communion from my father's hand. I remember it as communion, and I believe that's what it was.

I can't tell you what that day in the rain has meant to me. I can't tell myself what it has meant to me. But I know how many things it put altogether beyond question, for me.

Now all the old women have their hair cut short and colored blue, which is fine, I suppose.

Whenever I have held a Bible in my hands, I have remembered the day they buried those ruined Bibles under the tree in the rain, and it is somehow sanctified by that memory. And I think of the old reverend himself preaching in the ruins of his church, with all the windows open so the few that were there could hear "The Old Rugged Cross" drifting up the hill from the Methodist meeting. And my own church is sanctified by the story that was told to me. I remember my father said when the two of them first came home, they found the roof of the church in such disrepair that there were buckets and pans set in the aisle and on the benches. He said the women had planted climbing roses against the building and along the fence, so it looked prettier than it had ever looked before. Prairie had come into the fields and the orchards again, and there were sunflowers growing in the roads between the ruts. The women had their prayer meetings and their Bible studies even though the church was falling into ruin around them. I think about that, and it is strong and lovely in my mind. I truly believe it is waste and ingratitude not to honor such things as visions, whether you yourself happen to have seen them or not.

That said, we were always a little careful about approaching the old man from the right side. It was his right eye he was missing, and we had the impression that it was on that side his visions came to him. He never spoke to us about them very much, since he felt our attitude on the subject was more or less entirely wrong. Nevertheless, we tried to be properly respectful. Sometimes when I came home from school my mother would meet me at the back porch and whisper, "The Lord is in the parlor." Then I'd come creeping in in my socks and I'd just glance in through the parlor door and there my grandfather would be, sitting on the left end of the sofa, looking attentive and sociable and gravely pleased. I would hear a remark from time to time, "I see your point," or "I have often felt that way myself." And for a few days afterward the old man would be radiant and purposeful and a little more flagrant in his larcenies.

Once he told us at supper, "This afternoon I met the Lord over by the river, and we fell to talking, you know, and He made a suggestion I thought was interesting. He said, 'John, why don't you just go home and be old?' But I had to tell him I wasn't sure I was up to the traveling."

"Papa," my mother said, "you *are* home. He probably just meant you should ease up on yourself a little."

"Well," the old man said, "well . . . ," and sank back into his radiance, thinking whatever it was he thought.

My father would say afterward that if the old man was persuaded the Lord wanted him back in Kansas, nothing we said would have any influence one way or another. It was important to him to believe that, though I doubt he ever really did.

Once when I was walking to school I saw some children teasing my grandfather, as if he were just any scrawny old fellow picking blackberries into his hat, nodding a little and talking a little as he did it. They were coming up to him on that right side and touching his arm, tugging his coat. When they did, it would set him to nodding and talking, and they would clap their hands over their mouths and run away.

Now, I was astonished at this. I realize how much I did, in some sense, believe that there was a sort of sacredness just to the right of him, and it really shocked me that those children could violate it as they were doing. I was standing there, taking it in, trying to decide what to do, when the old man wheeled around and planted that stare on me. How he knew I was there I don't know, and why he looked at me that way is a thing I never have understood, as if I were the betrayer. It felt unfair to me at the time, but I never could dismiss it. I never could tell myself that it was just an error, that there was nothing in it.

Well, I'll confess I did feel a certain embarrassment about him. It may even have been shame. And it was not the first time I had felt it, either. But I was a child at the time, and it seems to me he might have made some allowance. These people who can see right through you never quite do you justice, because they never give you credit for the effort you're making to be better than you actually are, which is difficult and well meant and deserving of some little notice.

I might as well say this, too. It hurt us all something dreadful that he left the way he did. We knew there was judgment in it, and whatever we might say for ourselves, for our reasonableness and our good intentions, we knew they were trivial by his lights, and that made them a little bit trivial by our lights. He took so much away with him when he left.

My father said when he walked into his father's church after they came back from the army the first thing he saw was a piece of needlework hanging on the wall above the communion table. It was very beautifully done, flowers and flames surrounding the words "The Lord Our God Is a Purifying Fire." I suppose that is why I always think of my grandfather's church as the one struck by lightning. As in fact it was.

My father said it was that banner that had sent him off to sit with the Quakers. He said the very last word he would have applied to war, once he had had a good look at it, was "purifying," and the thought that those women could believe the world was in any way purer for the loss of their own sons and husbands was appalling to him. He stood there looking at it, visibly displeased by it, apparently, because one of the women said to him, "It's just a bit of Scripture."

He said, "I beg your pardon, ma'am. No, that is not Scripture."

"Well," she said, "then it certainly ought to be."

And of course that was terrible to his mind, that she could have thought such a thing. And yet if those precise words don't occur in the Bible, there are passages they could be said to summarize fairly well. That may have been all she meant.

I have always wished I could have seen it, that tapestry they made, if that's what it was. He said there were cherubim to either side of it, with their wings thrown forward the way they are in the old pictures, and then, where the Ark of the

Covenant would have been, those incendiary words, and flowers and flames around them and above them. I don't know how those women managed to find the material for it, how much snipping and raveling of their few best clothes they'd have to have done to make such a thing as that. And I've always wondered what happened to it. Material things are so vulnerable to the humiliations of decay. There are some I dearly wish might be spared.

One after another, when those women learned they were widows, they went back to their families in the East. Not all of them, but a good many. Some of them had buried their husbands and their children beside the church, so they felt they couldn't leave. And some of those who left came back, even years later. Still, that congregation dwindled away finally, and the Methodists bought the land and burned the old building down because it was past saving.

My father spoke once in a sermon about how he regretted the times after the war that he'd gone off to sit with the Quakers while his father struggled to find words of comfort to say to his poor remnant of a flock. He said in those days his father opened all the windows that still would open, so they could hear the Methodists singing by the river, and that some of the women would join in if the song was "The Old Rugged Cross" or "Rock of Ages," even in the middle of the sermon, and he'd just stop preaching and listen to them. The wind, he said, smelled like turned earth because of the new graves, and yet people afterward remembered those Sunday mornings and those Wednesday evenings as something strangely wonderful. There was a tenderness in the way they told about them. My father said he had regretted and repented his whole life since that time but never sufficiently, because at first staying away had seemed an act of principle almost. His father had preached his people into the war, saying while there was slavery there was no peace, but only a war of the armed and powerful against the captive and defenseless. He would say, Peace will come only when that war ends, so the God of peace calls upon us to end it. He said all this with that gun in his belt. And everyone there always shouted amen, even the littlest children.

I came home for lunch today and found you playing catch in the street with Jack Boughton. You had his mitt, a fine new fielder's mitt that reached almost to your elbow, and he had that old glove of Edward's that I keep on my desk. No webbing at all, no pocket to speak of. It's an oversight of mine that I haven't gotten you a glove of your own. I'll see to that.

Young Boughton was teaching you to scoop up grounders, probably to cover for the fact that you weren't likely to actually catch anything on the fly. You were being very earnest about it all, running hither and thither on those clever child legs of yours, and he was saying, "Come on, come on," and pounding his glove, and then, in a sportscaster's voice, "He's rounding second, folks. Will the throw be in time?" And you would lose the ball again, and he would say, "This is amazing, folks. The runner appears to have tripped on his shoelace! He's down! He's taking a while to catch his breath! Now he's up, he's headed for the plate!" He would say, "He's dragging his left leg, folks, he's hopping on one foot!" And by then you were giggling considerably, but you got the ball to him finally, and he said, "Well, folks, that runner's out!" It was beautiful to watch you two in the flickering shade.

I remember watching Louisa skipping rope in that street in a bright red coat with her pigtails jumping in the cold. It was early spring, so she didn't raise any dust to speak of. The trees were just budding their leaves. They still had that slight, brave look young trees have. I don't know whose idea it was to plant all these elms around town, but whoever it was did us a world of good. Old Boughton and I used to toss the ball of an evening under those same trees, till his joints began to bother him, which was before he was into his forties, as I recall. His health has been another great trial for him. This Jack Boughton could be his father, to look at him.

I'm trying to make the best of our situation. That is, I'm trying to tell you things I might never have thought to tell you if I had brought you up myself, father and son, in the usual companionable way. When things are taking their ordinary course, it is hard to remember what matters. There are so many things you would never think to tell anyone. And I believe they may be the things that mean most to you, and that even your own child would have to know in order to know you well at all. I remember that day in my childhood when I lay under the wagon with the other little children, watching them pull down the ruins of that Baptist church, and my father brought me a piece of biscuit for my lunch, and I crawled out and knelt with him there, in the rain. I remember it as if he broke the bread and put a bit of it in my mouth, though I know he didn't. His hands and his face were black with ash— he looked charred, like one of the old martyrs—and he knelt there in the rain and brought a piece of biscuit out from inside his shirt, and he did break it, that's true, and gave half to me and ate the other half himself. And it truly was the bread of affliction, because everyone was poor then. There had been drought for a few years and times were hard. Though we didn't notice it so much when they were hard for everybody. And I guess that must have been why no one minded the rain. There had been so little of it. One thing I do always remember is how the women let their hair fall down and their skirts trail in the mud, even the old women, as if none of it mattered at all. And then the singing, which was very beautiful as I remember it, though I'm pretty sure it could not have been. It would just rise up with the sound of the rain. "Beneath the Cross of Jesus." All the lovely, sad old tunes. The bitterness of that morsel has meant other things to me as the years passed. I have had many occasions to reflect on it.

It is not surprising that I remember that day as if my father had given me communion, taking that bread from his side and breaking it for me with his ashy hands. But it is strange that I remember receiving it the way I do, since it has never been our custom for the minister to place the bread in the communicant's mouth, as they do in some churches. I think of this because, on the morning of communion when your mother brought you forward and said, "You ought to give him some of that," I broke the bread and fed a bit of it to you from my hand, just the way my father would not have done except in my memory. And I know what I wanted in that moment was to give you some version of that same memory, which has been very dear to me, though only now do I realize how often it has been in my mind.

> Time, like an ever-rolling stream,
> Bears all its sons away;
> They fly forgotten, as a dream
> Dies at the opening day.

Good old Isaac Watts. I've thought about that verse often. I have always wondered what relationship this present reality bears to an ultimate reality.

> A thousand ages in Thy sight
> Are like an evening gone . . .

No doubt that is true. Our dream of life will end as dreams do end, abruptly and completely, when the sun rises, when the light comes. And we will think, All that fear and all that grief were about nothing. But that cannot be true. I can't believe we will forget our sorrows altogether. That would mean forgetting that we had lived, humanly speaking. Sorrow seems to me to be a great part of the substance of human life. For example, at this very moment I feel a kind of loving grief for you as you read this, because I do not know you, and because you have grown up fatherless, you poor child, lying on your belly now in the sun with Soapy asleep on the small of your back. You are drawing those terrible little pictures that you will bring me to admire, and which I will admire because I have not the heart to say one word that you might remember against me.

I will tell you some more old stories. So much of what I know about those old days comes from the time my father and I spent wandering around together lost in Kansas. I don't know if I ever actually cried, but I know I spent a lot of time trying not to. The soles of my shoes wore through and the dust and sticks and gravel came in and wore out my socks and got to work on my feet. O the filth! O the blisters! Time weighs on children. They struggle just to get through church, as you know. And there I was, trudging through the same old nowhere, day after day, always wanting to slow down, to sit down, to lie down, with my father walking on ahead, no doubt a little desperate, as he had every right to be. Once or twice I did sit down. I just sat there in the heat and the weeds with the grasshoppers flying around my head and watched him walk away, and he'd keep walking till he was almost out of my sight, which is a long way in Kansas. Then I'd go running to catch up. He'd say, "You're going to make yourself thirsty." Well, it seemed to me I'd been thirsty half my life.

But the pleasant thing was that when I did stay alongside him he would tell me remarkable things I'm pretty sure he would never have told me otherwise. If there was supper he'd tell stories to celebrate, and if there wasn't supper he'd tell stories to make up for the lack of it. Once, some owls woke us with that caviling they get into sometimes, and he told me the story of being awakened by sounds in the night and of walking outside and seeing old John Brown's mule coming out through the doors of his father's church, being coaxed down those wooden steps in the dark of the moon. He heard the noise of balking and a sad, grave voice saying, "Doing fine now. Doing just fine." Then four horses after it, abrupt and agile, all with their saddles already cinched on. The men mounted, two men on one horse leading the other horse along behind them—one of the men was wounded and had to be held—and they rode away without a word. Then, in a few minutes, he heard the barn door open and he heard their horse breathing and stepping and his father speaking to it, and then his father rode away, too.

He told me that he went up to the church and sat there in the dark, wondering what he should do. He wasn't even ten years old at the time. He said the church smelled like horses and gunpowder and it smelled like sweat. (In those days they didn't have bullets like the ones we have, so they'd have been using the time to load up their weapons with powder and shot.) They'd pushed the benches and the communion table against the walls to make room for the animals. No doubt the men had slept on the benches. Certainly the wounded man had, because there was a good deal of blood on one of them, and on the floor beside it. My father said, "That was the first thing I saw when the light began to come."

So he dragged that bench out back of the church and stood it on end so it would fall into the deep grass on its side. That was to trouble the surface of the grass as little as possible. Then he took a shovel and a broom and cleaned up after the horses as well as he could. He got a bucket of water and a piece of soap to scrub down that bloodstain, but that just made it bigger. So he ended up sloshing water over the whole floor to make that spot less conspicuous. His thought was that if the men who slept in the church were being pursued, their pursuers might come at any time and they would be looking for things like mule droppings in a church or blood on a pew. And of course they were things that would have to be seen to in any case, and especially since that was a Saturday.

But those same pursuers would surely be curious to find him scrubbing out a church before the sun was well up. Then it occurred to him how unlike his father it was to leave at such a time, making no arrangements whatever for putting things right, leaving no instructions whatever for how they should be put right, leaving him to wander from his bed into this ridiculous situation, in which it seemed there was no right thing to be done. He was thinking these things and lugging a bucket of water up into the church, and he saw a man in a U.S. Army uniform sitting there in the twilight on a bench against the wall, with his hat in his hands and his gun lying on the bench beside him.

"You've got it looking right nice in here," the soldier said. Then he plucked at the ripped knee of his trousers and said, "My dang horse bolted on me. An owl hooted or something, and off she went. You folks wouldn't have a horse I could requisition. It would only be for a day or two."

"You'd have to speak to my father."

The soldier said, "Your father isn't here. I'd guess he's ridden off somewhere on the very horse I was hoping to borrow." Then he said, "You heard of Osawatomie John Brown? Of course you have. Everybody has. I can see you're a fine boy. Don't worry, I'm not going to make you go telling lies right here in a church, little brother. You know the kinds of things John Brown has been up to."

My father said he had heard stories.

The soldier nodded. "There are decent folks around here who'd help him any chance they got. Ministers of the Gospel. They'd let him bring his old mule right into their church if he asked them to. They'd deem it an honor. I find that remarkable. Those fugitives would come in with their weapons and their wounds and their dirty boots, they'd come in bleeding on the floor, and that would be just fine. Then a soldier of the United States government comes along looking for them, as he is paid to do, and nobody even offers him a cup of coffee."

My father said, "We have coffee. I'm pretty sure we do."

The soldier stood up. He said, "My platoon left me about two miles from here and took off east. They knew where those fellows would likely be off to next as soon as the moon was down. They didn't have to find those road apples you left out there on the front step to get a general sense of the situation. So if your father's gone with them, he might be seeing a world of trouble right about now." He said, "I thought I should tell you that before I drank your coffee."

My father said his lips were so numb he couldn't move them to speak. The soldier said, "I'll just get myself a drink at your well." And he walked out of the church and got his drink and walked away up the road, favoring that one leg a little. My father hated to believe he was the man my grandfather shot, but he did believe it. I don't mean to suggest that he killed him outright, but in those days in that place a man could die of a whole lot of things besides a bullet wound.

He had walked to the next farm and requisitioned their horse and taken off in the general direction he thought his platoon had gone, though, if it was the same man, he drifted somewhat to the south of it. Brown and the others had circled back and to the south, knowing they would be followed and making for the hills. And my grandfather was ambling along toward home with that big gun in his belt and those two bloody shirts under his arm, which was very foolish. And he was bare-chested under his coat, since he had swapped his own shirt for the two he had brought back with him. But he was never really a practical man again after that day, my father said. I would not have known where to find the origins of his impracticality, but I am certainly willing to vouch for the fact of it. In any case, a lone soldier did approach him and did hail him down, and he was indeed riding a chestnut horse that could have been the neighbor's. The soldier began to question him, and my grandfather was caught without a lie. But he had that gun, and the gun was loaded.

"Well, I did, I winged him," my grandfather said. "Then his horse bolted. He took quite a spill." And he left him there on the ground. "Old Brown asked if I'd be willing to cover their retreat if occasion arose. I said I would, and I did." He said, "What *was* I to do with him, bring him back here?" His point was that the congregation had put a lot of thought and effort into hollow walls and hidden cellars in their various cabins and outbuildings, tunnels that started from false-bottomed potato bins and opened up under haystacks a hundred yards away and so forth. There was a false-bottomed coffin they kept in the church, and an open grave with a floor of burlap stretched over a couple of boards and covered with dirt, opening on a tunnel that came up in the woodshed. All that effort was for freeing the captives, and it had to be protected for their sake. The soldier could only have concluded that my grandfather was in serious cahoots with John Brown, and attention of that kind could destroy everything.

The old man told my father what had happened only because my father told him about finding the soldier in the church. "Dark fellow, you say? Kind of a drawl to his speech?" He told my father that it was a mortally serious business, life and death. He should never speak a word about it to anyone, and he should be ready with a lie in case someone came inquiring. So, waking and sleeping, he thought about that wounded soldier by himself out there on the plains, and tried to imagine himself saying he had not seen such a man, had not spoken to him.

Well, the authorities never did come to talk to them about that soldier, so my father thought he probably had died out there. He said, "The relief I suffered every day they didn't come was horrible." Of course the odds are fairly high that the day of a man's death will be the worst day of his life. But my father said, "When he told me the horse had bolted, my heart sank." So there we were, lying in the loft of somebody's barn they'd abandoned, hearing the owls, and hearing the mice, and hearing the bats, and hearing the wind, with no notion at all when the dawn might come. My father said, "I never did forgive myself not going out there to look for him." And I felt the truth of that as I have never felt the truth of any other human utterance. He said, "It was the very next Sunday the old devil preached in one of those shirts, with that gun in his belt. And you would not have believed how the people responded, all the weeping there was, and the shouting." And after that, he said, his father would be gone for days sometimes. There were Sundays when he would ride his horse right up to the church steps just when it was time for service to begin and fire that gun in the air to let the people know he was back. They'd find him standing in the pulpit, with his eyes red and his face pale and dust in his beard, all ready to preach on judgment and grace. My father said, "I never dared to ask him what he'd been up to. I couldn't risk the possibility of knowing things that were worse than my suspicions."

I lay there against my father's side with my head pillowed on his arm, hearing the wind, and feeling a pity that was far too deep to have any particular object. I pitied my mother, who might have to come looking for us and would never, never find us. I pitied the bats and the mice. I pitied the earth and the moon. I pitied the Lord.

It was the next day that we came to the Maine lady's farmstead.

I spent this morning in a meeting with the trustees. It was pleasant. They respectfully ignored a few suggestions I made about repairs to the building. I'm pretty sure they'll build a new church once I'm gone. I don't mean this unkindly—they don't want to cause me grief, so they're waiting to do what they want to do, and that's good of them. They'll pull the old church down and put up something bigger, sturdier. I hear them admiring what the Lutherans have done, and it is impressive, red brick and a porch with white columns and a fine big door and a handsome steeple. The inside is very beautiful, I'm told. I've been invited to the dedication, and I'll go, if I'm still around and still up to that sort of thing. God willing, in other words. I'd like to see our new church, but they're right, I'd hate to see the old one come down. I believe seeing that might actually kill me, which would not be such a terrible thing for a person in my circumstances. A stab of grief as coup de grâce—there'd be poetry in it.

Am I impatient? Can that be? Today there has been no hint of a thorn in my flesh, of a thorn in my heart, more particularly. The thump in my chest goes on and on like some old cow chewing her cud, that same dull endlessness and contentment, so it seems to me. I wake up at night, and I hear it. Again, it says. Again, again, again. "For Preservation is a Creation, and more, it is a continued Creation, and a Creation every moment." That is George Herbert, whom I hope you have read. *Again*, all any heart has ever said, and just as the word is said the moment is gone, so there is not even any sort of promise in it.

> Wherefore each part
> Of my hard heart
> Meets in this frame,
> To praise thy Name:
> That, if I chance to hold my peace,
> These stones to praise thee may not cease.

Yet awhile.

Well, if Herbert is right, this old body is as new a creation as you are yourself. I mean as you are now, playing under my window on the swing Dan Boughton put up for you. You must remember it. He tied fishing line to an arrow and shot it over the bough and then used the fishing line to hoist the rope, and so on. It took him the whole day, but he did it. He's a clever, good-hearted young fellow. He was a great comfort to his father and mother. Now he's teaching school somewhere in Michigan, I'm told. He didn't choose the ministry, though for a long time he was expected to.

You are standing up on the seat of your swing and sailing higher than you really ought to, with that bold, planted stance of a sailor on a billowy sea. The ropes are long and you are light and the ropes bow like cobwebs, laggardly, indolent. Your shirt is red—it is your favorite shirt—and you fly into the sunlight and pause there brilliantly for a second and then fall back into the shadows again. You appear to be altogether happy. I remember those first experiments with fundamental things, gravity and light, and what an absolute pleasure they were. And there is your mother. "Don't go so high," she says. You'll mind. You're a good fellow.

I did not mean to criticize the trustees. I do understand the reluctance to make any *substantial* investment in the church building at this point. But if I were a little younger, I tell you, I'd be up on that roof myself. As it is, I might drive a few nails into the treads on the front steps. I don't see the point in letting the old place look too shabby in its last year or so. It's very plain, but the proportions of it really are quite pleasing, and when it has a fresh coat of paint, it's all the church anyone could need, in terms of appearance. It is inadequate in other ways, I recognize that.

I did remember to mention to them that that weather vane on the steeple was brought from Maine by my grandfather and stood above his church for many years. He gave it to my father on the day of his ordination. The people in Maine used to put those roosters on their steeples, he told me, to remind themselves of the betrayal of Peter, to help them repent. They really didn't use crosses much at all in those days. But once I mentioned that there was a rooster on the steeple, which most of them had never noticed before, they became a little uneasy with the fact that there wasn't a cross up there. I believe they will put one up, now that it's on their minds. That's the one thing they'll get around to. They said they will mount the weather vane on a wall somewhere, in the foyer, probably, where people can appreciate it. I don't care what they do. I only mentioned it at all because I didn't want it to be discarded with everything else. It is very old. This way at least you can get a good look at it.

It has a bullet hole at the base of its tail feathers. There were a good many stories about how it got there. I was told once that, since my grandfather had no bell or any other respectable way to call a meeting, and almost nobody had a working timepiece, he would fire a rifle in the air, and one time he wasn't paying enough attention where he pointed it. There was a story, too, that a man from Missouri who was passing by just as the people were gathering fired one shot and set the rooster spinning around to try to dishearten them a little, since he knew they were Free Soilers. And there was a story that the church had taken delivery of a crate of Sharps rifles and somebody wanted to find out if they were really as accurate as they were said to be.

A Sharps is a very fine rifle, but I suspect the first story is the true one, because in my experience that degree of precision is only achieved accidentally. My grandfather could be very quiet about his embarrassments, so he might just have let people speculate, invent. I told my committee the story about the Missourian because it has a certain Christian character— dinging the weather vane would have been an act of considerable restraint, because feelings ran high in those days. That story has the most historical interest, too, I think, and it could well be true, for all I know to the contrary. It is hard to make people care about old things. So I thought I should do what I could for that poor old rooster.

Often enough these settlers' churches were only meant to keep the rain off until there were time and resources to put up something better. So they don't have the dignity of age. They just get shabby. They were never meant to become venerable. I remember that old Baptist church that my father helped to pull down, all black in the rain, looking ten times as formidable as it would have before the lightning struck. That was always a major part of my idea of a church. When I was a child I actually believed that the purpose of steeples was to attract lightning. I thought they must be meant to protect all the other houses and buildings, and that seemed very gallant to me. Then I read some history, and I realized after a while that not every church was on the ragged edge of the Great Plains, and not every pulpit had my father in it. The history of the church is very complex, very mingled. I want you to know how aware I am of that fact. These days there are so many people who think loyalty to religion is benighted, if it is not worse than benighted. I am aware of that, and I know the charges that can be brought against the churches are powerful. And I know, too, that my own experience of the church has been, in many senses, sheltered and parochial. In every sense, unless it really is a universal and transcendent life, unless the bread is the bread and the cup is the cup everywhere, in all circumstances, and it is a time with the Lord in Gethsemane that comes for everyone, as I deeply believe. That biscuit ashy from my father's charred hand. It all means more than I can tell you. So you must not judge what I know by what I find words for. If I could only give you what my father gave me. No, what the Lord has given me and must also give you. But I hope you will put yourself in the way of the gift. I am not speaking here of the ministry as such, as I have said.

I did a strange thing this morning. They were playing a waltz on the radio, and I decided I wanted to dance to it. I don't mean that in the usual sense. I have a general notion of waltzing but no instruction in the steps, and so on. It was mostly a matter of waving my arms a little and spinning around a little, pretty carefully. Remembering my youth makes me aware that I never really had enough of it, it was over before I was done with it. Whenever I think of Edward, I think of playing catch in a hot street and that wonderful weariness of the arms. I think of leaping after a high throw and that wonderful collaboration of the whole body with itself and that wonderful certainty and amazement when you know the glove is just where it should be. Oh, I will miss the world!

So I decided a little waltzing would be very good, and it was. I plan to do all my waltzing here in the study. I have thought I might have a book ready at hand to clutch if I began to experience unusual pain, so that it would have an especial recommendation from being found in my hands. That seemed theatrical, on consideration, and it might have the perverse effect of burdening the book with unpleasant associations. The ones I considered, by the way, were Donne and Herbert and Barth's *Epistle to the Romans* and Volume II of Calvin's *Institutes*. Which is by no means to slight Volume I.

There's a mystery in the thought of the re-creation of an old man as an old man, with all the defects and injuries of what is called long life faithfully preserved in him, and all their claims and all their tendencies honored, too, as in the steady progress of arthritis in my left knee. I have thought sometimes that the Lord must hold the whole of our lives in memory, so to speak. Of course He does. And "memory" is the wrong word, no doubt. But the finger I broke sliding into second base when I was twenty-two years old is crookeder than ever, and I can interpret that fact as an intimate attention, taking Herbert's view.

———

This morning I strolled over to Boughton's. He was sitting in the screened porch behind the trumpet vines, dozing. He and his wife were fond of those vines because they attract hummingbirds. They've pretty well taken over now, so the house looks sort of like a huge duck blind. Boughton corrected me when I told him that. "A hummingbird blind," he said. "There are times when a little bird shot would bring down a thousand of them." But, he says, since that's not enough yet to season a cup of broth, he's going to bide his time.

All his gardens have more or less gone to brush, but as I came up the road I saw young Boughton and the daughter Glory clearing out the iris beds. Boughton owns his house. I used to think that was an enviable thing, but there's been no one but him to see to it, and things have gotten a little out of hand these last years.

He seemed in excellent spirits. "The children," he said, "are putting things to rights for me."

I talked to him some about the baseball season and about the election, but I could tell he was listening mainly to the voices of his children, who did sound very happy and harmonious. I remember when they played in those gardens with their cats and kites and bubbles. It was as pretty a sight as you're likely to see. Their mother was a fine woman, and such a one to laugh! Boughton says, "I miss her something dreadful." She knew Louisa when they were girls. Once, I remember, they put hard-boiled eggs under a neighbor's setting hen. What the point was I never knew, but I remember them laughing so hard they just threw themselves down on the grass and lay there with the tears running down into their hair. One time Boughton and I and some others took a hay wagon apart and reassembled it on the roof of the courthouse. I don't know what the point of that was, either, but we had a grand time, working under cover of darkness and all that. I wasn't ordained yet, but I was in seminary. I don't know what we thought we were up to. All that laughter. I wish I could hear it again. I asked Boughton if he remembered putting that wagon on the roof and he said, "How could I forget it?" and chuckled to please me, but he really wanted to sit there with his chin propped on the head of his cane and listen to the voices of his children. So I walked home.

You and your mother were making sandwiches with peanut butter and apple butter on raisin bread. I consider such a sandwich a great delicacy, as you are clearly aware, because you made me stay on the porch until everything was ready, the milk poured and so on. Children seem to think every pleasant thing has to be a surprise.

Your mother was a little upset because she didn't know where I was. I didn't tell her I might go to Boughton's. She's afraid I'll just drop dead somewhere, and that's reasonable enough. It seems to me worse things could happen, actually, but that's not how she looks at it. Most of the time I feel a good deal better than the doctor led me to expect, so I'm inclined to enjoy myself as I can. It helps me sleep.

I was thinking about old Boughton's parents, what they were like when we were children. They were a rather somber pair, even in their prime. Not like him at all. His mother would take tiny bites of her food and swallow as if she were swallowing live coals, stoking the fires of her dyspepsia. And his father, reverend gentleman that he was, had something about him that bespoke grudge. I have always liked the phrase "nursing a grudge," because many people are tender of their resentments, as of the thing nearest their hearts. Well, who knows what account these two old pilgrims have made of themselves by now. I always imagine divine mercy giving us back to ourselves and letting us laugh at what we became, laugh at the preposterous disguises of crouch and squint and limp and lour we all do put on. I enjoy the hope that when we meet I will not be estranged from you by all the oddnesses life has carved into me. When I look at Boughton, I see a funny, generous young man, full of vigor. He's on two canes now, and he says if he could sprout a third arm there would be three. He hasn't stood in a pulpit these ten years. I conclude that Boughton has completed his errand and I have not yet completed mine. I hope I am not presuming on the Lord's patience.

I've started *The Trail of the Lonesome Pine*. I went over to the library and got a copy for myself, since your mother can't part with hers. I believe she's reading through it again. I'd forgotten it entirely, if I ever read it at all. There's a young girl who falls in love with an older man. She tells him, "I'll go with ye anywhar." That made me laugh. I guess it's a pretty good book. He isn't old like I am, but then your mother isn't young like the girl in the book is, either.

This week I intend to preach on Genesis 21:14–21, which is the story of Hagar and Ishmael. If these were ordinary times—if I were twenty years younger—I'd be making an orderly passage through the Gospels and the Epistles before I turned to Genesis again. That was my custom, and I have always felt it was effective as teaching, which is really what all this is about. Now, though, I talk about whatever is on my mind—Hagar and Ishmael at the moment.

The story of Hagar and Ishmael came to mind while I was praying this morning, and I found a great assurance in it. The story says that it is not only the father of a child who cares for its life, who protects its mother, and it says that even if the mother can't find a way to provide for it, or herself, provision will be made. At that level it is a story full of comfort. That is how life goes—we send our children into the wilderness. Some of them on the day they are born, it seems, for all the help we can give them. Some of them seem to be a kind of wilderness unto themselves. But there must be angels there, too, and springs of water. Even that wilderness, the very habitation of jackals, is the Lord's. I need to bear this in mind.

Young Boughton came by to see if you felt like a game of catch. You did. He was sunburned from working in the garden. It gave him a healthy, honest look. He's teaching you to throw overhand. He said he couldn't stay for supper. You were disappointed, as I believe your mother was also.

The moon looks wonderful in this warm evening light, just as a candle flame looks beautiful in the light of morning. Light within light. It seems like a metaphor for something. So much does. Ralph Waldo Emerson is excellent on this point.

It seems to me to be a metaphor for the human soul, the singular light within the great general light of existence. Or it seems like poetry within language. Perhaps wisdom within experience. Or marriage within friendship and love. I'll try to remember to use this. I believe I see a place for it in my thoughts on Hagar and Ishmael. Their time in the wilderness seems like a specific moment of divine Providence within the whole providential regime of Creation.

Just before suppertime yesterday evening Jack Boughton came strolling by. He sat himself down on the porch step and talked baseball and politics—he favors the Yankees, which he has every right to do—until the fragrance of macaroni and cheese so obtruded itself that I was obliged to invite him in. You and your mother still regard him as a fairly wonderful surprise, this John Ames Boughton with his quiet voice and his preacherly manner, which, by the way, he has done nothing to earn, or to deserve. To the best of my knowledge, at any rate. He had it even as a child, and I always found that disturbing. Maybe it's something he isn't conscious of, growing up the way he did. But it seems to me sometimes that there's an element of parody in it. I wonder if he acts that way everywhere, or if he does it only around me, and around his father. What do I mean by preacherly? There's a way of being formal and deferential and at the same time cordial, while maintaining an air of dignified authority, which is preacherly. I never mastered this myself, but my father had it and Boughton had it. My grandfather, that old Nazirite, was impressive in another style. But of sheer and perfect preacherliness I have never seen a finer example than this Jack Boughton, heathen that he is, or was. Your mother asked him if he would like to say grace, and he did, with an elegant simplicity that seemed almost wasted on macaroni and cheese.

He mentioned that I had not been to see his father in a few days, which is the truth, and which is no coincidence either. I thought he might be at his father's only a few days. It has been one of the great irritations of my life, seeing the two of them together. I hoped to stay away till he left, but clearly he is not about to do that.

In the old days I used to come into the kitchen and look around in the pantry and the icebox, and generally I'd find a pot full of soup or stew or a casserole of some kind, which I would warm up or not depending on my mood. If I didn't find anything, I'd eat cold baked beans and fried-egg sandwiches—which, by the way, I enjoyed. I'd find pie or biscuits on the table sometimes. When I was at the church or up in my study, one of the women would just step in the door and leave dinner there for me and go away, and then another day she'd come back and take her pan and her tea towels or whatever and go away. I'd find jam and pickles and smoked fish. Once I found liver pills. It was a strange life, with its own pleasures.

Then, when your mother and I got married, it was a little hard for people to learn that they couldn't just come and go anymore. They suspected she was not a cook, I believe, and in fact she was not, so they kept coming in the door with their casseroles until I realized it upset her, and then I spoke with them about it. I found her crying in the pantry one evening. Someone had come in and changed the pull cord on the light and put new paper down on the shelves. It was kindly intended, but not considerate, I understand that.

I mention this because it seemed so strange to me to be sitting there with the two of you and young Boughton, of all people. Because not so many years ago I was sitting at that table in the dark eating cold meat loaf from the pan it came in, listening to the radio, when old Boughton let himself in the door and sat down at the table and said, "Don't put the light on." So I turned the radio off and we sat there together and talked and prayed, about John Ames Boughton, for John Ames Boughton.

But that story may be more than you need to know, more than I ought to tell you. If things have come right, what is the point? There's nothing very remarkable in the story, in fact it is very commonplace. Which is not an extenuation by any means. So often people tell me about some wickedness they've been up to, or they've suffered from, and I think, Oh, *that* again! I've heard of churches in the South that oblige people to make a public confession of their graver sins to the whole congregation. I think sometimes there might be an advantage in making people aware how worn and stale these old transgressions are. It might take some of the shine off them, for those who are tempted. But I have no evidence to suggest it has that effect. Of course there are special and extenuating circumstances. They were fairly special in young Boughton's case and by no means extenuating, if I am any judge. Which I am not, or ought not to be, according to Scripture.

Transgression. That is legalism. There is never just one transgression. There is a wound in the flesh of human life that scars when it heals and often enough seems never to heal at all.

Avoid transgression. How's that for advice.

I have to decide what to tell your mother. I know she is wondering. He's very nice to her, and to you. And to me. No "Papa" this evening, thank goodness. He's so respectful I feel like telling him I'm not the oldest man in the world yet. Well, I know I'm touchy about some things. I have to try to be fair with him.

You look at him as if he were Charles Lindbergh. He keeps calling you little brother, and you love that.

I hope there's some special providence in his turning up just when I have so many other things to deal with, because he is a considerable disruption when peace would have been especially appreciated.

I'm not complaining. Or I ought not to be.

I've been thinking about my funeral sermon, which I plan to write to save old Boughton the trouble. I can do a pretty good imitation of his style. He'll get a laugh out of that.

————

Young Boughton came by again this morning, with some apples and plums from their trees. He and Glory have things looking pretty nice over there. They've done a lot of work.

I'm trying to be a little more cordial to him than I have been. He sort of steps back and smiles a little, and looks at me as though he's thinking, "Today we're cordial! What can account for that?" And he looks me right in the face, as though he wants me to know he knows it is a performance and he's amused by it. I suppose an attempt is a performance, in some sense. But what else can I do? Most people will go along with you in these situations, whatever their private thoughts might be. I hesitate to call it devilment, but it certainly does make me uncomfortable, and I'm fairly sure that is what he intends. And I believe he truly is amused as well. So I abandoned the attempt at cordiality for today and excused myself and went off to look after some things at the church.

I spent several hours in meditation and prayer over John Ames Boughton, and also over John Ames, the father of his soul, as Boughton once called me, though I can't endorse the phrase, any soul's father being the Lord only. There's much for me to ponder in that fact. Better that I should offend or reject my own son—which God forbid—but you are the Lord's child also, as am I, as we all are. I must be gracious. My only role is to be gracious. Clearly I must somehow contrive to *think* graciously about him, also, since he makes such a point of seeing right through me. I believe I have made some progress on that front through prayer, though there is clearly much more progress to be made, much more praying to be done.

———

This is an important thing, which I have told many people, and which my father told me, and which his father told him. When you encounter another person, when you have dealings with anyone at all, it is as if a question is being put to you. So you must think, What is the Lord asking of me in this moment, in this situation? If you confront insult or antagonism, your first impulse will be to respond in kind. But if you think, as it were, This is an emissary sent from the Lord, and some benefit is intended for me, first of all the occasion to demonstrate my faithfulness, the chance to show that I do in some small degree participate in the grace that saved me, you are free to act otherwise than as circumstances would seem to dictate. You are free to act by your own lights. You are freed at the same time of the impulse to hate or resent that person. He would probably laugh at the thought that the Lord sent him to you for your benefit (and his), but that is the perfection of the disguise, his own ignorance of it.

I am reminded of this precious instruction by my own great failure to live up to it recently. Calvin says somewhere that each of us is an actor on a stage and God is the audience. That metaphor has always interested me, because it makes us artists of our behavior, and the reaction of God to us might be thought of as aesthetic rather than morally judgmental in the ordinary sense. How well do we understand our role? With how much assurance do we perform it? I suppose Calvin's God was a Frenchman, just as mine is a Middle Westerner of New England extraction. Well, we all bring such light to bear on these great matters as we can. I do like Calvin's image, though, because it suggests how God might actually enjoy us. I believe we think about that far too little. It would be a way into understanding essential things, since presumably the world exists for

God's enjoyment, not in any simple sense, of course, but as you enjoy the *being* of a child even when he is in every way a thorn in your heart. "He has a mind of his own," Boughton used to say when that son of his was up to something. And he meant it as praise, he really did. Now, Edward, for example, *did* have a mind of his own, a mind worthy of respect.

I'm not sure that's true, either. Worthy of respect, of course. But the fact is that his mind came from one set of books as surely as mine has come from another set of books. But that can't be true. While I was at seminary I read every book he had ever mentioned and every book I thought he might have read, if I could put my hand on it and it wasn't in German. If I had the money, I ordered books through the mail that I thought he might be about to read. When I brought them home my father began to read them, too, which surprised me at the time. Who knows where any mind comes from. It's all mystery. Still, Boughton is right. Jack Boughton is a piece of work.

Much more prayer is called for, clearly, but first I will take a nap.

My impulse is strong to warn you against Jack Boughton. Your mother and you. You may know by now what a fallible man I am, and how little I can trust my feelings on this subject. And you know, from living out years I cannot foresee, whether you must forgive me for warning you, or forgive me for failing to warn you, or indeed if none of it turned out to matter at all. This is a grave question for me.

That paragraph would itself amount to a warning. Perhaps I can say to your mother only that much. He is not a man of the highest character. Be wary of him.

If he continues to come around, I believe I'll do that.

I have not been writing to you for a day or two. I have passed some fairly difficult nights. Discomfort, a little trouble breathing. I have decided the two choices open to me are (1) to torment myself or (2) to trust the Lord. There is no earthly solution to the problems that confront me. But I can add to my problems, as I believe I have done, by dwelling on them. So, no more of that. The Yankees are playing the Red Sox today. This is providential, since it should be a decent game and I don't care at all who wins. So there should be no excess of emotion involved in my watching it. (We have television now, a gift from the congregation with the specific intent of letting me watch baseball, and I will. But it seems quite two-dimensional beside radio.)

Your mother has sent you off to the neighbors, so you won't pester me, she says, but it makes me wonder about the impression I must be making on her this morning. The poor woman is very pale. She has not slept any better than I have. They put the television set in the parlor yesterday and spent the afternoon scrambling around on the roof rigging up an antenna. The young men are terribly interested in these things. It makes them happy to do a kindness so perilous and exotic in nature. I remember, I remember.

Your mother has brought down my writing materials and the books she found on my desk, and someone has brought in a TV tray for my pills and spectacles and water glass. In case this is as serious as everyone seems to think. I don't believe it myself, but maybe I'm wrong.

I fell asleep in my chair and woke up feeling so much better. I missed eight and a half innings, and nothing happened in the bottom of the ninth (4 to 2, Yankees), but the reception was good and I look forward to watching the rest of the season, if God wills. Your mother was asleep, too, kneeling on the floor with her head against my knees. I had to sit very still for a long time, watching a movie about Englishmen in trench coats who were up to something morose involving Frenchmen and trains. I didn't really follow it. When she woke up, she was so glad to see me, as if I had been gone a long time. Then she went and fetched you and we ate our supper in the parlor—it turns out that whoever brought the trays brought one for each of us. Since supper was three kinds of casserole with two kinds of fruit salad, with cake and pie for dessert, I gathered that my flock, who lambaste life's problems with food items of just this kind, had heard an alarm. There was even a bean salad, which to me looked distinctly Presbyterian, so anxiety had overspilled its denominational vessel. You'd have thought I'd died. We saved it for lunch.

We had a fine time, we three, watching television. There were jugglers and monkeys and ventriloquists, and there was a lot of dancing around. You asked for bites off my plate so you could decide which casserole and salad you wanted—you have the child's abhorrence of mingling foods on your plate. So I gave you a bite of one after another, (guessing) Mrs. Brown, Mrs. McNeill, Mrs. Pry, then Mrs. Dorris, Mrs. Turney, feeding you with my fork. You would say, "I *still* can't decide!" and we'd do it all again. That was your joke, eating it all up. It was a wonderful joke. I thought of the day I gave you communion. I wonder if you thought of it also.

I went up to the church for a few hours this morning, and when I came home I found a great many of my books moved into the parlor, with my desk and chair, and the television set moved upstairs. This was your mother's idea, but I knew it was young Boughton who did the lifting and carrying for her, or helped her with it. I am not angry about this. At my time of life, I refuse to be angry. It was kindly meant. And it had to be done sooner or later. It's true that if I have to spend my twilight stranded with somebody or other, I'd prefer Karl Barth to Jack Benny. Still. I have my study. I don't feel I need to give it up yet. Jack Boughton in my study. He may have carried this very journal down the stairs. After some fairly anxious looking around, which involved two trips upstairs, I found it down here, in the bottom drawer of my desk, where I never put it. That seemed like a sort of taunt, as if he had made a point of hiding it from me. I know I am not being reasonable.

I gave the sermon on Hagar and Ishmael today. I departed from my text a little more than I do ordinarily, which may not have been wise, since sleep was a struggle last night. Not that I couldn't sleep. I would have very much preferred to have been awake. I just lay there, helplessly subject to my anxieties. A good many of them I could have put out of my mind, if I'd had the use of my mind. But as it was, I had to endure a kind of dull paralysis. To struggle within paralysis is a strange thing—I doubt I stirred a limb, but when I woke up I was exhausted, weary at heart.

Then young Boughton came to the service. That was nothing I would have expected. You saw him and waved and patted the pew next to you, and he came down the aisle and sat with you. Your mother looked at him to say good morning, and then she did not look at him again. Not once.

I began my remarks by pointing out the similarity between the stories of Hagar and Ishmael sent off into the wilderness and Abraham going off with Isaac to sacrifice him, as he believes. My point was that Abraham is in effect called upon to sacrifice both his sons, and that the Lord in both instances sends angels to intervene at the critical moment to save the child. Abraham's extreme old age is an important element in both stories, not only because he can hardly hope for more children, not only because the children of old age are unspeakably precious, but also, I think, because any father, particularly an old father, must finally give his child up to the wilderness and trust to the providence of God. It seems almost a cruelty for one generation to beget another when parents can secure so little for their children, so little safety, even in the best circumstances. Great faith is required to give the child up, trusting God to honor the parents' love for him by assuring that there will indeed be angels in that wilderness.

I noted that Abraham himself had been sent into the wilderness, told to leave his father's house also, that this was the narrative of all generations, and that it is only by the grace of God that we are made instruments of His providence and participants in a fatherhood that is always ultimately His.

At this point I departed from my text to say that an old pastor's anxiety for his church is likewise a forgetfulness of the fact that Christ is Himself the pastor of His people and a faithful presence among them through all generations. I thought this was a good point, but it started some of the women crying, so I tried to change the subject. I put the question why the Lord would ask gentle Abraham to do two things that were so cruel on their face—sending a child and his mother into the wilderness, and taking a child to be bound on an altar as if for sacrifice. This came to my mind because I had often wondered about it. Then I had to attempt an answer.

It had occurred to me that these were the only two instances in Scripture where a father is even apparently unkind to his child. The Lord can ask, "What man of you, if his son asked for bread, would give him a stone?" and it is a rhetorical question. Anyone knows from experience that among us there are a good many fathers who mistreat their children, or abandon them. And it was at that point I noticed young Boughton grinning at me. White as a sheet, and grinning. The text was one I would never have chosen if I'd thought he might be there, though if I'd kept to the sermon as I wrote it, everything would have been better.

About the cruelty of those narratives I said that they rendered the fact that children are often victims of rejection or violence, and that in these cases, too, which the Bible does not otherwise countenance, the child is within the providential care of God. And this is no less true, I said, if the angel carries her home to her faithful and loving Father than if He opens the spring or stops the knife and lets the child live out her sum of earthly years.

I don't know how sufficient that is to the question. It is such a difficult question that I hesitate to raise it at all. My only preparation for dealing with it has been the many times people have asked me to explain it to them. Whatever they may have thought, I have not succeeded to my own satisfaction even once.

I have always worried that when I say the insulted or the downtrodden are within the providence of God, it will be taken by some people to mean that it is not a grave thing, an evil thing, to insult or oppress. The whole teaching of the Bible is explicitly contrary to that idea. So I quoted the words of the Lord: "If anyone offend these little ones, it would be better for him if a millstone were put around his neck and he were cast into the sea." That is strong language, but there it is.

Young Boughton just sat there grinning. That's one thing that has always been strange about him. He treats words as if they were actions. He doesn't listen to the *meaning* of words, the way other people do. He just decides whether they are hostile, and how hostile they are. He decides whether they threaten him or injure him, and he reacts at that level. If he reads chastisement into anything you say, it's as if you had taken a shot at him. As if you had nicked his ear.

Now, as I have said, I did not expect him to be at that service. Furthermore, there are plenty of people whose behavior toward their children falls far short of what it should be, so, even when I departed from my text, and even though I will concede that my extemporaneous remarks might have been influenced by his sitting there with that look on his face, right beside my wife and child, still it was considerable egotism on his part to take my words as directed at him only, as he clearly did.

Your mother looked anxious. That might have been because I seemed to her to be talking about my own situation, and hers and yours, or it might have been because I did struggle a little to organize my thoughts, or it might have been because my emotions ran higher than they normally do. And if I looked at all the way I felt, even half as weary, there'd be grounds for concern in that, too.

But the thought occurred to me that young Boughton had told her some version of events, enough so she saw the implications, from his point of view, of my sermon. I don't know when he might have spoken to her. If he wanted the opportunity, he could have found it, I suppose. It did strike me as strange that she didn't look at him even one time. If she wished not to seem at all to recognize him in the sermon, that would explain it. I felt perhaps others in the congregation might have thought the sermon was directed at him. It was all most unfortunate. I must hope some good can come of it. I just don't know why he isn't worshipping with the Presbyterians.

Now I will pray. First I think I'll sleep. I'll try to sleep.

Another morning, thank the Lord. A good night's sleep, and no real discomfort to speak of. A woman in my flock called just after breakfast and asked me to come to her house. She is elderly, recently a widow, all by herself, and she has just moved from her farm to a cottage in town. You can never know what troubles or fears such people have, and I went. It turned out that the problem was her kitchen sink. She told me, considerably amazed that a reversal so drastic could occur in a lawful universe, that hot water came from the cold faucet and cold water from the hot faucet. I suggested she might just decide to take C for hot and H for cold, but she said she liked things to work the way they were supposed to. So I went home and got my screwdriver and came back and switched the handles. She said she guessed that would do until she could get a real plumber. Oh, the clerical life! I think this lady has suspected me of a certain doctrinal sloughing off, and now she will be sure of it. The story made your mother laugh, though, so my labors are repaid.

Last night I finished *The Trail of the Lonesome Pine*. It gave me a sort of turn there for a while. The old man sees the girl with someone her own age and remarks how well suited they are, and then he starts getting old and shabby and broke, and she's still very beautiful, of course. But it all turns out fine. She loves him only and forever. I doubt the book would have kept my interest if that particular matter had not arisen. And then I did want to know what there was in it your mother liked so much. God bless her, she's a dear woman. I read most of it yesterday evening, and then I couldn't sleep, wondering about it, so I crept off to my study and read till almost dawn. And then

I went up to the church to watch the dawn come, because that peace does restore me better than sleep can do. It is as though there were a hoard of quiet in that room, as if any silence that ever entered that room stayed in it. I remember once as a child dreaming that my mother came into my bedroom and sat down in a chair in the corner and folded her hands in her lap and stayed there, very calm and still. It made me feel wonderfully safe, wonderfully happy. When I woke up, there she was, sitting in that chair. She smiled at me and said, "I was just enjoying the quiet." I have that same feeling in the church, that I am dreaming what is true.

It strikes me that your mother could not have said a more heartening word to me by any other means than she did by loving that unremarkable book so much that I noticed and read it, too. That was providence telling me what she could not have told me.

I wish I could be like one of the old Vikings. I'd have the deacons carry me in and lay me down at the foot of the communion table, and then torch the old ship, and it and I would sail into eternity together. Though in fact I hope they will save that table. Surely they will.

Even the Holy of Holies was broken open. The deep darkness vanished into ordinary daylight, and the mystery of God was only made more splendid. So my dear hoard of silence can be scattered, too, and the great silence will not be any poorer for it. And yet thank God they are waiting till I die.

Sometimes I almost forget my purpose in writing this, which is to tell you things I would have told you if you had grown up with me, things I believe it becomes me as a father to teach you. There are the Ten Commandments, of course, and I know you will have been particularly aware of the Fifth Commandment, Honor your father and your mother. I draw attention to it because Six, Seven, Eight, and Nine are enforced by the criminal and civil laws and by social custom. The Tenth Commandment is unenforceable, even by oneself, even with the best will in the world, and it is violated constantly. I have been candid with you about my suffering a good deal at the spectacle of all the marriages, all the households overflowing with children, especially Boughton's—not because I wanted them, but because I wanted my own. I believe the sin of covetise is that pang of resentment you may feel when even the people you love best have what you want and don't have. From the point of view of loving your neighbor as yourself (Leviticus 19:18), there is nothing that makes a person's fallenness more undeniable than covetise—you feel it right in your heart, in your bones. In that way it is instructive. I have never really succeeded in obeying that Commandment, Thou shalt not covet. I avoided the experience of disobeying by keeping to myself a good deal, as I have said. I am sure I would have labored in my vocation more effectively if I had simply accepted covetise in myself as something inevitable, as Paul seems to do, as the thorn in my side, so to speak. "Rejoice with those who rejoice." I have found that difficult too often. I was much better at weeping with those who weep. I don't mean that as a joke, but it is kind of funny, when I think about it.

If I had lived, you'd have learned from my example, bad as well as good. So I want to tell you where I have failed, if the failures were important enough to have had real consequences, as this one certainly was.

But to return to the matter of honoring your mother. I think it is significant that the Fifth Commandment falls between those that have to do with proper worship of God and those that have to do with right conduct toward other people. I have always wondered if the Commandments should be read as occurring in order of importance. If that is correct, honoring your mother is more important than not committing murder. That seems remarkable, though I am open to the idea.

Or they may be thought of as different kinds of law, not comparable in terms of their importance, and honoring your mother might be the last in the sequence relating to right worship rather than the first in the series relating to right conduct. I believe this is a very defensible view.

The apostle says, "Outdo one another in showing honor," and also "Honor everyone." The Commandment is much narrower. The old commentators usually say "your father and mother" means anyone in authority over you, but that is the way people thought for a long time and a lot of harm came from it—slavery was "patriarchal," and so on. Anyone who happens to have authority over you is your parent! Then there have been some vicious, brutal parents in this world. "What do you mean, grinding the faces of the poor!" Does the text anywhere say, "Children will be given good things and *parents* will be sent empty away"? No, because parents are not equated with the rich or those in authority. Nowhere in Scripture is there a father who behaves wickedly toward his child, but the rich and powerful in Scripture are wicked much more often than not. And if honoring authority means only that you don't go out of your way to defy it, that really cheapens the notion of honoring as it would apply to an actual mother. It would not be anything beautiful or important enough to be placed right at the center of the Ten Commandments, for goodness' sake.

I believe the Fifth Commandment belongs in the first tablet, among the laws that describe right worship, because right worship is right perception (see especially Romans 1), and here the Scripture commands right perception of people you have a real and deep knowledge of. How you would honor someone differs with circumstances, so you can only truly fulfill a general obligation to show honor in specific cases of mutual intimacy and understanding. If all this seems lopsided in favor of parents, I would point out again that it is the consistent example of parents in the Bible that they honor their children. I think it is notable in this connection that it is not Adam but the Lord who rebukes Cain. Eli never rebukes his sons, or Samuel his. David never rebukes Absalom. At the very end, poor old Jacob rebukes his sons as he blesses them. A remarkable thing to consider.

There's a sermon here. The Prodigal Son as the Gospel text. I should ask Boughton if he has noticed this. But of course he has, of course he has. I must give that more thought.

My point here is that the great kindness and providence of the Lord has given most of us someone to honor—the child his parent, the parent his child. I have great respect for the uprightness of your character and the goodness of your heart, and your mother could not love you more or take greater pride in you. She has watched every moment of your life, almost, and she loves you as God does, to the marrow of your bones. So that is the honoring of the child. You see how it is godlike to love the *being* of someone. Your *existence* is a delight to us. I hope you never have to long for a child as I did, but oh, what a splendid thing it has been that you came finally, and what a blessing to enjoy you now for almost seven years.

As for the child honoring the parent, I believe that had to be commanded because the parent is a greater mystery, a stranger in a sense. So much of our lives has passed, and that is true even for your mother, who is a good generation younger than I am but who had a considerable life before she came to me—by which I mean only that she was well into her thirties when we were married. As I have said, I think she experienced a good deal of sorrow in those years. I have never asked, but one thing I have learned in my life is what settled, habitual sadness looks like, and when I saw her I thought, Where have you come from, my dear child? She came in during the first prayer and sat in the last pew and looked up at me, and from that moment hers was the only face I saw. I heard a man say once that Christians worship sorrow. That is by no means true. But we do believe there is a sacred mystery in it, it's fair to say that. There is something in her face I have always felt I must be sufficient to, as if there is a truth in it that tests the meaning of what I say. It's a fine face, very intelligent, but the sadness in it is engrafted into the intelligence, so to speak, until they seem one thing. I believe there is a dignity in sorrow simply because it is God's good pleasure that there should be. He is forever raising up those who are brought low. This does not mean that it is ever right to cause suffering or to seek it out when it can be avoided, and serves no good, practical purpose. To value suffering in itself can be dangerous and strange, so I want to be very clear about this. It means simply that God takes the side of sufferers against those who afflict them. (I hope you are familiar with the prophets, particularly Isaiah.)

Now, your mother never talks about herself, really, and she never admits to having felt any sort of grief in her life at all. That's her courage, her pride, and I know you will be respectful of it, and remember at the same time that a very, very great gentleness is called for, a great kindness. Because no one ever has that sort of courage who hasn't needed it. But you might not realize that, when you are young. I have often worried a little about the way the people in the church act toward her. She is distant, but she can't help that. So they are distant, too. On the other hand, I have often thought that she and I are well suited, no matter how we appear, because I have seen enough of life to understand her. They are not unkind, and they will give her whatever help she will accept. But most of them cannot see her youth in her as I do. I believe she may even seem a little hard to them.

I have written a letter to her, with instructions. I will add this to it—I have given money to people over the years, not a large amount, but a fair portion of my salary. Generally, I made up stories about forgotten funds and anonymous donations. Whether most of them believed me I doubt. At the time I had no idea that I would ever have a wife or a child, so I didn't think much about it, as I have said. I didn't keep any record, and I have no certain memory of individuals or circumstances. I have also paid for things around the church, paint and windowpanes and so on. We had some bleak times when I couldn't bring myself to ask anyone to provide what I could provide myself. I say this only because I want you to know that any help you receive, even to a fairly substantial amount, may be thought of by you not as charity but as *repayment*. I have never thought of the congregation as being in my debt, but the fact is that I have cast considerable bread upon those waters, and whatever bread returns you will be receiving as from my own hand. By the grace of God, of course.

But I wished to say certain things about the Fifth Commandment, and why it should be thought of as belonging to the first tablet. Briefly, the right worship of God is essential because it forms the mind to a right understanding of God. God is set apart—He is One, He is not to be imagined as a thing among things (idolatry—this is what Feuerbach failed to grasp). His name is set apart. It is sacred (which I take to be a reflection of the sacredness of the Word, the creative utterance which is not of a kind with other language). Then the Sabbath is set apart from other days, for the enjoyment of time and duration, perhaps, over and above the creatures who inhabit time. Because "the beginning," which might be called the seed of time, is the condition for all the creation that follows. Then mother and father are set apart, you see. It seems to me almost a retelling of Creation—First there is the Lord, then the Word, then the Day, then the Man and Woman—and after that Cain and Abel—Thou shalt not kill—and all the sins recorded in those prohibitions, just as crimes are recorded in the laws against them. So perhaps the tablets differ as addressing the eternal and the temporal.

What the reading yields is the idea of father and mother as the Universal Father and Mother, the Lord's dear Adam and His beloved Eve; that is, essential humankind as it came from His hand. There's a pattern in these Commandments of setting things apart so that their holiness will be perceived. Every day is holy, but the Sabbath is set apart so that the holiness of time can be experienced. Every human being is worthy of honor, but the conscious discipline of honor is learned from this setting apart of the mother and father, who usually labor and are heavy-laden, and may be cranky or stingy or ignorant or over-bearing. Believe me, I know this can be a hard Commandment to keep. But I believe also that the rewards of obedience are great, because at the root of real honor is always the sense of the sacredness of the person who is its object. In the particular instance of your mother, I know that if you are attentive to her in this way, you will find a very great loveliness in her. When you love someone to the degree you love her, you see her as God sees her, and that is an instruction in the nature of God and humankind and of Being itself. That is why the Fifth Commandment belongs on the first tablet. I have persuaded myself of it.

I slept decently. I stay at home Mondays when I can—my day of rest—so I had the morning to think and pray and also to do a little reshelving, and while I was doing that, it came to my mind that I should consider what I would say to myself if I came to myself for counsel. In fact, I do that all the time, as any rational person does, but there is a tendency, in my thinking, for the opposed sides of a question to cancel each other more or less algebraically—this is true, but on the other hand, so is that, so I discover a kind of equivalency of considerations that is interesting in itself but resolves nothing. If I put my thinking down on paper perhaps I can think more rigorously. Where a resolution is necessary it must also be possible. Not deciding is really one of the two choices that are available to me, so decision must be allowed its moment, too. That is, as behavior, not deciding to act would be identical with deciding not to act. If I were to put deciding not to act at one end of a continuum of possibility and deciding to act at the other end, the whole intervening space would be given over to not deciding, which would mean not acting. I believe this makes sense.

My point in any case is that I must put special, corrective emphasis on the possibility of doing the thing I dread doing, which is telling your mother what I think I ought to tell her.

Question: What is it you fear most, Moriturus?

Answer: I, Moriturus, fear leaving my wife and child unknowingly in the sway of a man of extremely questionable character.

Question: What makes you think his contact with them or his influence upon them will be considerable enough to be damaging to them?

Now, that really is an excellent question, and one I would not have thought to put to myself. The answer would be, he has come by the house a few times, he has come to church once. Not an impressive reply. The truth is, as I stood there in the pulpit, looking down on the three of you, you looked to me like a handsome young family, and my evil old heart rose within me, the old covetise I have mentioned elsewhere came over me, and I felt the way I used to feel when the beauty of other lives was a misery and an offense to me. And I felt as if I were looking back from the grave.

Well, thank God I thought that through.

And while I am being honest, I will add here that for perhaps two months I have felt a certain change in the way people act toward me, which could be a simple reflex of the way I act toward them. Maybe I don't understand as much as I should. Maybe I don't make as much sense as I should.

The fact is, I don't want to be old. And I certainly don't want to be dead. I don't want to be the tremulous coot you barely remember. I bitterly wish you could know me as a young man, and not really so young, either, necessarily. I was trim and fit into my sixties. That was one way I took after my grandfather and my father. I was never rangy like them, but I was very strong, very sound. Even now, if I could trust my heart, there's a lot I could do.

I don't have to fault myself for feeling this way. The Lord wept in the Garden on the night He was betrayed, as I have said to people in my situation many times. So it isn't just some unredeemed paganism in me that I dread what I should welcome, though clearly my sorrow is alloyed with discreditable emotions, emotions of other kinds. Of course, of course. "Who will free me from the body of this death?" Well, I know the answer to that one. "We shall not all sleep, but we shall all be changed, in a moment, in the twinkling of an eye." I imagine a kind of ecstatic pirouette, a little bit like going up for a line drive when you're so young that your body almost doesn't know about effort. Paul couldn't have meant something *entirely* different from that. So there's that to look forward to.

I say this because I really feel as though I'm failing, and not primarily in the medical sense. And I feel as if I am being left out, as though I'm some straggler and people can't quite remember to stay back for me. I had a dream like that last night. I was Boughton in the dream, for all purposes. Poor old Boughton.

This morning you came to me with a picture you had made that you wanted me to admire. I was just at the end of a magazine article, just finishing the last paragraph, so I didn't look up right away. Your mother said, in the kindest, saddest voice, "He doesn't hear you." Not "He didn't" but "He doesn't."

That article was very interesting. It was in *Ladies' Home Journal*, an old issue Glory found in her father's study and brought over for me to look at. There was a note on it. *Show Ames.* But it ended up at the bottom of a stack of things, I guess, because it's from 1948. The article is called "God and the American People," and it says 95 percent of us say we believe in God. But our religion doesn't meet the writer's standards, not at all. To his mind, all those people in all those churches are the scribes and the Pharisees. He seems to me to be a bit of a scribe himself, scorning and rebuking the way he does. How do you tell a scribe from a prophet, which is what he clearly takes himself to be? The prophets love the people they chastise, a thing this writer does not appear to me to do.

The oddness of the phrase "believe in God" brings to my mind that first chapter of Feuerbach, which is really about the awkwardness of language, not about religion at all. Feuerbach doesn't imagine the possibility of an existence beyond this one, by which I mean a reality embracing this one but exceeding it, the way, for example, this world embraces and exceeds Soapy's understanding of it. Soapy might be a victim of ideological conflict right along with the rest of us, if things get out of hand. She would no doubt make some feline appraisal of the situation, which would have nothing to do with the Dictatorship of the Proletariat or the Manhattan Project. The inadequacy of her concepts would have nothing to do with the reality of the situation.

That's a drastic way of putting it, and not a very precise one. I don't wish to suggest a reality that is simply an enlarged or extrapolated version of this reality. If you think how a thing we call a stone differs from a thing we call a dream—the degrees of unlikeness within the reality we know are very extreme, and what I wish to suggest is a much more absolute unlikeness, with which we exist, though our human circumstance creates in us a radically limited and peculiar notion of what existence is. I gave a sermon on this once, the text being "Your thoughts are not our thoughts." That was a good deal longer than two months ago. I believe it was last year. I thought at the time it might have puzzled a few people, but I was pleased with it. I even wished Edward could have heard it. I felt I'd clarified some things. I remember one lady did ask me, as she was going out the door, "Who is Feuerbach?" And that made me aware of that tendency of mine to live too much in my own thoughts. Your mother wanted to name the cat Feuerbach, but you insisted on Soapy.

It could be true that my interest in abstractions, which would have been forgiven first on grounds of youth and then on grounds of eccentricity, is now being forgiven on grounds of senility, which would mean people have stopped trying to see the sense in the things I say the way they once did. That would be by far the worst form of forgiveness. I used to have one of those books with humorous little sermon anecdotes in it somewhere. It was a gift, I remember, no name on it. How many years ago did I get that? I've probably been boring a lot of people for a long time. Strange to find comfort in the idea. There have always been things I felt I must tell them, even if no one listened or understood. And one of them is that many of the attacks on belief that have had such prestige for the last century or two are in fact meaningless. I must tell *you* this, because everything else I have told you, and them, loses almost all its meaning and its right to attention if this is not established.

If I were to go through my old sermons, I might find some in which I deal with this subject. Since I am presumably somewhere near the end of my time and my strength, that might be the best way to make the case for you. I should have thought of this long ago.

This afternoon we walked over to Boughton's to return his magazine. You held my hand a fair part of the way. There were milkweed seeds drifting around which you had to try to catch, but you'd come back and take my hand again. It's a hard thing to be patient with me, the way I creep along these days, but I'm trying not to get my heart in a state. There have been so many fine days this summer that I've begun to hear talk of a drought. Dust and grasshoppers are fine in their way, too, within limits. Whatever is coming, I'd be sorry to miss it.

Boughton was on his porch, "listening to the breeze," he said. "Feeling the breeze." Glory brought out some lemonade for us and sat down with us, and we talked a little bit about television. Your mother has been looking at it, too. I don't enjoy it myself. It's not the last impression I want to have of this world.

It turns out that when Glory found that article and asked her father if he still wanted me to see it, he asked her to read it over to him, and then he laughed and said, "Oh yes, yes, Reverend Ames will want to have a look at that." He knows what will exasperate me, and he was laughing in anticipation as soon as I mentioned it.

We agreed it must have been fairly widely read in both our congregations, because on one page there's a recipe for that molded salad of orange gelatin with stuffed green olives and shredded cabbage and anchovies that has dogged my ministerial life these last years, and which appears at his house whenever he so much as catches cold. There should be a law to prevent recipes for molded salad from appearing within twenty pages of any article having to do with religion. I ended up bringing the magazine back home because I thought I might want to use it in a sermon.

There are two insidious notions, from the point of view of Christianity in the modern world. (No doubt there are more than two, but the others will have to wait.) One is that religion and religious experience are illusions of some sort (Feuerbach, Freud, etc.), and the other is that religion itself is real, but *your* belief that *you* participate in it is an illusion. I think the second of these is the more insidious, because it is religious experience above all that authenticates religion, for the purposes of the individual believer.

But people of any degree of religious sensitivity are always vulnerable to the accusation that their consciousness or their understanding does not attain to the highest standards of the faith, because that is always true of everyone. St. Paul is eloquent on this subject. But if the awkwardness and falseness and failure of religion are interpreted to mean there is no core of truth in it— and the witness of Scripture from end to end discourages this view—then people are disabled from trusting their thoughts, their expressions of belief, and their understanding, and even from believing in the essential dignity of their and their neighbors' endlessly flawed experience of belief. It seems to me there is less meanness in atheism, by a good measure. It seems that the spirit of religious self-righteousness this article deplores is precisely the spirit in which it is written. Of course he's right about many things, one of them being the destructive potency of religious self-righteousness.

Here is a sentence Boughton and I got a laugh out of: "One might ask how many Christians can define Christianity." In twenty-five volumes or less, I said.

Boughton said, "Fewer," and winked at Glory, and she said, "Ever the stickler," which is true.

(Of course I was simply using contemporary idiom, and he was aware of that. He just doesn't approve of it. I don't use it often. But I think it's perfectly fine for making a little joke now and then.)

Here is a paragraph we lingered over: "There is indeed a note of sinful pride in the confidence with which the majority of people expressed their ideas about heaven. For although the Bible has much to say about final judgment, it offers no definitive picture of life after death. Yet fewer than one third of the American people—29 percent—admit they have no ideas on what is one of the most ambiguous subjects in Biblical revelation."

Now, that is a kind of interpretation I would call fraudulent. To say a subject is ambiguous is not to say one cannot form ideas on it, or shouldn't, nor is it to say even that it is possible to *avoid* forming ideas on it. Any concept that exists in the mind at all exists in some form, among some set of associations. I'd like to talk to that 29 percent who have no ideas, to see how they do it. I bet they just didn't like the question.

Boughton says he has more ideas about heaven every day. He said, "Mainly I just think about the splendors of the world and multiply by two. I'd multiply by ten or twelve if I had the energy. But two is much more than sufficient for my purposes." So he's just sitting there multiplying the feel of the wind by two, multiplying the smell of the grass by two. "I remember when we put that old wagon on the courthouse roof," he said. "Seems to me the stars were brighter in those days. Twice as bright."

"And we were twice as clever."

"Oh, more than that," he said. "Much more than that."

Jack came out and sat down with us. He asked if he could look at the article, and I gave it to him. He said, "I thought he made the point in here somewhere that Americans' treatment of the Negro indicated a lack of religious seriousness."

Boughton said, "It is very easy to judge."

Jack smiled and handed the magazine back to me. "True," he said.

That was the first I'd seen of him since Sunday, since the service. He went out through the chancel and the side door, to avoid shaking hands with me, I believe. I've been feeling some discomfort on that account as well as others. I was even a little embarrassed to meet his eyes, to tell the truth. I believe returning the magazine was mainly a pretext for looking in on Boughton and Glory, to see if they were upset with me. I wasn't done with that article. I meant all along to bring it back with me. I conceal my motives from myself pretty effectively sometimes. I had even imagined, lying awake Sunday night, that Jack might go away again because I had brought up the old catastrophe right there in church, or so he seemed to believe. I thought of apologizing, but that would only confirm in his mind that my meaning and my intention were what he took them to be, which I do not wholly believe, and which would deprive him of the possibility of making a less damaging interpretation of them. At any rate, it would raise the issue between us, perhaps unnecessarily. Finally, I was hesitant to go to the house at all, fearing that my mere presence might be an irritant or a provocation, as I feared my staying away might be also. Then Glory came by to say hello. She seemed in fine spirits. And I was mightily relieved. If there is one thing I don't want to do in the time that remains to either one of us, it is offend Boughton. I fell to thinking what a pleasure it must be to him to have Jack there, and it occurred to me that it might be a remarkable generosity on Jack's part to come home to the poor old man, and perhaps to Glory also, considering her troubles. I was downright ashamed to remember how impatient I was for him to leave, thinking only of my own life, I admit. The thought had even occurred to me that he might be there to start moving his father out of the house, so to speak, since he and the other children will inherit it. The place really did need to be put right, and there was much more to do than Glory could have done alone. Sitting there on the porch with Jack, I was struck by how much he had aged. Of course he's old enough to have aged, he's in his forties somewhere. Angeline would be fifty-one, so he's forty-three. There is gray in his hair, and he looks tired around the eyes. Well, he looked tense, as he always does, and he also looked sad, it seemed to me.

Your mother came up the road to tell us our supper was ready. It was a cold supper, she said, so there was no hurry. She agreed to sit with us for a few minutes. She always has to be coaxed to stay in company even a little while, and then it's all I can do to get a word from her. I believe she worries about the way she talks. I love the way she talks, or the way she talked when I first knew her. "It don't matter," she would say, in that low, soft voice of hers. That was what she said when she meant she forgave someone, but it had a sound of deeper, sadder resignation, as if she were forgiving the whole of the created order, forgiving the Lord Himself. It grieves me that I may never hear just those words spoken by her again. I believe Boughton made her self-conscious with that little trick of his of correcting people. Not that he ever corrected her.

"It don't matter." It was as if she were renouncing the world itself just in order to make nothing of some offense to her. Such a prodigal renunciation, that empty-handed prodigality I remember from the old days. I have nothing to give you, take and eat. Ashy biscuit, summer rain, her hair falling wet around her face. If I were to multiply the splendors of the world by two—the splendors as I feel them—I would arrive at an idea of heaven very unlike anything you see in the old paintings.

So Jack Boughton is forty-three. I have no idea what sort of life he has had since he left here. There has never been any mention of marriage or children or of any particular kind of work. I always felt it was best not to inquire.

I was sitting there listening to old Boughton ramble along (he uses the expression himself) about a trip he and his wife made once to Minneapolis, when Jack broke in and said to me, "So, Reverend, I would like to hear your views on the doctrine of predestination."

Now, that is probably my least favorite topic of conversation in the entire world. I have spent a great part of my life hearing that doctrine talked up and down, and no one's understanding ever advanced one iota. I've seen grown men, God-fearing men, come to blows over that doctrine. The first thought that came to my mind was, Of *course* he would bring up predestination!

So I said, "That's a complicated issue."

"Let me simplify it," he said. "Do you think some people are intentionally and irretrievably consigned to perdition?"

"Well," I said, "that may actually be the kind of simplification that raises more questions than it avoids."

He laughed. "People must ask you about this all the time," he said.

"They do."

"Then I suppose you must have some way of responding."

"I tell them there are certain attributes our faith assigns to God: omniscience, omnipotence, justice, and grace. We human beings have such a slight acquaintance with power and knowledge, so little conception of justice, and so slight a capacity for grace, that the workings of these great attributes together is a mystery we cannot hope to penetrate."

He laughed. "You say it in those very words."

"Yes, I do. More or less those very words. It's a fraught question, and I'm careful with it."

He nodded. "I take you to mean that you do believe in predestination."

"I dislike that word. It's been put to crude uses."

"Can you propose a better word?"

"Not offhand." I felt he was deviling me, you see.

"I would like your help with this, Reverend," he said, so seriously that I began to think he might be serious. "This is a grave issue, isn't it? We're not really dealing here with a mere word, a mere abstraction."

"You're right," I said. "That's true."

"I assume predestination does not, in your understanding,

mean that a good person will go to hell simply because he was consigned to hell from the beginning."

Glory said, "Excuse me. I've heard this argument a thousand times and I hate it."

Old Boughton said, "I hate this conversation a good deal myself and I've never seen it go anywhere. I wouldn't really call this an argument, though, Glory."

"Wait five minutes," she said. She got up and walked into the house, but your mother sat still, listening.

Jack said, "I'm the amateur here. I suppose if I had your history with the question I'd be sick of it, too. Well, actually I believe I do have a history with it. I have had reason to wonder fairly often about it. I hoped you would instruct me a little."

"I don't believe a person can be good in any meaningful sense and also be consigned to perdition. Nor do I believe that a person who is sinful in any sense is necessarily consigned to perdition. Scripture clearly says otherwise in both cases."

"I'm sure it does. But are there people who are simply born evil, live evil lives, and then go to hell?"

"On that point Scripture is not so clear."

"What does your own experience suggest, Reverend?"

"Generally, a person's behavior is consistent with his nature. Which is only to say his behavior is consistent. The consistency is what I mean when I speak of his nature." I recognized a redundancy there, a circularity. He smiled.

"People don't change, then," he said.

"They do, if there is some other factor involved—drink, or some sort of personal influence. That is, their behavior changes. Whether that means their nature changes or that another aspect of it becomes visible is hard to say."

He said, "For a man of the cloth, you're pretty cagey."

That made old Boughton laugh. "You should have seen him thirty years ago."

"I did."

"Well," his father said, "you should have been paying attention."

Jack shrugged. "I was."

Now, that got to me a little. I don't know why Boughton would have led him on like that. Cagey at checkers, maybe.

I said, "I'm just trying to find a slightly useful way of saying there are things I don't understand. I'm not going to force some theory on a mystery and make foolishness of it, just because that is what people who talk about it normally do."

Your mother looked at me, so I knew I must have sounded upset. I *was* upset. Nine-tenths of the time when some smart aleck starts in on theological questions he's only trying to put me in a false position, and I'm just too old to see the joke in it anymore. Then Glory came to the door and said, "Your five minutes aren't up yet," as if anyone needed to underscore the futility.

But your mother spoke up, which surprised us all. She said, "What about being saved?" She said, "If you can't change, there don't seem much purpose in it." She blushed. "That's not what I meant."

"You've made an excellent point, dear," Boughton said. "I worried a long time about how the mystery of predestination could be reconciled with the mystery of salvation. I remember thinking about that a great deal."

"No conclusions?" Jack asked.

"None that I can remember." Then he said, "To conclude is not in the nature of the enterprise."

Jack smiled at your mother as if he was looking for an ally, someone to share his frustration, but she just sat very still and studied her hands.

"I should think," he said, "that the question Mrs. Ames has raised is one you gentlemen would approach with great seriousness. I know you have attended tent meetings only as interested observers, but— Excuse me. I don't believe anyone else wants to pursue this, so I'll let it go."

Your mother said, "I'm interested."

Old Boughton, who was getting a little ruffled, said, "I hope the Presbyterian Church is as good a place as any to learn the blessed truths of the faith, including redemption and salvation first of all. The Lord knows I have labored to make it so."

"Pardon me, Father," Jack said. "I'll go find Glory. She'll tell me how to make myself useful. You always said that was the best way to keep out of trouble."

"No, stay," your mother said. And he did.

There was an uneasy silence, so I remarked that he might find Karl Barth a help, just for the sake of conversation.

He said, "Is that what you do when some tormented soul arrives on your doorstep at midnight? Recommend Karl Barth?"

I said, "It depends on the case," which it does. I have found Barth's work to be full of comfort, as I believe I have told you elsewhere. But in fact, I don't recall ever recommending him to any tormented soul except my own. That is what I mean about being put in a false position.

Your mother said, "A person can change. Everything can change." Still never looking at him.

He said, "Thanks. That's all I wanted to know."

So that was the end of the conversation. We went home to supper.

I was left wondering what he was referring to when he mentioned tent meetings. And I have thought a lot about that word "cagey." I have always dreaded having to talk theology with

people who have no sympathy for it. I've been evasive from time to time, that's true. I see the error of *assuming* a person is not speaking with you in good faith. It's not respectful, I know that, and I don't do it often. Nor do I have much occasion to around here, where it seems as if I've baptized half the people I pass on the street and taught them all the theology they will ever know.

But it is hard for me to see good faith in John Ames Boughton, and that's a terrible problem. As we were walking home, your mother said, "He was only asking a question," which was almost a rebuke, coming from her. Then, after we'd walked a little farther, she said, "Maybe some people aren't so comfortable with themselves." Now, that *was* a rebuke. And she was quite right. What need had an old soldier like me to defend himself even from mockery, if that was what he was up to? There was no question of need, there was only habit.

I believe I have tried never to say anything Edward would have found callow or naïve. That constraint has been useful to me, in my opinion. It may be a form of defensiveness, but I hope it has at least been useful on balance. There is a tendency among some religious people even to invite ridicule and to bring down on themselves an intellectual contempt which seems to me in some cases justified. Nevertheless, I would advise you against defensiveness on principle. It precludes the best eventualities along with the worst. At the most basic level, it expresses a lack of faith. As I have said, the worst eventualities can have great value as experience. And often enough, when we think we are protecting ourselves, we are struggling against our rescuer. I know this, I have seen the truth of it with my own eyes, though I have not myself always managed to live by it, the Good Lord knows. I truly doubt I would know how to live by it for even a day, or an hour. That is a remarkable thing to consider.

———

I believe it will put my mind at ease to tell you straightfor-
wardly what is at issue here. Sleep has become a great problem, elusive, and then pretty grueling when it comes. Prayer
has not been equal to quieting these perturbations. If I feel
that what I tell you is untrue in some way, or that I simply
ought not to tell it, I can just destroy these pages. They certainly won't be the first I've destroyed. Back when I had a
woodstove, it was a satisfyingly easy thing to do. There was a
rightness to seeing nonsense and frustration fall into the
flames. I'm thinking we should have somebody build us a bar-
becue, like the Muellers did.

Let me say first of all that the grace of God is sufficient to any
transgression, and that to judge is wrong, the origin and
essence of much error and cruelty. I am aware of these things,
as I hope you are also.

Let me say, too, that there are bonds which oblige me to
special tolerance and kindness toward this young man, John
Ames Boughton. He is the beloved child of my oldest and
dearest friend, who gave him to me, so to speak, to compensate
for my own childlessness. I baptized him in Boughton's congregation. I remember the moment very clearly, Boughton and
Mrs. Boughton and all the little ones there at the font, watching to see my joyful surprise, which I hope they did see, because my feelings at the time were a little more complex than
I'd have wished. I had not been warned.

All this being the case, it offends my conscience to bear witness against him. Nevertheless, there is a very real sense in
which people are fairly and appropriately associated with their
histories, for human purposes. To say a thief is a brother man

and beloved of God is true. To say therefore a thief is not a thief is an error. I don't wish to imply that young Boughton ever, to the best of my knowledge, stole anything of significance in any conventional sense of the word "stole." It is only to explain why I feel I may speak to you of his past, or at least of what little I know of it and what is to the point.

As I said before, the basic circumstances themselves are so commonplace that they can be dealt with in a very few words. About twenty years ago, while he was still in college at any rate, he became involved with a young girl, and the involvement produced a child. This sort of thing happens, and it is sorted out one way or another, as any clergyman can tell you.

In this instance, however, there were aggravating circumstances. For one thing, the girl was very young. For another, her family situation was desolate, even squalid. In other words, to say the least, she enjoyed none of the protections a young girl needs. How Jack Boughton even found her has never been clear to me. She and her family lived in an isolated house with a lot of mean dogs under the porch. It was a sad place and she was a sad child. And there he was with his college airs and his letter sweater and that Plymouth convertible he got somewhere for a song, he said, when he was asked about it. (Boughton had so many children to educate, they all had to work, Jack too, and a car was out of the question even for old Boughton. His congregation gave him a used Buick in 1946, because by then it was too hard for him to walk anywhere.)

Jack Boughton had no business in the world involving himself with that girl. It was something no honorable man would have done. However I turn it over in my mind, that fact remains. And here is a prejudice of mine, confirmed by my lights through many years of observation. Sinners are not all dishonorable people, not by any means. But those who are dishonorable never really repent and never really reform. Now, I may be wrong here. No such distinction occurs in Scripture. And repentance and reformation are matters of the soul which only the Lord can judge. But, in my experience, dishonor is recalcitrant. When I see it, my heart sinks, because I feel I have no help to offer a dishonorable person. I know the deficiency may be my own altogether.

In any case, young Boughton never acknowledged the child, to make any provision for it at all. But he did tell his father about it. As if confessing a transgression, as his father saw it, though to me it seemed like pure meanness, because he must have known that grandchild would weigh on old Boughton's mind something terrible, as it did. He even told Boughton where the young girl lived, and Glory drove the old man out there in that foolish convertible. Boughton hoped to baptize the child—it was a little girl—or at least to satisfy himself that she would be baptized, but the people were hostile to him, as if he were the one at fault. So he left some money and went away, very dejected and humiliated. He was so obviously miserable that Mrs. Boughton made Glory tell her what the problem was, and then she was so miserable that Glory drove them both out in the country. Mrs. Boughton had to see the baby, and she had to hold her. It was probably unwise for her to do that. Well, I held her, too. Where wisdom could have found a place in a situation like that one I don't claim to know. They brought diapers and clothes and they left money. This went on for a long time. It went on for several years, in fact. Glory used to come to me and cry about it, because nothing ever got better. The baby was always too dirty and too small.

She took me out to see the situation for myself, and I can tell you it was very bad. People have a right to live as they see fit, but that was no place for an infant. There were tin cans and broken glass all over the yard and dirty old mattresses on the floor, and who knows what all. Dogs everywhere. How could young Boughton have taken advantage of that girl? And then to have abandoned her? Glory said when she asked her brother if he planned to marry the girl he just said, "You've seen her." On the way there Glory told me how I must try to persuade the family to let the girl and her baby come into town and live in a nice Christian family. I tried that, but her father spat on the floor and said, "She's already got a nice Christian family."

Then all the way home Glory described a plan she had come up with to kidnap the child. The baby, that is. She knew some stories about the old days when they used to smuggle fugitives up from Missouri, and she thought one small infant would be a much easier thing to conceal. Several houses in town have hidden cellars or cabinets where people could be put out of sight for a day or two. The church has one in the attic. I'll have to remember to show it to you. It will involve climbing a ladder. Well, we'll see.

I told her that in the old days towns like ours were a conspiracy. Lots of people were only there to be antislavery by any means that came to hand. Persuading someone to take a child from her mother, to steal it, was a very different thing, especially since Glory had no evidence of any claim on the child. She said she had written again and again to young Boughton asking him to acknowledge the child for his parents' sake. She had washed the baby and dressed her up and sent him smiling photographs. She had photographed the baby in his father's arms. Jack sent Glory cards on her birthday and boxes of chocolate and made no reference whatever to his child or to the misery he had caused in their household. She was crying so hard she had to pull off the road. "They're so sad!" she said. "They're so ashamed!" (Young Boughton did have the decency to leave his convertible and take the train back to school, so that Glory could drive her parents out to see that poor croupy, rashy child every week or so.)

Well, here is the end of the story. The little girl lived about three years. She was turning into a spry, wiry little thing, a source of sullen pride to her mother and her nice Christian family. But she cut her foot somehow and died of the infection. The last time they visited her, they saw she was in bad shape. So Glory went and found a doctor, but by then there was nothing to be done. The grandfather said, "Her lot was very hard," and Glory slapped him. He threatened to press charges, but I guess he never got around to it. He let the Boughtons bury the little girl in their family plot, since they agreed to pay the expenses and a little more beside. So there she is. The stone says Baby, three years (her mother had never really settled on a name), and then: "Their angels in Heaven always see the face of My Father in Heaven."

It is a bitter story, and left us all with much to regret. I suppose we really should have stolen her. The fact is, though, that Glory's scheme would probably have ended with her and some of the rest of us in jail, the baby back with its mother, and young Boughton under a tree somewhere, reading Huxley or Carlyle, his convertible at last restored to him. I don't know the right and wrong of a situation like that. I suppose we could have bought the child if we'd somehow managed to raise the money. But that's a crime, too. And those people had a sort of blackmail situation, with the baby as hostage. If the Lord hadn't taken her home, it could have gone on for decades. Glory said, "If we could have had her *just one week!*" Then what, I wonder. I know exactly why she would say that, but I wonder what it means. I have often thought the same about that other child of mine.

Now they have penicillin, and so many things are different. In those days you could die of almost anything, almost nothing. "We brought her shoes," Mrs. Boughton said. "Why was she barefoot?" The girl said, "Savin' 'em." The poor little girl, her mother. She was white and sullen, about to die of sadness, by the look of her. What to do with all the frustration and regret that builds up in this life? She had left school, and all we ever knew of her was that she ran off to Chicago.

That's all I think I need to tell you about Jack Boughton. When his mother died he didn't come home, as I have said. Maybe he wanted to spare us all having to deal with him.

They loved that baby the way they did because they loved Jack so much. She looked just like him. And now here he is at home, and Glory as glad to be with him as if no shadow had ever fallen between them at all. I have no idea why he is at home. Nor do I know what reconciliation they have worked out among themselves. If my sermon had disturbed it, I would not feel equal to the regret that would have cost me.

Twenty years is a long time. I know nothing about those years, and I believe that I would know—if anything had happened that redounded at all to his credit. He doesn't have the look of a man who has made good use of himself, if I am any judge.

I found a couple of my sermons under the Bible on the night table, which I take to mean that your mother recommends them to my attention. She has brought down a number of those sermons, fetched them down in the laundry basket, and she really is reading them. She says that I should use some of them, to spare myself effort that I might otherwise spend writing to you. That is a much more persuasive notion than her earlier one, that I should use them to spare myself effort. If I really thought I wasn't up to writing a sermon, I'd have to resign my pulpit. But the thought of having more time with you is a different thing altogether.

One of the sermons is on forgiveness. It is dated June 1947. I don't know what the occasion was. I might have been thinking of the Marshall Plan, I suppose. I don't find much in it to regret. It interprets "Forgive us our debts as we forgive our debtors" in light of the Law of Moses on that subject. That is, the forgiveness of literal debt and the freeing of slaves every seventh year, and then the great restoration of the people to their land, and to themselves if they were in bondage, every fiftieth year. And it makes the point that, in Scripture, the one sufficient reason for the forgiveness of debt is simply the existence of debt. And it goes on to compare this to divine grace, and to the Prodigal Son and his restoration to his place in his father's house, though he neither asks to be restored as son nor even repents of the grief he has caused his father.

I believe it concludes quite effectively. It says Jesus puts His hearer in the role of the father, of the one who forgives. Because if we are, so to speak, the debtor (and of course we are that, too), that suggests no graciousness in us. And grace is the great gift. So to be forgiven is only half the gift. The other half is that *we* also can forgive, restore, and liberate, and therefore we can feel the will of God enacted through us, which is the great restoration of ourselves to ourselves.

That still seems right to me. I think it is a sound reading of the text. Well, in 1947 I was almost seventy, so my thinking should have been fairly mature at that point. And your mother would have heard me preach that sermon, come to think of it. She first came to church on Pentecost of that year, which I think was in May, and never missed a Sunday after it except the one.

It rained, as I have said, but we had a good many candles lighted, which has always been our custom for that service, when we could afford them. And there were a good many flowers. And when I saw there was a stranger in the room, I do remember feeling pleased that the sanctuary should have looked as cheerful as it did, that it should have been such a pleasant place to step into out of the weather. I believe that day my sermon was on light, or Light. I suppose she hasn't found it, or she doesn't remember it, or she doesn't think it was especially good. I'd like to see it, though.

I do enjoy remembering that morning. I was sixty-seven, to be exact, which did not seem old to me. I wish I could give you the memory I have of your mother that day. I wish I could leave you certain of the images in my mind, because they are so beautiful that I hate to think they will be extinguished when I am. Well, but again, this life has its own mortal loveliness. And memory is not strictly mortal in its nature, either. It is a strange thing, after all, to be able to return to a moment, when it can hardly be said to have any reality at all, even in its passing. A moment is such a slight thing, I mean, that its abiding is a most gracious reprieve.

Once, I went out with Glory to take some things to that little baby. The family lived just across the West Nishnabotna, and when we came to the bridge we saw the two children, the baby and her mother, playing there in the river. We drove on to the house and set the food we had brought by the fence. We didn't approach the house, because that pack of dogs came roaring out to the gate and no one appeared to call them off—we always brought canned ham, canned milk, and so on, things the dogs couldn't get into. The little girl must have heard the car passing and the dogs barking and known that we had come to her house, since it was a Monday. She would have ignored us if she did. She loyally reflected her father's view of us. She was offended by our concern and our helpfulness and let us know as much by ignoring us as often as we gave her the chance.

And I must say I do not find that hard to understand. Her father clearly assumed that we were going to so much bother
and expense in order to keep Jack out of trouble. And while no
one ever said such a thing or even hinted at such an idea, I
can't say he was altogether wrong. Nor can I say that it was no
part of Jack's motive in confessing to his father, that he knew
poor old Boughton would respond to the situation as he did.
That would explain why he left the Plymouth.

In any case, Glory and I parked the car along the road a
hundred yards beyond the bridge and walked back and stood
on the bridge and watched those children. The baby, who had
just begun to walk, didn't have a stitch on, and the little girl
was wearing a dress that was soggy to her waist. It was late
summer. The river is very shallow at that time of year, and the
bottom was half exposed and braided like water. There were
sandbars right across, the bigger ones small jungles of weedy
vegetation weedily in bloom, with butterflies and dragonflies
attending on them like spirits. The little girl was practicing the
maternal imperative from time to time, the way children
sometimes do when they are playing. Maybe she knew she was
being overheard. She was trying to dam a rivulet with sticks
and mud, and the baby was trying to understand the project
well enough to help. She would bring her mother handfuls of
mud and handfuls of water, and her mother would say, "Now,
don't you go stepping on it. You're just messing up all my
work!"

After a while the baby cupped her hands and poured water
on her mother's arm and laughed, so her mother cupped her
hands and poured water on the baby's belly, and the baby
laughed and threw water on her mother with both hands, and
the little girl threw water back, enough so that the baby whim-
pered, and the little girl said, "Now, don't you go crying! What
do you expect when you act like that." And she put her arms

163

around her and settled her into her lap, kneeling there in the water, and set about repairing her dam with her free hand. The baby made a conversational sound and her mother said, "That's a leaf. A leaf off a tree. Leaf," and gave it into the baby's hand. And the sun was shining as well as it could onto that shadowy river, a good part of the shine being caught in the trees. And the cicadas were chanting, and the willows were straggling their tresses in the water, and the cottonwood and the ash were making that late summer hush, that susurrus.

After a while we went on back to the car and came home. Glory said, "I do not understand one thing in this world. Not one."

This came to my mind because remembering and forgiving can be contrary things. No doubt they usually are. It is not for me to forgive Jack Boughton. Any harm he did to me personally was indirect, and really very minor. Or say at least that harm to me was probably never a primary object in any of the things he got up to. That one man should lose his child and the next man should just squander his fatherhood as if it were nothing—well, that does not mean that the second man has transgressed against the first.

I don't forgive him. I wouldn't know where to begin.

You and Tobias are out in the yard. You have put your Dodgers cap on a fence post, and the two of you are chucking pebbles at it. Accuracy will come, probably. "Ah, man!" says T., and screws up his face and does a tightfisted dance of frustration, as if he had achieved a near miss. Now off you go to gather more pebbles, Soapy tagging after at a fastidious distance, as if she had some business of her own that happened to be taking her in more or less the same direction.

I was trying to remember what birds did before there were telephone wires. It would have been much harder for them to roost in the sunlight, which is a thing they clearly enjoy doing.

And here comes Jack Boughton with his bat and his glove. You and T. are running up the street to meet him. He has set his glove on top of your head and you think that is a very good thing. You are holding it on with both hands and striding straight-legged along beside him, barefoot and bare-bellied like some primordial princeling. I can't see the Popsicle streaks down your belly, but I know they're there. T. is carrying the bat. Since Jack never looks entirely at ease, it should not surprise me that he looks a little tense. But here he is, coming through the gate. I can hear him speaking with your mother on the porch. It sounds pleasant. I believe my heart would prefer that I stay here in this chair, at least for the time being.

You three have come out in the side yard. He's batting fungo. You and T. are running hither and yon as if to catch the ball. When you get anywhere near the ball, you put up your gloves to protect yourselves from it, and it thumps on the ground somewhere nearby. But you're getting the idea of throwing overhand. It's pretty to watch you, the three of you. I believe I will just step outside and see what he has on his mind. I know there's something.

He wanted to know if I would be in my study at church tomorrow. I said in the morning, yes. So he will come by to talk with me.

I wish I had more pictures of myself as a younger man, I suppose because I believe that as you read this I will not be old, and when I see you, at the end of your good long life, neither of us will be old. We will be like brothers. That is how I imagine it. Sometimes now when you crawl into my lap and settle against me and I feel that light, quick strength of your body and the weightiness of your head, when you're cold from playing in the sprinkler or warm from your bath at night, and you lie in my arms and fiddle with my beard and tell me what you've been thinking about, that is perfectly pleasant, and I imagine your child self finding me in heaven and jumping into my arms, and there is a great joy in the thought. Still, the other is better, and more likely to be somewhere near the reality of the situation, I believe. We know nothing about heaven, or very little, and I think Calvin is right to discourage curious speculations on things the Lord has not seen fit to reveal to us.

Adulthood is a wonderful thing, and brief. You must be sure to enjoy it while it lasts.

I believe the soul in Paradise must enjoy something nearer to a perpetual vigorous adulthood than to any other state we know. At least that is my hope. Not that Paradise could disappoint, but I believe Boughton is right to enjoy the imagination of heaven as the best pleasure of this world. I don't see how he can be entirely wrong, approaching it that way. I certainly don't mind the thought of your mother finding me a strong young man. There is neither male nor female, they neither marry nor are given in marriage, but, *mutatis mutandis*, it would be a fine thing. That *mutandis*! Such a burden on one word!

> Grant me on earth what seems Thee best,
> Till death and Heav'n reveal the rest.

> —Isaac Watts

And John Ames adds his amen.

This morning I woke early, which is really a way of saying last night I hardly slept at all. I had it in my mind that I would dress a little more carefully than has been my habit lately. I have a good head of hair, not as evenly distributed as it might be, but pretty thick where it grows and a good white. My eyebrows are white, too, and quite thick. I mean the hairs grow long and spiral off in every direction. The irises of my eyes have begun to melt at the edges a little. They never were any particular color, and now they're a lighter shade. My nose and ears are definitely larger than they were in my prime. I know I'm a perfectly passable old fellow with regard to my appearance, for what that's worth. Age is strange, though. Yesterday you stood by my chair and toyed with my eyebrow, pulling the hairs out to their full length and watching them curl back again. You thought it was funny, and it is.

Well, but I shaved carefully and put on a white shirt and buffed my shoes a little, and so on. I think such preparations can be the difference between an elderly gentleman and a codger. I know the former is a more suitable consort for your lovely mother, but sometimes I forget to go to the necessary trouble, and that's an error I mean to correct.

And after all that, I went up to the church and waited in the sanctuary for the light to come and fell asleep in the pew, upright, which is a good thing, because young Boughton came in looking for me when he found I wasn't in my study. I felt just the way I imagine the shade of poor old Samuel must have felt when the witch dragged him up from Sheol. "Why hast thou disquieted me, to bring me up?" In fact, I had spent the morning darkness praying for the wisdom to do well by John Ames Boughton, and then when he woke me, I was immediately aware that my sullen old reptilian self would have handed him over to the Philistines for the sake of a few more minutes' sleep. I really despise the pathos of being found asleep at odd times in odd places. Your mother always tells people I'm just up the whole night reading and writing, and sometimes that is true. And sometimes I'm just up the whole night wishing I weren't.

(I do recommend prayer at such times, because often they mean something is in need of resolving. I had arrived at a considerable equanimity, there in the dark, and I believe that is what permitted me to sleep. The problem was that I slept too deeply. The physical body can crave sleep with an animal greed, as everybody knows. Then it is snappish when it is disturbed, as I would have been if I hadn't had the memory, at least, of praying for tranquillity. At that moment I cannot claim to have had tranquillity itself.)

So Jack Boughton's first words to me were "I'm very sorry." He sat down in the pew, allowing me time to gather myself, which was good of him. I noticed that he also was dressed with special care, that he was wearing a jacket and a tie and that his shoes had a good shine on them. He studied the room, taking in the simplicity of it, which I know is naked simplicity, not the elegant, ornamental kind you see in some of the finer old churches, since this one was always meant to be temporary.

"Your father preached here," he said.

"For a good many years. It hasn't changed much since then."

"It's like the church I grew up in."

The Presbyterians did have a church very much like this one, but they replaced it several years ago with a fairly imposing building of brick and stone. It already has a good deal of ivy clinging to it. Boughton says if he could just get them to dilapidate the bell tower a little they would have a real antiquity. He has suggested that we out-antiquate the Presbyterians by modeling our new building on the catacombs. I believe I'll propose it.

Jack said, "It's an enviable thing, to be able to receive your identity from your father."

I have a dreadful habit of taking the measure of a conversation early, in terms of the pleasure or benefit I can expect from it or what I might accomplish through it, and at that point my hopes were not high. I said, "My vocation was the same as my father's. I assume that if I'd had another father entirely the Lord would still have called me." I'll admit I'm a little touchy on that point.

Jack was quiet for a minute, and then he said, "I always seem to give offense. I don't always intend to." Then he said, "I hope you will understand that I don't wish to offend you. Reverend."

I said, "I'll bear that in mind."

He said, "Thank you." Then after a minute he said, "I wish I could have been like my father," and he glanced up at me as though he thought I might laugh.

I said, "Your father has been an example to us all."

He gave me a look, then covered his eyes with his hand. There were elements of grief and frustration in the gesture, and of weariness as well. And I knew what it meant. I said, "I'm afraid I offend you."

"No, no," he said. "But I do wish we could speak more—directly."

There was a silence. Then he said, "But I thank you for your time," and stood up to leave.

I said, "Sit down, son. Sit down. Let's give this another try."

So we were just quiet there for a while. He took off his necktie and wound it around his hand and showed it to me as though there were something amusing about it and slipped it into his pocket. Finally he said, "When I was small I thought the Lord was someone who lived in the attic and paid for the groceries. That was the last form of religious conviction I have been capable of." Then he said, "I don't mean to be rude."

"I understand."

"Why would that happen, do you think? I mean, that I could never believe a word my poor old father said. Even as a child. When everyone I knew thought it was all, well, everyone thought it was the Gospel."

"Do you believe any of it now?"

He shook his head. "I can't say that I do." He glanced up at me. "I'm trying to be honest."

"I can see that."

He said, "I'll tell you another strange thing. I lie quite a lot, because when I do people believe me. It's when I try to tell the truth that things go wrong for me." He laughed and shrugged. "So I know the risk I'm running here." Then he said, "And in fact, things also go wrong when I lie."

I asked him what exactly it was that he wanted to tell me.

"Well," he said, "I believe I put a question to you."

He had every right to point that out. He had asked a question, and I had avoided responding to it. That's true. I couldn't help but notice the edge of irritation in his voice, considering how earnest he seemed to be about keeping the conversation civil.

I said, "I just don't know how to answer that question. I truly wish I did."

He folded his arms and leaned back and twitched his foot for a minute. "Does it seem right to you," he said, "that there should be no common language between us? That there should be no way to bring a drop of water to those of us who languish in the flames, or who will? Granting your terms? That between us and you there is a great gulf fixed? How can capital-T Truth not be communicable? That makes no sense to me."

"I am not sure those are my terms. I would speak of grace in that context," I said.

"And never of the absence of grace, which would in fact seem to be the issue here. If your terms are granted. I don't mean to be disrespectful."

"I understand that," I said.

"So," he said, after a silence, "you have no wisdom to share with me on this subject."

I said, "Well, I don't know quite how to approach it in this case. Do you want to be persuaded of the truth of the Christian religion?"

He laughed. "I'm sure if I were persuaded of it, I would be grateful in retrospect. People generally are, as I understand."

"Well," I said, "that doesn't give me much to work with, does it?"

He just sat there for a while, and then he said, "A friend of mine—no, not a friend, a man I met in Tennessee—had heard about this town, and he had also heard of your grandfather. He told me some stories about the old days in Kansas that his father had told him. He said that during the Civil War Iowa had a colored regiment."

"Yes, we did. And a graybeard regiment, and a Methodist regiment, as they called it. They were teetotalers, at any rate."

"I was interested to learn that there was a colored regiment," he said. "I wouldn't have thought there were ever that many colored people in this state."

"Oh yes. Quite a few colored people came up from Missouri in the days before the war. And I think quite a few came up the Mississippi Valley, too."

He said, "When I was growing up, there were some Negro families in this town."

I said, "Yes, there were, but they left some years ago."

"I remember hearing about a fire at their church."

"Oh yes, but that was *many* years ago, when I was a boy. And it was only a small fire. There was very little damage."

"So they're all gone now."

"Yes, they are. It's a pity. We have several new Lithuanian families. Of course they're Lutheran."

He laughed. He said, "It is a pity that they're gone." And he seemed to ponder it for a while.

Then he said, "You admire Karl Barth." And I believe it was here he began to speak out of that anger of his, that sly, weary anger I have never been able to deal with. He was always smart as the devil, and serious as the devil, too. I should have known he'd have read Karl Barth.

I said, "Yes, I do admire him. Very much."

"But he seems to have very little respect for American religion. Don't you agree? He is quite candid about it."

"He has been very critical of European religion also," I said, which is true. And yet even at the time I recognized that my reply was somewhat evasive. So did young Boughton, as I could tell by his expression, which was not exactly a smile.

He said, "He takes it seriously, though. He thinks it's worth quarreling with."

"Granted." That is certainly true, too.

Then he asked, "Do you ever wonder why American Christianity always seems to wait for the real thinking to be done elsewhere?"

"Not really," I said, which surprised me, since I have wondered about that very thing any number of times.

Now, at that point I did feel that Jack Boughton was, so to speak, winning the conversation, and furthermore, that he was no happier about it than I was, maybe even a little disgusted. Certainly I found myself in a false position yet again. I felt like pleading old age. But I was sitting there in my church, with the sweet and irrefragable daylight pouring in through the windows. And I felt, as I have often felt, that my failing the truth could have no bearing at all on the Truth itself, which could never conceivably be in any sense dependent on me or on anyone. And my heart rose up within me—that's exactly what it felt like—and I said, "I have heard any number of fine sermons in my life, and I have known any number of deep souls. I am well aware that people find fault, but it seems to me to be presumptuous to judge the authenticity of anyone's religion, except one's own. And that is also presumptuous."

And I said, "When this old sanctuary is full of silence and prayer, every book Karl Barth ever will write would not be a feather in the scales against it from the point of view of profundity, and I would not believe in Barth's own authenticity if I did not also believe he would know and recognize the truth of that, and honor it, too."

I was tired and I was feeling more beleaguered than a man my age should feel, and that is the only way I can explain the tears. I was almost as surprised as young Boughton.

He said, "I can't tell you how sorry I am," and he said it convincingly.

There I was, wiping tears off my face with my sleeve, just the way you do it. It was embarrassing, believe me. He said something that sounded like "Forgive me," and he went away.

Now what? My present thought is that I will write him a letter. I have no idea what it will say.

There have been heroes here, and saints and martyrs, and I want you to know that. Because that is the truth, even if no one remembers it. To look at the place, it's just a cluster of houses strung along a few roads, and a little row of brick buildings with stores in them, and a grain elevator and a water tower with Gilead written on its side, and the post office and the schools and the playing fields and the old train station, which is pretty well gone to weeds now. But what must Galilee have looked like? You can't tell so much from the appearance of a place.

Those saints got old and the times changed and they just

seemed like eccentrics and nuisances, and no one wanted to listen to their fearsome old sermons or hear their wild old stories. I say it to my shame—it got so I didn't really like to be with my grandfather, and that's the truth. It wasn't just the shabbiness, and it wasn't just that whenever some useful object turned up missing, the owner happened by our house to mention the fact. That eye of his always seemed to me to be full of expectation and disappointment, both at once, and I began to dread the moments when it would fall on me. The old men called people who failed to embrace the great cause "doughfaces." There is a lot of contempt in that phrase. They were harsh in their judgments. With reason, I believe.

I particularly remember one time when my grandfather was asked to say a few words at the Fourth of July celebration. I remember because it caused us all anxiety in anticipation, and then embarrassment enough to justify some part of our worrying. The idea was that since he was a sort of founder of the place in a general sense and a veteran, it would be a fitting thing to have him speak. The mayor at that time had lived in Gilead only about twenty years, and he was Swedish and a Lutheran, so he may not have heard the stories about the old times. And my grandfather rarely stole except from his family. The exceptions were pretty well limited to our own congregation and, very rarely, the most openhanded Presbyterians and Methodists, all of whom were good about keeping the matter quiet out of respect for his age and for the purity of his intent. My mother said you could tell where a Congregationalist lived by the padlock on the shed door, and there was an element of truth in that. In any case, the mayor most likely had no notion of the degree of the old man's eccentricity when he sent the invitation.

My grandfather had a gleam in his eye from the moment he read that letter. My parents were trying to make the best of it all. My mother searched the house for his army uniform, but of course nothing was left of it but the hat, which had survived, I suppose, because it was fairly useless. "The gristle, the hooves, and the snout," my mother would say, that being what remained of anything that in any wise came into his hands. My mother found the cap in a closet and did what she could to shape it up a little. But the old man said, "I'm preaching," and put it back in the closet again. I have the sermon, the *ipsissima verba*, because it was among the things my father buried and unburied that day in the garden. It is very brief, so I'll copy it here as he wrote it. My father encouraged him to write it out, I remember, probably to discourage rambling, and most likely in the hope that he or my mother might get a look at it and discuss it a little with my grandfather if need be. But he kept it very close, dropping his drafts into the kitchen stove and keeping the text on his unapproachable Nazirite person.

Here is what he wrote and what he said:

Children—

When I was a young man the Lord came to me and put His hand just here on my right shoulder. I can feel it still. And He spoke to me, very clearly. The words went right through me. He said, Free the captive. Preach good news to the poor. Proclaim liberty throughout the land. That is all Scripture, of course, and the words were already very familiar to me at the time. But it is clear enough why He would feel they needed special emphasis. No one lives by them, unless the Lord takes him in hand. Certainly I did not, until the day He stood beside me and spoke those words to me.

I would call that experience a vision. We had visions in those days, a number of us did. Your young men will have visions and your old men will dream dreams. And now all those young men are old men, if they're alive at all, and their visions are no more than dreams, and the old days are forgotten. We fly forgotten as a dream, as it says in the old hymn, and our dreams are forgotten long before we are.

The President, General Grant, once called Iowa the shining star of radicalism. But what is left here in Iowa? What is left here in Gilead? Dust. Dust and ashes. Scripture says the people perish, and they certainly do. It is remarkable. For all this His anger is not turned away, but His Hand is stretched out still.

The Lord bless you and keep you, etc.

Only a few people seemed to have been paying attention. Those who did came very near taking offense at the notion that they were perishing even though the terrible drought had begun to set in that would bankrupt and scatter so many families, even whole towns. There was a little laughter of the kind you hear when the outlandishness of a thing is being generally agreed on. But that was the worst of it. My grandfather stood there on the stage in his buzzard-black preacher's clothes, eyeing the crowd with the dispassionate intensity of death itself, with the banners flying around him. Then the band struck up, and my father went to him and put his hand on his left shoulder, and brought him down to us. My mother said, "Thank you, Reverend," and my grandfather shook his head and said, "I doubt it did much good."

I have thought about that very often—how the times change, and the same words that carry a good many people into the howling wilderness in one generation are irksome or meaningless in the next. You might think I am under some sort of obli gation to try to "save" young Boughton, that by inquiring into these things he is putting me under that obligation. Well, I have had a certain amount of experience with skepticism and the conversation it generates, and there is an inevitable futility in it. It is even destructive. Young people from my own flock have come home with a copy of *La Nausée* or *L'Immoraliste*, flummoxed by the possibility of unbelief, when I must have told them a thousand times that unbelief is possible. And they are attracted to it by the very books that tell them what a misery it is. And they want me to defend religion, and they want me to give them "proofs." I just won't do it. It only confirms them in their skepticism. Because nothing true can be said about God from a posture of defense.

From the time my father began receiving those long letters from Germany, he began watching me more, or otherwise, than he ever had before. For the first time in my life we were not quite at ease with each other, my father and I. I had to be careful what I said to him, because he would note any possible tinge of heterodoxy and lecture me solemnly on the nature of the error my thinking might have brought me to. Even days later he would come to me with new refutations of things I had not said. No doubt he was speaking to Edward; certainly he was speaking to me as, so it must have seemed, the next Edward. Then, too, he was clearly rehearsing for his own sake the defenses he could make of his beliefs. They had never till that moment struck me as vulnerable, nor him, I suspect.

Then, when he began reading those books I brought home, it was almost as if he wanted to be persuaded by them, and as if any criticism I made of them was nothing more than recalcitrance. He used phrases like "forward-looking." You'd have thought a bad argument could be put beyond question by its supposed novelty, for heaven's sake. And a lot of the newness of this new thinking was as old as Lucretius, which he knew as well as I did. In that letter he sent me which I burned he spoke of "the courage required to embrace the truth." I never forgot those words because of the way they irritated me. He just assumed that his side of the question was "the truth" and only cowardice could be preventing me from admitting as much. All that time, though, I think he was just finding his way to Edward, and I can't really blame him for it. He did try to take me along with him.

In the matter of belief, I have always found that defenses have the same irrelevance about them as the criticisms they are meant to answer. I think the attempt to defend belief can unsettle it, in fact, because there is always an inadequacy in argument about ultimate things. We participate in Being without remainder. No breath, no thought, no wart or whisker, is not as sunk in Being as it could be. And yet no one can say what Being is. If you describe what a thought and a whisker have in common, and a typhoon and a rise in the stock market, excluding "existence," which merely restates the fact that they have a place on our list of known and nameable things (and which would yield as insight: being equals existence!), you would have accomplished a wonderful thing, still too partial in an infinite degree to have any meaning, however.

I've lost my point. It was to the effect that you can assert the existence of something—Being—having not the slightest notion of what it is. Then God is at a greater remove altogether—if God is the Author of Existence, what can it mean to say God exists? There's a problem in vocabulary. He would have to have had a character before existence which the poverty of our understanding can only call existence. That is clearly a source of confusion. Another term would be needed to describe a state or quality of which we can have no experience whatever, to which existence as we know it can bear only the slightest likeness or affinity. So creating proofs from experience of any sort is like building a ladder to the moon. It seems that it should be possible, until you stop to consider the nature of the problem.

So my advice is this—don't look for proofs. Don't bother with them at all. They are never sufficient to the question, and they're always a little impertinent, I think, because they claim for God a place within our conceptual grasp. And they will likely sound wrong to you even if you convince someone else with them. That is very unsettling over the long term. "Let your works so shine before men," etc. It was Coleridge who said Christianity is a life, not a doctrine, words to that effect. I'm not saying never doubt or question. The Lord gave you a mind so that you would make honest use of it. I'm saying you must be sure that the doubts and questions are your own, not, so to speak, the mustache and walking stick that happen to be the fashion of any particular moment.

No sleep this night. My heart is greatly disquieted. It is a strange thing to feel illness and grief in the same organ. There is no telling one from the other. My custom has always been to ponder grief; that is, to follow it through ventricle and aorta to find out its lurking places. That old weight in the chest, telling me there is something I must dwell on, because I know more than I know and must learn it from myself—that same good weight worries me these days.

But the fact is, I have never found another way to be as honest with myself as I can be by consulting with these miseries of mine, these accusers and rebukers, God bless them all. So long as they do not kill me outright. I do hope to die with a quiet heart. I know that may not be realistic.

Well, I close my eyes and I see Jack Boughton, and it seems to me that more than he has matured or aged he has wearied. And I think, Why must I always defend myself against this sad old youth? What is the harm I fear from him?

Well, that really is not a purely rhetorical question. This morning your mother gave me a note from him. It said, "I am very sorry that I offended you yesterday. I will not trouble you again." He writes a good hand. In any case, I felt from her manner that your mother knew what lay behind the note. It was just a folded slip of paper, but she would never have read it if he had not shown it to her. Perhaps he told her what it said. Or simply that it was an apology. I heard them talking on the porch before she brought it in to me. She looked sorry and concerned—for me, for him perhaps, or for both of us. They do talk, I know that. Not much and not often. But I sense a kind of understanding between them.

"Understanding" might be the wrong word, since I have never spoken to her about him, and it is precisely the fact of her knowing so little about him that worries me. Or "understanding" might be exactly the right word, no matter what she knows or does not know. I can't decide which thought worries me more. Maybe neither one could worry me more.

I sent him a note. It said I was the one who should apologize, that my health has not been perfect lately, and so on, that I hoped we might have a chance to speak again soon. And your mother carried the note back to him.

I was thinking about the time when he was just ten or twelve and he filled my mailbox with wood shavings and set them on fire. He rigged up a sort of fuse of twine dipped in paraffin. At that time the mailbox was on a post by the gate. It was that loaf-shaped kind people use in the country. I was walking home from a meeting at the church in the dark of a winter evening. I heard a poof and looked up, and just then flames came pouring out of the mouth of that box. It gave me quite a turn. But I didn't doubt for a minute whose prank it was.

That boy was always alone, always grinning, always intent on some piece of devilment. He wasn't more than ten when he took off in a Model T he saw idling in the street downtown. Cars were still pretty rare around here in those days, so his interest was understandable. He drove it straight west for a number of miles, until it ran out of gas, and then he just walked home. A couple of young fellows with a team of horses happened upon the car and towed it off to Wilkinsburg and traded it for a hunting rifle. I think half the people in the county owned the thing for a day or so over the couple of months it stayed missing. Then a good-sized family who had traded a heifer for it came sailing into Gilead to enjoy the Fourth of July and got themselves arrested. The authorities traced it back through any number of swaps and IOUs and poker games, but never found the original thief. As it turned out, there were so many people involved in minor criminality having to do with buying that car and selling it that the resources of the law were in no way sufficient, so the whole thing was forgotten officially and remembered for a long time afterward because it made such a good story. People clearly knew the car was stolen, but they couldn't resist owning it for a little while, even though they didn't have the nerve to keep it—which kept the price very reasonable and the temptation that much greater.

It was Jack himself who told me what he had done. He'd kept the handle from the glove box as a souvenir and he showed it to me, but I would have believed him anyway. Shrewd as he was even as a youngster, he knew I would never speak to anyone about it, and I never did. Of course, I thought his parents should know, and still, I never had the heart to say a word. I was always a little in awe of a child who could keep a secret like that, when it would have been the perfection of the tale to know that a ten-year-old boy had incriminated half a county.

There is a sadness in all this I do not wish to obscure. I mean a sadness in the child. I remember coming out of the house one morning and finding my front steps painted with molasses. The ants were so thick they were piling over each other. They were just absolutely solid. Now, you have to ask yourself, How lonely would a child have to be to have time to make such a nuisance of himself? He developed some method for breaking my study windows so that the whole pane would shatter altogether. It was remarkable. I will ask him how he did that, someday when our souls are at peace and we can laugh about it.

That is the sort of thing he did as a young boy, mischief only bordering on harm, generally speaking. That is my belief, though certain harmful things were done which I have never wished to ascribe to him but which, in the privacy of my thoughts, I always did. For example, there was a barn fire, and some animals were lost in it. I may be wrong in blaming him for that.

His transgressions were sly and lonely, and this became truer as he grew up. I believe I said earlier that he did not steal in any conventional sense, but by that I meant he stole things of no value except to the people he stole them from. There was no sense in what he did, unless his purpose was to cause a maximum of embarrassment and risk a minimum of retribution. When he was fifteen or sixteen, he'd come into the house while I was at the church and pocket one thing or another. It was the most irritating trick you could imagine. Once, he took that old

Greek Testament right off my desk. If ever there was a thing on earth so little worth the trouble of stealing I don't know what it would be. Once, he stole my reading glasses. Once, I came in when he was standing right there in the parlor. He just laughed and said, "Hello, Papa," cool and charming as you please. He made some small talk, in that precocious way he had, smiling as if there were a joke between us. It took me a while to figure out what was missing that time. Then I realized—it was a little photograph in a velvet case of Louisa, taken when she was a child. I was as angry about that as I have ever been in my life. Just the sheer meanness of it. And how could I tell Boughton that he had done such a thing? How could I say the words?

Things would drift back sooner or later. The Greek Testament was left on the doormat. The photograph appeared on Boughton's hall table, mysteriously, and was brought back to me. That penknife with the word "Chartres" pressed into the handle, which was made from a shell casing, was left on the kitchen table, plunged through an apple. I found that disconcerting at the time.

Then he started doing the things that got his name in the newspaper, stealing liquor and joyriding, and so on. I've known young fellows who spent time in jail or got themselves sent off to the navy for behavior that wasn't any worse. But his family was so well respected that he got away with it all. That is to say, he was allowed to go right on disgracing his family.

I notice I have said he seemed lonely. That was one very strange thing about him, because, as I have said also, the Boughtons really loved him. All of them did. His brothers and sisters would stand up for him no matter what. When he was little, he'd slip out, run off, and they'd come by looking for him, anxious beyond their years, all business, hoping to find him and exert their respectable influence on him before he could get into too much trouble. I remember one summer I had planted a row of sunflowers along the back fence. There must have been twenty of them. One afternoon the other little Boughtons came to the door asking for Johnny, as they called him in those days. I went out to help them look around a little, and darned if those sunflowers hadn't been pulled back, bent over the fence so their heads were hanging down on the other side of it. Glory said, "It could have been the wind that did that." I said, Yes, maybe it was the wind.

If I had to choose one word to describe him as he is now, it might be "lonely," though "weary" and "angry" certainly come to mind also. Once during the time I was missing Louisa's picture I went over to Boughton's to borrow a book, and we sat on the porch and talked awhile, and that boy sat on the steps, fiddling with a slingshot, I remember, and listening to every word, and from time to time he would look up at me and smile, as if we were in on a joke together, some interesting conspiracy. I found that extremely irritating. He almost provoked me into mentioning the photograph then and there. I had to leave to stop myself. He said, "Goodbye, Papa!" I went home just trembling. Maybe you can see why, when the business with the young girl came up, I was chiefly struck by the meanness of it.

I don't think I do my heart much good by remembering these things. My point is that he was always a mystery, and that's why I worry about him, and that's why I know I can't judge him as I might another man. That is to say, I can't assign a moral valuation to his behavior. He's just mean. Well, I don't know that that is true of him now. But I do see what he might injure. That is very clear to me. While I was standing there in the pulpit, the thought came to me that I was looking back from the grave and there he was, sitting beside you, grinning up at me—

This is not doing me any good at all. I'd better pray.

I woke up this morning to the smell of pancakes, which I dearly love. My heart was a sort of clayey lump midway up my esophagus, and that after much earnest prayer. Your mother found me sleeping in my chair and slipped my shoes off and put a quilt over me. I do sometimes sleep better sitting up these days. Breathing is easier. I was careful to put this diary away before I turned the light out last night. I know I still have thinking to do on this matter of Jack Boughton.

It is my birthday, so there were marigolds on the table and my stack of pancakes had candles in it. There were nice little sausages besides. And you recited the Beatitudes with hardly a hitch, two times over, absolutely shining with the magnitude of the accomplishment, as well you might. Your mother gave a sausage to Soapy, who slunk off with the unctuous thing and hid it who knows where. She is beyond doubt the descendant of endless generations of vermin eaters, fat as she is, domesticated as she ought to be.

I hate to think what I would give for a thousand mornings like this. For two or three. You were wearing your red shirt and your mother was wearing her blue dress.

And your mother has found that sermon I was wondering about, that Pentecost sermon, the one I gave the first time I saw her. It was beside my plate, wrapped in tissue paper, with a ribbon on it. "Now, don't you go revising that," she said. "It don't need revising." And she kissed me on the top of the head, which, for her, was downright flamboyant.

So now I am seventy-seven.

Yesterday was very fine altogether. Glory came by in her car and took us for a picnic over by the river. Tobias came along, Tobias the good. There were balloons and even firecrackers, and there was a chocolate cake with chocolate frosting. The river was low but pretty, with the first yellow leaves drifting down to it. I was sorry I had not slept better the night before, that there was so much unease in the region of my heart. But the party went on cheerfully enough anyway. Glory and your mother are good friends now, and you and T. would have happily spent forever racing leaves down that river and generally puddling around in it.

Last night I slept fairly well.

It bothers me to think I might be bothered to death, if you see what I mean. Jack Boughton is home, to the delight of his father, my dear friend. For all I know, he has done no harm, and for all I know, he intends no harm. And yet the mere fact of him troubles me.

You asked if he was not coming along on the birthday jaunt. You were disappointed. Glory made some sort of excuse, and your mother said nothing. The tact was audible. I have to wonder what they know, what they have talked about. How could they not pity him? I pity him. I regret absolutely that I cannot speak with him in a way becoming a pastor, knowing as I do what an uneasy spirit he is. That is disgraceful.

It is one of the best traits of good people that they love where they pity. And this is truer of women than of men. So they get themselves drawn into situations that are harmful to them. I have seen this happen many, many times. I have always had trouble finding a way to caution against it. Since it is, in a word, Christlike.

He has not replied to the note I sent him.

I wrote another note, telling him how deeply I felt any fault lay with me, and so on, and carried it over to Boughton's myself. I was just going to slip it in the mailbox, but Jack was out in the garden and he saw me and so I took it over to him. He actually seemed to shy from it a little. I told him it was another apology, more considered than the first one had been, and then he thanked me for it, and I am sure I saw genuine relief in his expression. I suspect he had not read the earlier note, perhaps thinking there might be some sort of rebuke in it. He did open the one I handed him and he read it over and then he thanked me again.

I said, "If you would like to talk, I would be happy to see you anytime."

And he said, "Yes, I do want to talk with you, if you're sure it's all right." So we'll see what comes of that.

I was pleased that it all fell out so agreeably. It took a weight from my heart. I'll admit it was one part of my motive in writing the second note that I didn't want your mother pitying him for any hurt I had done him. Still, I felt good about it. I enjoyed seeing his face change the way it did then. He looked young for a moment.

Again no sleep. I have been thinking of the morning I baptized Jack Boughton. I had one of the deacons begin the service without me so that I could be there in Boughton's church.

We'd talked it over. The child's name was to be Theodore Dwight Weld. I thought that was an excellent name. My grandfather had heard Weld preach every night for three weeks until he had converted a whole doughface settlement to abolitionism, and the old man numbered it among the great experiences of his life. But then when I asked Boughton, "By what name do you wish this child to be called?" he said, "John Ames." I was so surprised that he said the name again, with the tears running down his face.

It simply was not at all like Boughton to put me in a position like that. It was so un-Presbyterian, in the first place. I could hear weeping out in the pews. It took me a while to forgive him for that. I'm just telling you the truth.

If I had had even an hour to reflect, I believe my feelings would have been quite different. As it was, my heart froze in me and I thought, This is *not* my child—which I truly had never thought of any child before. I don't know exactly what covetise is, but in my experience it is not so much desiring someone else's virtue or happiness as rejecting it, taking offense at the beauty of it.

That's interesting. There is certainly a sermon there. "Blessed is he who takes no offense at me." That would be the primary text. I hope I have time to think it through.

I'll tell you a perfectly foolish thing. I have thought from time to time that the child felt how coldly I went about his christening, how far my thoughts were from blessing him. Now, that's just magical thinking. That is superstition. I'm ashamed to have said such a thing. But I'm trying to be honest. And I do feel a burden of guilt toward that child, that man, my namesake. I have never been able to warm to him, never.

I am glad I said that. I am glad to see it in my own words, in my own hand. Because now I realize it isn't true. And that is a great relief to me.

I do wish I could christen him again, for my sake. I was so distracted by my own miserable thoughts I didn't feel that sacredness under my hand that I always do feel, that sense that the infant is blessing me. Now that is a pity.

John Ames Boughton is my son. If there is any truth at all in anything I believe, that is true also. By "my son" I mean another self, a more cherished self. That language isn't sufficient, but for the moment it is the best I can do.

I fell to thinking about the passage in the *Institutes* where it says the image of the Lord in anyone is much more than reason enough to love him, and that the Lord stands waiting to take our enemies' sins upon Himself. So it is a rejection of the reality of grace to hold our enemy at fault. Those things can only be true. It seems to me people tend to forget that we are to love our enemies, not to satisfy some standard of righteousness, but because God their Father loves them. I have probably preached on that a hundred times.

Not that I mean to call young Boughton my enemy. That is more than I know. Calvin is simply making the most extreme case: *a fortiori*, how much more readily should I forget transgressions which generally amounted to nothing more than annoyances, insofar as they even affected me? Jack has grieved his father terribly and he has been forgiven always, instantly, and I have only grieved Boughton myself when he has felt I was slow to forgive Jack, too. I believe most of that grief was just old Boughton's loneliness for the boy, who has been such a stranger to him and to all of us.

Now here is the point I wish to make, because this is the thought that came to me as I was putting all this before the Lord. Existence is the essential thing and the holy thing.

If the Lord chooses to make nothing of our transgressions, then they *are* nothing. Or whatever reality they have is trivial and conditional beside the exquisite primary fact of existence. Of course the Lord would wipe them away, just as I wipe dirt from your face, or tears. After all, why should the Lord bother much over these smirches that are no part of His Creation?

Well, there are a good many reasons why He should. We human beings do real harm. History could make a stone weep. I am aware that significant confusion enters my thinking at this point. I'm tired—that may be some part of the problem. Though I recall even in my prime foundering whenever I set the true gravity of sin over against the free grace of forgiveness. If young Boughton is my son, then by the same reasoning that child of his was also my daughter, and it was just terrible what happened to her, and that's a fact. As I am a Christian man, I could never say otherwise.

Having looked over these thoughts I set down last night, I realize I have evaded what is for me the central question. That is: How should I deal with these fears I have, that Jack Boughton will do you and your mother harm, just because he can, just for the sly, unanswerable meanness of it? You have already asked after him twice this morning.

Harm to you is not harm to me in the strict sense, and that is a great part of the problem. He could knock me down the stairs and I would have worked out the theology for forgiving him before I reached the bottom. But if he harmed you in the slightest way, I'm afraid theology would fail me.

That may be one great part of what I fear, now that I think of it.

———

Well, I hear him out on the porch talking with you and your mother. You're laughing, all of you. That's actually a relief. To me he always looks like a man standing too close to a fire, tolerating present pain, knowing he's a half step away from something worse. Even when he laughs he looks that way, at least when it's me he's dealing with, though I truly believe I have always tried not to offend him. Oh, I am a limited man, and old, and he will still be his inexplicable mortal self when I am dust.

I have wandered to the limits of my understanding any number of times, out into that desolation, that Horeb, that Kansas, and I've scared myself, too, a good many times, leaving all landmarks behind me, or so it seemed. And it has been among the true pleasures of my life. Night and light, silence and difficulty, it seemed to me always rigorous and good. I believe it was recommended to me by Edward, and also by my reverend grandfather when he made his last flight into the wilderness. I may once have fancied myself such another tough old man, ready to dive into the ground and smolder away the time till Judgment. Well, I am distracted from that project now. My present bewilderments are a new territory that make me doubt I have ever really been lost before.

Though I must say all this has given me a new glimpse of the ongoingness of the world. We fly forgotten as a dream, certainly, leaving the forgetful world behind us to trample and mar and misplace everything we have ever cared for. That is just the way of it, and it is remarkable.

Jack brought gourds, a whole sack of them. Your mother sent him back with green tomatoes. Oh, these late, strange riches of the summer, these slab-sided pumpkins and preposterous zucchinis. Every wind brings a hail of acorns against the roof. Still, it is mild. For a while the spiders were building webs everywhere, and now those webs are all blown to shreds and tatters, so I suppose we can imagine well-fed spiders tucked up in the detritus of old leaves, drowsing away the very thought of toil.

I remember once my father and my grandfather were sitting on the porch together cracking and shelling black walnuts. They loved each other's company when they weren't at each other's throats, which meant when they were silent, as they were that day.

My grandfather said, " 'The summer is ended and still we are not saved.' "

My father said, "That is the Lord's truth."

Then silence again. They never looked up from their work. It was the drought they were speaking of, which had already set in and which would go on for years, a true calamity. I remember a sweet, soft wind like there is today. There is no work more tedious than shelling black walnuts, and the two of them did it every autumn of the world. My mother said they tasted like furniture, and I'm not sure anyone disagreed. But she always had them, so she used them.

You and Tobias are on the porch steps sorting gourds by size and color and shape, choosing favorites, assigning names. Some of them are submarines and some of them tanks, and some of them are bombs. I suppose I should be expecting another visit from T.'s father shortly. All the children play at war now. All of them make those sounds of airplanes and bombs and crashing and exploding. We did the same things, playing at cannon fire and bayonet charges.

There is certainly nothing in that fact to reassure.

Cataract that this world is, it is remarkable to consider what does abide in it.

I fell to thinking about a sermon my father gave, after the breach with Edward had become known and he had had a little while to reflect on it. It was not at all like him to refer to anything private or personal except in the most abstract terms. But that morning he thanked the Lord for letting him know finally in some small degree what defection was, for allowing him to understand what it was he himself had done to his father in those days after the war when he had gone off to the Quakers and left his father to carry his terrible burden alone. He said a thing I had never heard before, that his mother, though she had been too ill and in too much pain to come to church for months, did come when she learned that he was staying away. His sisters, who by then were always with her, carried her in their arms, one and then the other, up the road, which must have seemed very long to them. They were late because it was only that morning their mother had asked them to bring her, and they were hot and unkempt with haste, haste in the slow work of gentleness, because by then their mother could hardly bear to be touched. Their mother was white and shorn, much too small for the dress they had to ease her into with such painful care. They walked in in the middle of the sermon in their wash dresses, sweaty and unbonneted, Amy, the eldest, carrying their mother in her arms as she might have carried a half-grown child. My father said the old reverend stopped preaching and stood looking at them, then took up his text again, which was about the profound mystery of suffering for others, as all his sermons were in those days. He preached a few minutes and prayed a few minutes and said the benediction, and then he went to his wife and took her up in his arms and kissed her forehead and carried her home, leaving his flock to the long Sabbath of the Methodists.

"I cannot describe the shame I felt," my father said. "My sisters spoke to me about what my mother had done because they were afraid she might insist on going to church again if I stayed away again. Amy told me, 'If you put us through that one more time, I will hate you till I die!' And of course I did not."

My father was telling himself and all the rest of us that Edward's transgressions were trivial beside his own. He was also saying, to himself and to the rest of us, that there was an aptness in this present embarrassment and disappointment which made it valuable and instructive to him—that there was a seeming design in it that might mark it in fact as the Lord's benevolence, a sort of parable meant to deepen his own understanding. This construction of the matter would certainly have forbidden, or at least discouraged, any impulse he might have felt to blame Edward. The thoughtlessness of any individual, when it is seen to be in service to the mindfulness of the Lord, cannot justify anger.

I have used this line of reasoning any number of times myself, when I have felt the need and found the occasion. And the fact is, it is seldom indeed that any wrong one suffers is not thoroughly foreshadowed by wrongs one has done. That said, it has never been clear to me how much this realization helps when it comes to the practical difficulty of controlling anger. Nor have I found any way to apply it to present circumstance, though I have not yet abandoned the effort.

———

This afternoon I came back from a fairly discouraging meeting at the church—just a few people came, and absolutely nothing was accomplished. That is the kind of thing that wears me out. So I took a nap and slept through supper. It was dark when I woke up and the house was empty so I went out to the porch. You and your mother were sitting on the swing, wrapped up in a quilt. She said, "This might be the last mild night." She made room for me beside her and spread the quilt across my lap and rested her head on my shoulder. It was just as pleasant as could be. This summer she planted what she calls her owl garden, I being the owl in question. She read somewhere that white flowers are most fragrant at night, so she planted every white flower she could think of along the front walk. Now there are just a few roses left, and alyssum and petunias.

So we sat there in the dark together for a while, you asleep, more or less, with your mother stroking your hair. Then we heard footsteps in the road. And sure enough, it was Jack Boughton. I believe he may have meant to say good evening and pass by, but your mother asked him to come visit a little, so he did. He came in the gate and sat down on the steps. I have noticed that toward her he is consistently obliging.

"We were just enjoying the quiet," she said.

He said, "No better place in the world to do that." Then, as though he was afraid he might be misunderstood, or at any rate that he might give offense, he said, "It really is good to be back for a while." He laughed. "There are people here now who don't know me from Adam. It's wonderful."

Then he put his hand to his face, his eyes. It was dark, but I could recognize that gesture. He has made it his whole life, I believe.

I said, "It has been a great happiness to your father, having you here."

He said, "The man's a saint."

"That might be true, but it was still good of you to come."

"Ah," he said, as a man might when a chasm has opened at his feet.

So there was a silence of a few minutes, and then your mother stood up and lifted you out of the quilt and carried you away to bed.

"I have been glad to see you, too," I said, because I really was, for old Boughton's sake.

To that he made no reply.

"I say that quite sincerely."

He stretched out his legs and leaned back against the porch pillar.

"No doubt," he said.

"Stack of Bibles."

He laughed. "How high?"

"A cubit or so."

"That'll do, I guess."

"Would two cubits put your mind at ease?"

"Entirely." And then, remembering his manners, "It has been good seeing you again. And meeting your wife. Your family."

Then we were quiet for a while.

I said, "I'm impressed that you know Karl Barth."

"Oh," he said. "From time to time I still try to crack the code."

"Well," I said, "I admire your tenacity."

He said, "You might not, if you understood my motives."

Of all people on this earth he must be the hardest one to have a conversation with.

So I said, "That's all right, I admire it anyway."

And he said, "Thanks."

So we were just quiet there for some time. Your mother came out with a pot of hot cider and cups, and she sat there quiet right along with us, the dear woman. And I spent the time thinking how it would be if Jack Boughton were indeed my son, and had come home weary from whatever life he had, and was sitting there still and at seeming peace in that peaceful night. There was a considerable satisfaction in that thought. The idea of grace had been so much on my mind, grace as a sort of ecstatic fire that takes things down to essentials. There in the dark and the quiet I felt I could forget all the tedious particulars and just feel the presence of his mortal and immortal being. And a sensation came over me, a sort of lovely fear, that made me think of Boughton's fear of angels.

Now, I may have been more than half asleep at that point, but a thought arose that abides with me. I wished I could sit at the feet of that eternal soul and learn. He did then seem to me the angel of himself, brooding over the mysteries his mortal life describes, the deep things of man. And of course that is exactly what he is. "For who among men knoweth the things of a man, save the spirit of the man, which is in him?" In every important way we are such secrets from each other, and I do believe that there is a separate language in each of us, also a separate aesthetics and a separate jurisprudence. Every single one of us is a little civilization built on the ruins of any number of preceding civilizations, but with our own variant notions of what is beautiful and what is acceptable—which, I hasten to add, we generally do not satisfy and by which we struggle to live. We take fortuitous resemblances among us to be actual likeness, because those around us have also fallen heir to the same customs, trade in the same coin, acknowledge, more or less, the same notions of decency and sanity. But all that really just allows us to coexist with the inviolable, untraversable, and utterly vast spaces between us.

Maybe I should have said we are like planets. But then I would have lost some of the point of saying that we are like civilizations. The planets may all have been sloughed from the same star, but still the historical dimension is missing from that simile, and it is true that we all do live in the ruins of the lives of other generations, so there is a seeming continuity which is important because it deceives us. I am old enough to remember when we used to go out in the brush, a lot of us, and spread out in a circle, and then close in, scaring the rabbits along in front of us, till they were trapped there in the center, and then we would kill them with sticks and clubs. That was during the Depression, and people were hungry, and we did what we could. I am not finding fault. (We didn't take the jackrabbits, only the cottontails. We all knew there was something objectionable about jackrabbits, though I don't remember anyone saying just what it was.) There were people eating groundhogs. The children would go to school with nothing in their lunch buckets but a boiled potato or a scrap of bread with lard smeared on it. In those days the windows of the church used to get so pelted with dust that I'd get up on a ladder and sweep them down with a broom so there would be light enough inside for people to read their hymnals.

The times were dreadful, but it was just how it was, and we got very used to it. That was our civilization. The valley of the shadow. And it might as well be Ur of the Chaldees for all people know about it now. For which I thank God, of course, though, since it had to happen, I don't regret having been here for it. It gives you another look at things. I have heard people say it taught them there is more to life than security and the material comforts, but I know a lot of older people around here who can hardly bear to part with a nickel, remembering those hard times. I can't blame them for it, though it has meant that the church is just now beginning to come out of its own Depression. "There is that scattereth, and increaseth yet more, and there is that withholdeth more than is meet, but it tendeth only to want." Much in this very town proves the truth of that proverb. Well, the church is shabby for the same reason it's still standing at all. So I shouldn't really complain. It is a good thing to know what it is to be poor, and a better thing if you can do it in company.

I believe they thought I had nodded off, as I do with fair frequency, I know. They began to talk. Your mother said, in a lowered voice, "Have you decided how long you will be staying here?"

He said, "I'm afraid it's already begun to seem long—not to me so much."

There was a silence, and then she said, "You'll be going back to St. Louis?"

"That's possible."

Another silence. He struck a match. I could smell the smoke of a cigarette.

"Would you care for one?"

"No, thank you." She laughed. "Sure I would. It just isn't seemly in a preacher's wife."

" 'It just isn't seemly'! I guess they've been after you."

"I don't mind," she said. "Somebody had to tell me a few things sooner or later. Now I been seemly so long I'm almost beginning to like it."

He laughed.

She said, "It did take me a while to get used to this place. That's a fact."

"Well, for me that's not the problem. It feels familiar to me, all right. It feels a little like returning to the scene of the crime."

After a moment she said, "Everybody speaks about you very kindly, you know."

"Really? Interesting. I suppose I believe you."

She laughed. "I haven't lied in years."

"Hmm. That sounds exhausting."

"They say you can get used to anything."

He said, "Reverend Ames still hasn't warned you about me?"

She found my hand and took it between her two warm hands. "He don't speak unkindly. He never does."

There was a silence. I was fairly uncomfortable with myself, as you can imagine, and I was about to show some signs of stirring, just to extricate myself from this discreditable situation I had put myself into, which seemed almost to be spying.

But your mother said, "I was in St. Louis once. Some of us went there looking for work." She laughed. "No luck."

He said, "It's a miserable place to be broke."

"If there's a good place to be broke, I sure never found it. And I tried 'em all."

They laughed.

He said, "When I was young I thought a settled life was what happened to you if you weren't careful."

She said, "I always knew better than that. It was the one thing I wanted. I used to look in people's windows at night and wonder what it was like."

He laughed. "That's how I was planning to spend this very evening."

There was a silence.

"Well," she said, and her voice was very gentle, "well, Jack, bless your heart."

And he said, "Why, I thank you for that, Lila." Then he stood up. "Tell the reverend good night for me." And he went away.

I lay awake the whole night, except for the part of it I spent sitting at my desk, writing this all out and thinking it over. Of course I was touched by your mother's pride in my tendency to avoid speaking evil. It is something I do in fact try to avoid, though you know very well what a struggle it has been for me in this case.

But I could only be struck by young Boughton's amazement that I had not yet, in his words, warned her about him. It was almost as if he thought I had been negligent. And who would be a better judge of that than he is? He might think I know things I don't know, assuming Boughton confided in me more than he ever did, or that talk about him would have reached me, as in fact it did only rarely. I always suspected people of a good deal of tact where he was concerned.

"The scene of the crime." That was a joke, I'm pretty sure. But it does lead me to wonder how much of the misery I feel in him comes from the fact that he *is* here, where things went on that still might cause him suffering, maybe shame.

I wish I could put my hand on his brow and calm away all the guilt and regret that is exaggerated or misplaced, or beyond rectification in the terms of this world. Then I could see what I'm actually dealing with.

Theologically, that is a completely unacceptable notion. It just happened to cross my mind. I apologize for it.

Since I am trying to tell the truth, there is one other thing. The edginess went out of his voice while he was talking with your mother. I would almost say he seemed to relax. He sounded like someone speaking with a friend. And so did she.

I believe I am beginning to see where the grace is for me in this. I have prayed considerably, and I have slept awhile, too, and I feel I am reaching some clarity.

I have never been to St. Louis, a fact I now regret.

I have been looking through these pages, and I realize that for some time I have mainly been worrying to myself, when my intention from the beginning was to speak to you. I meant to leave you a reasonably candid testament to my better self, and it seems to me now that what you must see here is just an old man struggling with the difficulty of understanding what it is he's struggling with.

I believe I may have found a way out of the cave of this tedious preoccupation, however. It's worth a try. So:

When I was sitting there on the porch last night more or less feigning sleep and your mother took my hand and held it in her hands, that was a great happiness to me. I see I did indicate this—"her two warm hands"—and I noted that at the same time she spoke of me much more kindly than I deserve. Only thinking back on it did I realize that she was speaking as if from that settled life she said she had always wanted and as if it could not be lost to her, though in every practical, material sense she knows it will be. That pleased me, too. Remembering when they said what they did about looking in windows and wondering about other people's lives made me feel companionable with them. I could have said that's three of us, because, as the Lord knows, for many years I did exactly the same thing. But in that moment, the way she spoke, it seemed that all the wondering about life had been answered for her, once and for all, and if that is true, it is wonderful. The notion is a source of peace for me.

I had a dream once that Boughton and I were down at the river looking around in the shallows for something or other—when we were boys it would have been tadpoles—and my grandfather stalked out of the trees in that furious way he had, scooped his hat full of water, and threw it, so a sheet of water came sailing toward us, billowing in the air like a veil, and fell down over us. Then he put his hat back on his head and stalked off into the trees again and left us standing there in that glistening river, amazed at ourselves and shining like the apostles. I mention this because it seems to me transformations just that abrupt do occur in this life, and they occur unsought and unawaited, and they beggar your hopes and your deserving. This came to my mind as I was reflecting on the day I first saw your mother, that blessed, rainy Pentecost.

That morning something began that felt to me as if my soul were being teased out of my body, and that's a fact. I have never told you how all that came about, how we came to be married. And I learned a great deal from the experience, believe me. It enlarged my understanding of hope, just to know that such a transformation can occur. And it has greatly sweetened my imagination of death, odd as that may sound.

Even though I told myself I had hardly noticed her that first morning, I spent the whole next week hoping she would come back. I rebuked myself considerably for forgetting to ask her name as she went out the door, thinking about it in terms of my obligations to "strayed sheep" and "lost souls," which are expressions I never do use, even in my thoughts, and which I would certainly never have applied to her. One interesting aspect of the whole experience was that I simply could not be honest with myself, and I couldn't deceive myself, either. It was terrible. I felt like such a fool. But you see, I was mindful of her youth and of my age, and I knew nothing about her, whether she might be married or not. So I couldn't admit to myself that I simply wanted to *see* her, to hear her voice again. She said, "Good morning, Reverend," that was all. But I remember trying to retain the sound of it, trying to hear it again in my mind.

I'll tell you, if my grandfather did throw his mantle over me, so to speak, he did it long before I came into this world. The holiness of his life imputed a holiness to mine, or to my vocation, that I have tried to diminish as little as I could. I have tried to be careful of my reputation and also of my character. I have tried to keep the Gospel before me as a standard for my life and my preaching. And yet there I was trying to write a sermon, when all I really wanted to do was try to remember a young woman's face.

If I had had this experience earlier in life, I would have been much wiser, much more compassionate. I really didn't understand what it was that made people who came to me so indifferent to good judgment, to common sense, or why they would say "I know, I know" when I urged a little reasonableness on them, and why it meant "It doesn't matter, I just don't care." That's what the saints and the martyrs say. And I know now that it is passion that moves them to their prodigal renunciations. I might seem to be comparing something great and holy with a minor and ordinary thing, that is, love of God with mortal love. But I just don't see them as separate things at all. If we can be divinely fed with a morsel and divinely blessed with a touch, then the terrible pleasure we find in a particular face can certainly instruct us in the nature of the very grandest love. I devoutly believe this to be true. I remember in those days loving God for the existence of love and being grateful to God for the existence of gratitude, right down in the depths of my misery. I realized many things I am at a loss to express. And of course those feelings become milder with time, which is a mercy.

Louisa and I were expected to marry almost from childhood. So nothing had prepared me to find myself thinking day and night about a complete stranger, a woman much too young, probably a married woman—that was the first time in my life I ever felt I could be snatched out of my character, my calling, my reputation, as if they could just fall away like a dry husk. I had never felt before that everything I thought I was amounted to the clothes on my back and the books on my shelves and the calendar I kept full of obligations waiting and obligations fulfilled. As I have said, it was a foretaste of death, at least of dying. And why should that seem strange? "Passion" is the word we use, after all.

Well, it got much worse. She was there every Sunday but one, and I wrote all those sermons, I confess, with the thought of pleasing her, impressing her. I struggled not to look at her too often or too long, but I would convince myself nevertheless that I saw disappointment of some kind in her face, and then I would spend the next week praying, right down on my knees, that she would give me another chance. I felt so ridiculous. But I would speak to the Lord about it just the same, asking Him to strengthen me in exercising my pastoral responsibilities, and not a word I said was true, because I was really just a foolish old man asking the Almighty to indulge his foolishness and I knew it at the time. And my prayers were answered, beyond anything I could have thought to ask. A wife, and a child. I would never have believed it.

There was the one terrible Sunday that she wasn't there. How dead and sad and airless that morning was, how shabby we all seemed, and the church, too. Of course my sermon that day was about welcoming the stranger because you might be welcoming "an angel unawares." I hated reading it. I felt everyone in the room knew I was standing there making a confession of my folly. It seemed inevitable to me that she would never come back again. So I spent a dreadful week resigning myself to the smallness of my life, the drabness of it, and thanking the Lord that I had never made a complete fool of myself, had never held her by the hand at the door and attempted conversation, though I had rehearsed in my mind what I might say to her and had even written it out. It must be said also that I hated myself for a fool that I had not held her hand, had not spoken to her. I spent that week trying to make myself describe what it was that attracted me to her so strongly—somehow thinking that because I could not, the attraction would be dispelled. And I spent the week missing her as if she were the only friend I had ever had on earth. (And I also gave some thought to the practical problem of learning her name and finding out where she lived, thinking to excuse this as a pastoral concern. What humiliation.)

The next Sunday there she was again. I was miserable with relief, afraid I might laugh for no reason, afraid I might look at her too long, trying to remind myself she *was* a stranger, though she had been my dearest and most inward thought for weeks, and that I must not startle her with some unaccountable familiarity. I had been to the barber and I was wearing a new shirt, since it seemed only prudent to suppose that my constant, passionate, and most unworthy prayers might be answered. And I'd made a little experiment with hair tonic. Boughton met me in the road, as he often did in those days, and he looked at me and chuckled, and I thought, What an utter and transparent fool I am.

When she left the church that day I did hold her hand and I did say a few words—"We missed you last week, it's good to have you here again."

"Oh," she said, and she blushed and looked away, as if the kindness had surprised her, though it was only the most basic and routine preacherly kindness, that being all I felt I could allow myself under the circumstances.

"I am sick with love." That's Scripture. It makes me laugh to remember this—I turned to the Bible in my crisis, as I have always done. And the text I chose was the Song of Songs! I might have learned from it that such miseries as mine were beautiful in the Lord's sight, if I had been younger and if I had known that your mother was not a married woman. As it was, the beauty of the poems just hurt my feelings.

Oh, but the *next* week I held her hand and I told her we had a Bible study that met on Sunday night and she would be most welcome. Then I went home and prayed that my wiliness would be rewarded, and shaved again, and tried to read until evening. I walked up early to the church, and there she was, waiting for me by the steps, hoping she might have a word with me. At that point I began to suspect, as I have from time to time, that grace has a grand laughter in it. She confided to this unworthy old swain with perfume in his hair that she came to me seeking baptism.

"No one seen to it for me when I was a child," she said. "I been feeling the lack of it." Oh, the sad, stark purity of her look.

I said, "Well, my dear, we will take care of you," and then, very conversationally, I asked her if she had family in the area.

She shook her head and said, very softly, "I don't have family at all." I felt a surge of sadness for her, and still, in my wretched heart, I thanked the Lord.

So I instructed your mother in the doctrines of the faith, and in due course I did indeed baptize her, and I became happily accustomed to the sight of her, her quiet presence, and I began to give thanks that I had lived through the worst of my passion without making a ruin and a desolation of my good name, without running after her in the street, as I nearly did once when I saw her step out of the grocery store and walk away. I scared myself so badly that time I broke into a sweat. That's how strong the impulse was. And I was *sixty-seven*. But I did always act consistently with my great respect for her youth and her loneliness, I can promise you that. I took great care about it. I thought it best to recruit some of the kindest older women to sit through her instruction with her, and I believe that made her shy about speaking, which I regretted very much.

Two or three of the ladies had pronounced views on points of doctrine, particularly sin and damnation, which they never learned from me. I blame the radio for sowing a good deal of confusion where theology is concerned. And television is worse. You can spend forty years teaching people to be awake to the fact of mystery and then some fellow with no more theological sense than a jackrabbit gets himself a radio ministry and all your work is forgotten. I do wonder where it will end.

But even that was for the best, because one of the ladies, Veda Dyer, got herself into a considerable excitement talking about flames, that is, perdition, so I felt obliged to take down the *Institutes* and read them the passage on the lot of the reprobate, about how their torments are "*figuratively* expressed to us by physical things," unquenchable fire and so on, to express "how wretched it is to be cut off from all fellowship with God." I have the passage in front of me. It is alarming, certainly, but it isn't ridiculous. I told them, If you want to inform yourselves as to the nature of hell, don't hold your hand in a candle flame, just ponder the meanest, most desolate place in your soul.

They all did ponder a good while, and I did, too, listening to the evening wind and the cicadas. I came near alarming myself with the thought of the loneliness stretching ahead of me, and the new bitterness of it, and how I hated the secretiveness and the renunciation that honor and decency required of me and that common sense enforced on me. But when I looked up, your mother was watching me, smiling a little, and she touched my hand and she said, "You'll be just fine."

How soft her voice is. That there should be such a voice in the whole world, and that I should be the one to hear it, seemed to me then and seems to me now an unfathomable grace.

She began to come to the house when some of the other women did, to take the curtains away to wash, to defrost the icebox. And then she started coming by herself to tend the gardens. She made them very fine and prosperous. And one evening when I saw her there, out by the wonderful roses, I said, "How can I repay you for all this?"

And she said, "You ought to marry me." And I did.

Here is my thought: If I were to put my hand on her brow and bless her purely, as if I were indeed and altogether a minister of the Lord, I would hope just such an experience for her as that one of mine. Oh, I know she is fond of me, and very loyal. But I could hope that sometime the Song of Songs would startle her, as if it spoke from her own heart. I cannot really make myself believe that her feelings could have been at all like mine. And why do I worry so much over this Jack Boughton? Love is holy because it is like grace—the worthiness of its object is never really what matters. I might well be leaving her to a greater happiness than I have given her, even granting every difficulty. Sometimes I think I have seen the beginnings of it in her. If the Lord is letting me momentarily be witness to a grace He intends for her, I should find in this a great kindness toward myself.

This morning a splendid dawn passed over our house on its way to Kansas. This morning Kansas rolled out of its sleep into a sunlight grandly announced, proclaimed throughout heaven—one more of the very finite number of days that this old prairie has been called Kansas, or Iowa. But it has all been one day, that first day. Light is constant, we just turn over in it. So every day is in fact the selfsame evening and morning. My grandfather's grave turned into the light, and the dew on his weedy little mortality patch was glorious.

"Thou wast in Eden, the garden of God; every precious stone was thy covering, the sardius, the topaz, and the diamond."

While I'm thinking of it—when you are an old man like I am, you might think of writing some sort of account of yourself, as I am doing. In my experience of it, age has a tendency to make one's sense of oneself harder to maintain, less robust in some ways.

Why do I love the thought of you old? That first twinge of arthritis in your knee is a thing I imagine with all the tenderness I felt when you showed me your loose tooth. Be diligent in your prayers, old man. I hope you will have seen more of the world than I ever got around to seeing—only myself to blame. And I hope you will have read some of my books. And God bless your eyes, and your hearing also, and of course your heart. I wish I could help you carry the weight of many years. But the Lord will have that fatherly satisfaction.

This has been a strange day, disturbing. Glory called and invited you and your mother to the movies. Then, when she came for you, she had old Boughton with her, and she helped him out of the car and up the walk and up the steps. He so rarely leaves his house now that I was really amazed to find him at my door. We sat him down at the kitchen table and gave him a glass of water, and then the three of you left. All the bother seemed to have worn him out, because he just sat there with a more or less sociable expression but with his eyes closed, clearing his throat from time to time as if he was about to speak but then thought better of it. I found something on the radio, and we listened awhile to that. He'd chuckle a little if anything interesting happened. I believe he had been there most of an hour before he started to speak.

Then he said, "You know, Jack's not right with himself yet. Still not right." And he shook his head.

I said, "We've talked about that."

"Oh yes, he talks," Boughton said. "But he's never told me why he's come back here. Never told Glory either. He was supposed to have some kind of job down in St. Louis. I don't know what's become of that. We thought he might be married. I believe he was, for a while. I don't know what became of that, either. He seems to have a little money. I don't know anything about it." He said, "I know he talks to you and Mrs. Ames. I know that."

Then he closed his eyes again. The effort of speaking seemed to have been considerable, and I think it was because he hated to have to say what he had just said. I took it as a warning. I don't know another way to look at it. And I took his coming to the house as a way of underscoring his words, as it certainly did. And now I am persuaded again that I must speak to your mother.

Young Boughton came walking up the porch steps while we were still sitting there. I said, Come in, and pushed a chair out for him, but he stood by the door for a minute or two taking us in and drawing conclusions, which were pretty near the mark, as I could see by his expression. He seems always to suspect that people are in some sort of league against him. And no doubt that's true, often enough, just as it was true at that moment. And there is an element of frustration and embarrassment in his manner, when he looks past the pretense, as he seems always to do, that makes me feel ashamed to be a part of it, and sorry for him, too. There is also anger, and that concerns me.

Jack said, "I came home and there was no one there. It was a bit of a shock."

Boughton said, in that hearty voice he can still muster when he wants to sound as though he's telling the truth, "I'm sorry, Jack! Ames and I have been looking after each other while the women are out at the movies! We thought you would be gone a little longer!"

"Yes. Well, no harm done," he said, and he sat down when I asked him to again, and he kept his eyes on me, with that half-smile he has when he wants you to know he knows what's really going on and he can't quite believe you persist in trying to fool him. Boughton sort of nodded off then, as he does when conversations get difficult, and I can't blame him, though I do have my heart to consider, too. Because it was a considerable strain on me to think what to say to Jack, as it always is and always has been, it seems to me. I felt sorry for him, and that's a fact. It seems almost a curse to me the way he can see through people. Of course, I couldn't be honest with him, so there I was being dishonest with him, and there he was watching me as if I were the worst liar in the world, as if I were insulting him, as I suppose in fact I was.

"Your father felt like he needed to get out of the house," I said.

He said, "Understandable."

In fact, that was a ridiculous thing for me to have said, considering that it's about all Boughton can do to walk from his bed to his chair on the porch.

I said, "I suppose he wanted to take advantage of the good weather while it lasts."

"I'm sure he did."

"Well," I said, after a minute, "this is some year for acorns!" which was perfectly pitiful. Jack laughed outright.

"The crows have made an impressive showing," he said. "And the gourds are particularly shapely and abundant, I think." And all that time he was looking at me as if to say, Let's just be honest with each other for five minutes.

Now, I excuse myself in that I don't know what the truth actually is. I do believe his father came here to, in effect, warn me about him, but I am not absolutely certain of it. And in any case, I can hardly betray a confidence, especially not one as inflammatory and injurious as that one, certainly not with poor old Boughton sitting there three feet from me, quite probably listening to the whole conversation. But dishonesty is dishonesty, a humiliating thing to be caught at, especially when you have no choice but to persist in it, and to salvage as much of the deception as you can, under the very eye of indignation, so to speak.

On the other hand, as an old man, his father's senior by a couple of years despite my relative vigor, such as it is, I feel I have a right not to be deviled in this way. If the point was to make me angry, I am angry as I write this. My heart is up to something that is alarming the rest of my body, in fact. I must go pray. I wonder what he knows about my heart.

Well, of course he must know a good deal about my heart, since your mother did enlist him in bringing my study downstairs.

When I pray about all this, it is a sense of the sadness in him that keeps coming to my mind. He is someone who must be forgiven a great deal on the grounds of that strange suffering.

And when the three of you came back, which you did fairly soon, things were much better. Glory seemed a little startled at first at finding Jack there, but your mother was pleased to see him, as she always is, I believe.

You liked the movie. Tobias isn't allowed to go to movies, so you brought him almost half your box of Cracker Jacks, which I thought was decent of you. I wonder whether you should go to movies. But with television in the house, there seems no point in forbidding them. Of course Tobias can't watch television, either. Your mother promised his mother we'd see to that whenever he comes over, which is often enough to make you miss the Cisco Kid a lot more frequently than you would like. You're not the most sociable child in the world, and I'm a little afraid that, given a choice, Tobias or television, your best chum would be on his own. As it is, he spends more time waiting on the porch than he should. From time to time, you have seemed so lonely to us, and here is Tobias, an estimable chap, an answer to our prayers, and you let him sit on the porch until some cartoon is over. But I'm not inclined to do much forbidding these days. T.'s father is young. He has years and years with his boys, God willing.

Well, the three of you came in, pleased with yourselves and smelling of popcorn, and I was so relieved I can't tell you. Then after a little talk your mother and Glory helped Boughton out to the car and took him home, which is the only place he is comfortable anymore, and then they made a supper for us all to have there. You went off to find Tobias so you could contaminate his good Lutheran mind with nonsense about gunslingers and federal marshals. And I sat there at the table with Jack Boughton, who didn't say a word. He just took a little time deciding to leave. He didn't come back to his father's house for dinner, and nobody said anything about it, but I know it worried us all. Your mother and Glory took a walk after the table was cleared, to enjoy the evening, they said, but when they came back, Glory said they had seen Jack, and he had told them he would come home later. I could tell they had found him down at the bar. They didn't offer particulars and Boughton didn't ask.

J ACK BOUGHTON HAS A WIFE AND A CHILD. He showed me a picture of them. He only let me see it for half a minute, and then he took it back. I was slightly at a loss, which he must have expected, and still I could tell it was an effort for him not to take offense. You see, the wife is a colored woman. That did surprise me.

I was over at the church yesterday morning, in my study, sorting through some old papers, thinking if I put aside the interesting ones, the actual records, they might not be discarded along with all the clutter. There are just boxes and boxes of memoranda and magazine articles and flyers and utility bills. It seems as if I never threw anything away. I'm afraid a new minister might not be patient enough to sort through it all, and that would be my fault.

Well, there I was, feeling a little dirty and cobwebby and also a little morose and, I must say, dreading interruption, too, since I may at any time stop feeling up to this sort of thing. I hadn't been at it half an hour and I was tired already.

And in came Jack Boughton, once again wearing the suit and necktie, once again kempt and shaved, but looking a little frayed for all that, weary about the eyes, God bless him. I was interested to see him, more interested than pleased, I admit. I couldn't very well talk to him with dirt all over my face and hands, so I excused myself to go wash, and when I came back, he was still standing by the door—I'd forgotten to offer him a chair, so he was just standing there. He was looking quite pale, and I was ashamed of myself for my thoughtlessness. But he is so afraid of offending unintentionally that he abides by manners most people forget as soon as they learn them, and that can make it seem almost as if he means to make you ashamed. That is how I felt, at least, and I know it was unfair of me.

Then when he sat down I went to lift some boxes from my desk and he stood up and took one of them right out of my hands, which was good of him, but irked me a little just the same. I'd rather drop dead doing for myself than add a day to my life by acting helpless. But he meant well. He moved both boxes onto the floor, and then his hands were grimy and the front of his jacket, so he took out his handkerchief and wiped himself down a little. I suggested we could go into the sanctuary, but he said the office was fine with him. So we sat there quiet for a while.

Then he said, "I stayed away from this town for a long time. As a courtesy to my father, mainly. I might never have come back."

I asked him what had made him change his mind. It took him a while to answer.

"For several reasons I felt I needed to speak with him. My father. But," he said, "somehow, when I came here, I didn't expect him to be so very old."

"The last few years have been hard on him."

He put his hand to his eyes.

I said, "It has done him good to have you here."

He shook his head. "You talked with him yesterday."

"Yes. He did seem a little worried about you."

He laughed. "A few days ago Glory said to me, 'He's fragile. We don't want to kill him.' We! It's true, though. I *don't* want to kill him. So I thought I might be able to speak with you. This will be my last attempt, I promise."

I almost reminded him my own health is not perfect, which

would have been foolish, since on second thought I could not really imagine that any revelation he might make would strike me down.

He took a little leather case out of his breast pocket and opened it and held it in front of me. His hand was not steady, and I had to put on my reading glasses, but then I could see it fairly well. It was posed like a portrait photograph—himself, a young woman, and a boy about five or six. The woman was seated in a chair with the child standing next to her, and young Boughton was standing behind them. It was Jack Boughton, a colored woman, and a light-skinned colored boy.

Boughton looked at the picture and then he snapped the case shut and slipped it back into his pocket. He said, "You see," and his voice was so controlled it sounded bitter, "you see, I also have a wife and child." Then he just watched me for a minute or two, clearly hoping he would not have to take offense.

"That's a fine-looking family," I said.

He nodded. "She's a fine woman. He's a fine boy. I'm a lucky man." He smiled.

"And you're afraid this might kill your father?"

He shrugged. "It came near enough killing *her* father. *And* her mother. They curse the day I was born." He laughed and touched his hand to his face. "As you know, I have considerable experience antagonizing people, but this is on another level entirely."

I was thinking my own thoughts, so he said, "Maybe not. Maybe that's just how it seems to me—" and then he sat there studying his hands.

So I said, "Well, how long have you been married?" And regretted the question.

He cleared his throat. "We are married in the eyes of God, as they say. Who does not provide a certificate, but who also does not enforce anti-miscegenation laws. The Deus Absconditus at His most benign. Sorry." He smiled. "In the eyes of God we have been man and wife for about eight years. We have lived as man and wife a total of seventeen months, two weeks, and a day."

I remarked that we have never had those laws here in Iowa, and he said, "Yes, Iowa, the shining star of radicalism."

So I asked him if he came here to be married.

He shook his head. "Her father doesn't want her to marry me. Her father is also a minister, by the way. I suppose that was inevitable. And there is a good Christian man down there in Tennessee, a friend of the family, who is willing to marry my wife and adopt my son. They think this is very kind of him. I suppose it is. They believe it would be best for everybody." He said, "And the fact is, I have had considerable difficulty looking after my family. From time to time they have gone back to Tennessee, when things were too difficult. That's where they are now." He said, "I can't really ask her to make a final break with her family under the circumstances." He cleared his throat.

We were just quiet. Then he said, "You know the chief thing her father has against me? He takes me for an atheist! Della says he thinks all white men are atheists, the only difference is that some of them are aware of it. Della is my wife."

I said, "Well, from certain things you have said, I have gotten the impression that you are an atheist."

He nodded. "It is probably truer to say I am in a state of categorical unbelief. I don't even believe God doesn't exist, if you see what I mean. Of course this is a matter of concern to my wife, too. Partly for my sake. Partly for the boy's. I lied to her about it for a little while. When I told her the truth, I believe she thought she could rescue me. As I said, when she first knew me, she took me for a man of the cloth. Many people make that mistake." He laughed. "I generally correct them. I did her."

Now, the fact is, I don't know how old Boughton would take all this. It surprised me to realize that. I think it is an issue we never discussed in all our years of discussing everything. It just didn't come up.

I said, "I take it you've talked to Glory."

"No. I can't do that. She'd just break her heart over it. She can tell there's something on my mind. She probably thinks I'm in trouble. I believe my father thinks so, too."

"I believe he does."

He nodded. "He was crying yesterday." He looked at me. "I have disappointed him again." And then he said, controlling his voice, "I haven't had any word from my wife since I left St. Louis. I have been waiting to hear from her. I have written to her a number of times— What is the proverb? 'Hope deferred maketh the heart sick.' " He smiled. "I have even found myself turning to liquor for solace."

I said, "So I understand," and he laughed.

" 'Give strong drink unto him that is ready to perish, and wine unto the bitter in soul.' Isn't that right?"

Word for word.

He said, "The first thing she ever said to me was 'Thank you, Reverend.' She was walking home in a rainstorm with an armful of books and papers—she was a teacher—and some of the papers fell onto the pavement, and the wind was scattering them, so I helped her gather them up, and then I walked her to her door, since I had an umbrella. I didn't think about what I was doing, particularly. My impeccable manners."

"You were well brought up."

"I was indeed." He said, "Her father told me that if I were a gentleman I'd have left her alone. I understand why he feels that way. She had a good life. And I am not a gentleman." He wouldn't let me object to that. "I know what the word means, Reverend. Though I can now say that the influence of my wife worked a change in me for the better, at least temporarily."

Then he said, "I don't want to tire you with this. I know I've interrupted you. I'll tell you why I have kept trying to talk to you."

I told him he was welcome to take all the time he wanted. He said, "That's very kind." And then he just sat there for a little while. "If we could find a way to live," he said, "I think she would marry me. That would answer her family's most serious objections, I believe. They say I can't provide a decent life for my family, and that has in fact been the case to this point."

He cleared his throat. "If you can really spare me the time, I will explain. Thank you. You see, I met Della during a fairly low point in my life. I won't go into that. Della was very nice to me, very pleasant. So I found myself now and then walking down that street at that hour, and sometimes I saw her and we spoke. I swear I had no intentions at all, honorable or otherwise. It was just pleasant to see her face." He laughed. "She would always say, 'Good afternoon, Reverend.' I was not at that time accustomed to being treated like a respectable man. I must say I enjoyed it. It got so that I would walk along her street with no thought of seeing her, just because there was a kind of comfort in being reminded of her. And then one evening I did meet her, and we spoke a little, and she asked me in for tea. She shared rooms with another woman who taught at the colored school. It was pleasant. We had our tea together, the three of us. I told her then I was not a minister. So she knew that. I believe she invited me in in the first place because she was under that impression, but I was honest with her. About that. It didn't seem to matter too much.

"I don't know just how it happened—I stopped by to lend her a book I had bought in order to lend it to her—as if from my library—I even dog-eared a few pages—and she invited me to come for Thanksgiving dinner. She knew I wasn't on excellent terms with my family, and she said she couldn't have me spending the holiday by myself. I said I was uncomfortable with strangers, and she promised me it would be all right. Still, I had a couple of drinks before I came and I was later than I had intended. I thought I would walk in on a gathering of some kind, but she was there all by herself, looking terribly unhappy.

"I apologized as well as I could and offered to go away, but she said, 'You just sit down!' So we sat there eating, neither one of us saying anything. I told her the dinner was delicious and she said, 'It probably was once.' Then she said, 'Two hours late, liquor on your breath—' speaking to me as if I were, well, what I was, and it came over me that I had no business there, I was no one she could respect, and the grief I felt was amazing to me. I stood up to thank her and excuse myself, and then I left.

"But when I had walked a few blocks I realized she was following along behind me. She came up beside me and she said, 'I just wanted to tell you not to feel so bad.'

"And I said, 'Now I will have to walk you back to your door.'

"And she laughed and said, 'Of course you will.'

"So I did. And then the other woman came home, Lorraine, the one who shared her rooms. There was a dinner at their church, but Della had made some excuse about not feeling well and having to stay home. I should have been long gone by then, but there we were, eating our pumpkin pie. What could have been more compromising?"

He laughed. "It was all so respectable. But word got to Tennessee somehow and her sister came to visit, with the clear intention of scaring me off. I'd come in the evenings with a book of poetry and we'd read to each other, while her sister sat there glaring at me. It was ridiculous. It was wonderful. But when the school year ended, her brothers came and took her back to Tennessee. She left a note for me with Lorraine, saying goodbye. I knew her father couldn't be hard to find, since he was a minister, so I went there, to Memphis, and I found his church, a very large African Methodist Episcopal church, and the next morning being Sunday, I went to hear him preach. Knowing Della would be there, of course. And I hoped to speak to him. I thought it might recommend me to him, if I could manage to seem forthright and manly, you know. I got my shoes shined and my hair trimmed.

"The church was full and I sat near the back, but I was the only white man there, and people noticed me. Della's sister was in the choir, so of course she saw me. And I could tell her father suspected who I was, by the way he watched me. He preached about those who come among you in sheep's clothing but inwardly they are ravening wolves. He also spoke about whited tombs, which inwardly are full of dead men's bones and all uncleanness. Looking at me the whole time, of course.

"But I still made myself speak to him at the door. I said, 'I only want to assure you that my friendship with your daughter has been entirely honorable.' And he said, 'If you were an honorable man, you would leave her alone.'

"I said, 'Yes, I will do that. I came here to assure you of that.' Which was a lie, of course. I did intend to stop seeing her, but it was an intention I had formed in his church that very morning. I thought that Della's standing with her family might be helped if I impressed him as a plausibly decent man, and my only chance of doing that was by going away. And I could see what a very good life she had. I'm not sure what my intentions had been in going there. Certainly I never thought I would leave without saying even one word to her. But I did. I left for St. Louis that same evening. I'm not sure he was impressed by my gallantry, but I do know it impressed Della. Then the fall came, and I happened to be walking down her street, as I happened to do every week or so, and there she was. I tipped my hat and she burst into tears. And from that moment we have considered ourselves man and wife.

"Word got back to Tennessee and she was more or less disowned, and then she got pregnant and the school dismissed her. I was selling shoes at the time—there's very little money in it, but you don't get arrested for it, either. So her mother came a few weeks before the baby was due and found us in a state of something like destitution, living in a residential hotel in an unpleasant part of town. It was humiliating. But of course we couldn't find respectable accommodations, and the hotel clerk where we got a room charged me a good deal extra for turning a blind eye, or words to that effect. He had a phrase for the law we were breaking—'pernicious cohabitation'? 'lascivious cohabitation'? Lewd. For some reason I always forget that word. You can't imagine how many ways they make things difficult.

"Then her father came and her brothers, and the five of us had an earnest talk about Della's well-being, which began with her father saying, 'You should be very glad that I am a Christian man.' He is an imposing figure. And he persuaded me that I should tell Della to go home where she could be cared for. I did that, and she went away with them. Ah, the desolation! The relief! I was so scared by the thought of that baby. I knew in my miserable heart that something would go wrong and I would be to blame for it. I tried to hide my relief from her, but she could see it, and she was hurt by it, I knew she was. I told her I would come to Memphis as soon as I had saved up the money. It took me weeks, because I had some debts and the fellows found me. I expected they would, and that was another reason I was glad to let her go, but of course I couldn't explain that to her. Finally, I wrote to my father and told him I needed money—he hadn't heard from me in a year at least—and he sent me three times as much as I asked for. And there was a note telling me that you were getting married.

"During those weeks there was a revival, a tent meeting, down by the river. I used to walk over there every night because there were crowds and noise and there wasn't much alcohol. One night a man standing just beside me, as close to me as you are, went down as if he'd been shot. When he came up again, he threw his arms around me and said, 'My burdens are gone from me! I have become as a little child!' I thought, If I'd been standing two feet to the left, that might have been me. I'm joking, of course, more or less. But it's a fact that if I could have traded places with him, my whole life would be different, in the sense that I might have been able to look Della's father in the eye, maybe even my father. That I would no longer be regarded as quite such a threat to the soul of my child. That man was standing there with sawdust in his beard, saying, 'I was the worst of sinners!' and he looked as if that might well be true. And there he was weeping with repentance and relief while I stood watching with my hands in my pockets, feeling nothing but anxiety and shame. And a certain amusement, if you will forgive me. But the next day my father's letter came and I got a decent coat and a bus ticket and I was all right then.

"When I got to Memphis the baby had just been born the day before, and the house was full of aunts and women from the church, coming and going. They let me come in and sit in a corner. I don't think anyone knew what to do with me till her father came home, so they just went on with their business. If the day had been warmer, I think I'd have been sitting on the stoop. One woman said to me, 'They're both just fine. They're sleeping.' And she brought me a newspaper, which was kind of her. It eased my embarrassment to have something to look at.

"When her father finally did come home, the room emptied and the house became completely still. I stood up, but he didn't offer to shake hands. The first words he said to me were 'I understand you are not a veteran.' Ah. I told him some lie about my heart, and then I regretted it instantly, because I felt I had made myself sound feeble, but I needn't have worried about that, because I could tell he didn't believe a word. As I recall, Deuteronomy says cowardice forbids one from going to the army. 'What man is there that is fearful and faint-hearted? Let him go and return unto his house, lest his brother's heart melt as his heart.' So I had scriptural warrant, though I chose not to mention it.

"He said, 'I understand you are descended from John Ames, of Kansas.' Of course anyone else would have put that right, but I thought there might be some advantage in letting him believe it—he was referring to your grandfather, of course. It was the first slightly positive thing he had ever said to me. He said he knew people whose families came north from Missouri before the war, and apparently they told some remarkable stories about him, about raids and ambushes. I told him I had heard stories about the old man while I was growing up, which is true. They were mainly stories about him running off with the laundry, but I didn't tell him that. I remember my father said once when he was a boy the old man came to our church and sat in the back, and when the collection plate came to him he just emptied it into his hat."

It's a fact that my grandfather always did suspect the Presbyterians of hoarding, so that's not at all unlikely. And he did make a world of use of that hat.

He said, "We had a few minutes of actual conversation, but I had to be cautious. I didn't know enough about the old times to risk telling lies, so I said my family had turned pacifist after the war. And didn't encourage discussion of it. That's correct, I believe?"

Absolutely.

"He knew my full name because that is what Della wanted to call the baby. I was so relieved when I heard that. Her father said, 'She's been waiting for you.' And I just sat there beside her bed all that afternoon, talking a little when she felt like it. Looking at the baby now and then. The women would take him away if he cried. They brought in some supper. I thought maybe things were improving, but they were all just being Christian. In the evening her father told me it would be best if I went away. He said, 'This time I make no appeal to your honor.' I suppose he had the right to say that. They were looking after her and I didn't see how I could, so my thought was to go back to St. Louis and find a decent job and save up some money and try to figure something out. Because she talked to me about bringing the baby home, and she meant St. Louis.

"I left what I could of my father's money with her. And three months later she came with her sister and the baby to the old place, Lorraine's place, where she lived when I met her. I had a new room at the time, very clean and cheap, and also very respectable, which is to say I'd have been out on the street if I'd brought home a colored wife and child. I couldn't afford the old squalor, if I was to save anything at all. As it is, I've never repaid my father. Not a dime.

"So over all these years we have been back and forth, with her going to Memphis when things were too difficult, for the boy's sake. He is a wonderful boy. I believe he has never really lacked anything. He has uncles and cousins, and his grandfather dotes on him. Della's father.

"My son's name is Robert Boughton Miles. He is very good to me, very respectful and polite. Not as much at ease with me as your boy is.

"I managed finally, about two years ago, to get a job that paid a little money. I made a down payment on a house in a mixed neighborhood, and Robert and Della came. It isn't much of a house, but I did some painting and found some rugs and chairs. And we had almost eight months there. But then we got careless and went to the park together, and my boss happened to be there with his family. And the next day he called me into his office and told me he had his good name to consider. I hit him, which was very stupid of me. I hit him twice. He fell against his desk and cracked a rib. I thought I had talked him out of going to the law, I promised to pay his doctor bills and something for his inconvenience, but that evening the police came to speak with us, to mention that law about cohabiting. It was humiliating, but I kept my head. I think it becomes a husband and father to stay out of jail when possible. I arranged to put my family on the bus to Memphis, rented the house. Gave the dog to a neighbor.

"And when I had sorted that out as well as I could, I came here, thinking I might find some way to live with my family here, I mean my wife and son. I have even thought it might be a pleasure to introduce Robert to my father. I would like him to know that I finally have something I can be proud of. He's a beautiful child, very bright. And believe me, he's being brought up in the church. He wants to be a preacher. But now I see how feeble my father is, and I don't want to kill him. I really don't. I have enough on my shoulders as it is."

He said, "You will not tell me this is divine retribution."

"Furthest thing from my mind."

"I was pretty sure I could trust you not to do that."

I said, "Thank you."

He drew a long breath. He said, "You know my father so well."

"But I can't give you any assurances about this, one way or the other. I'd hate to be wrong. You'll have to let me reflect on it."

Then he said, "If it were you, and not my father—"

Now, I could see his point in putting that question, since Boughton and I are in general very much of one mind. But it was not so simple a question as he might have thought, and I paused over it.

He watched me for a minute, and then he smiled and said, "You have made a somewhat—unconventional marriage yourself. You know a little bit about being the object of scandal. Unequally yoked and so on. Of course, Della is an educated woman." Those were his very words.

Now, that was just like him. That meanness. His remark was not even entirely to the point. And I never felt there was anything the least bit scandalous about my marriage. In her own way, your mother is a woman of great refinement. If a few people did make remarks, I just forgave them so fast it was as if I never heard them, because it was wrong of them to judge and I knew it and they should have known it.

But then that look of utter weariness came over him and he covered his face with his hands. And I could only forgive him.

My thought when I hesitated was that since I was so long in the habit of seeing meanness at the root of everything he did, I might well have doubted his motives in involving himself with this woman he did not marry, and bringing me this child. I'd have been wrong, I believe, but his question was not how I should react but how I would be liable to react. With Boughton this could be completely different, since he thought so much better of Jack, or so I had always believed.

I said, "I would love to know the child. Especially if you explained everything to me the way you just did." And then I said, "He certainly took to that other child."

Young Boughton gave me such a look as I have never seen in my life before. He went stark white. Then he smiled and said, " 'Children's children are the crown of old men.' "

I said, "You have to forgive me for that. That was such a foolish thing to say. I'm tired. I'm old."

"Yes," he said, and his voice was very controlled. "And I have taken far too much of your time. Thank you. I know I can trust your pastoral discretion."

I said, "We can't let the conversation end here," but I was just so weary and downhearted it was all I could do to get up from my chair. He stopped by the door and I went over to him and I put my arms around him. For a moment he actually let his head rest on my shoulder. "I am tired," he said. I could just feel the loneliness in him. Here I was supposed to be a second father to him. I wanted to say something to him to that effect, but it seemed complicated, and I was too tired to think through its possible implications. It might sound as if I were trying to establish some sort of equivalency between his failings and mine, when in fact I would have meant he was a better man than I ever thought he could be. So I said, "You are a good man," and he gave me a look, purely appraising, and laughed and said, "You can take my word for it, Reverend, there are worse."

But then he said, "What about this town? If we came here and got married, could we live here? Would people leave us alone?"

Well, I didn't know the answer to that one, either. I thought so.

He said, "There was a fire at the Negro church."

"That was a little nuisance fire, and it happened many years ago."

"And it has been many years since there was a Negro church."

Of course there wasn't much I could say to that.

He said, "You have influence here."

I said that might be true, but I couldn't promise to live long enough to make much use of it. I mentioned my heart.

He said, "I had no right to weary you with my troubles," which I took to mean there had been no point in it. I thought our conversation had been good, on balance, and I said that, and he nodded and said goodbye. And then after a minute he said, "No matter, Papa. I believe I've lost them, anyway."

I just sat there with my head on my desk and went over this in my mind and prayed until your mother came looking for me. She thought I had had some sort of episode and I let her think that. It seemed to me as if I ought to have had one. And there was nothing I could say to her in any case.

You might wonder about my pastoral discretion, writing this all out. Well, on one hand it is the way I have of considering things. On the other hand, he is a man about whom you may never hear one good word, and I just don't know another way to let you see the beauty there is in him.

That was two days ago. Now it's Sunday again. When you do this sort of work, it seems to be Sunday all the time, or Saturday night. You just finish preparing for one week and it's already the next week. This morning I read from one of those old sermons your mother keeps leaving around for me. It was on Romans I: "They became vain in their reasonings and their senseless heart was darkened, professing themselves to be wise they became fools," and so on. The Old Testament text was from Exodus, the plague of darkness. The sermon was a sort of attack on rationalism and irrationalism, the point being that both worship the creature rather than the Creator. I had glanced over it a little, but as I read it, it surprised me, sometimes because it seemed right and sometimes because it seemed embarrassingly wrong, and always because it seemed like something someone else must have written. Jack Boughton was there in that weary suit and tie, sitting beside you, and you were very pleased, and I believe your mother was, too.

Now, it does not at all agree with my notion of preaching, to stand there reading from a stack of yellowed pages full of what I must have thought once, trying to play down the certainty I had written into the language some black night half a lifetime ago. And there in the second pew was young Boughton, who always seems to see right through me. And I, being newly persuaded that he might come into a church with some however cynical hope of encountering a living Truth, was obliged to mouth these dead words while he sat there smiling at me. I do think there was a point in associating rationalism and irrationalism, that is, materialism and idolatry, and if I had had the energy to depart from the text I could have made something of that. As it was, I just read the sermon, shook all those hands, and came home and took a nap on the couch. I did have the feeling that young Boughton might actually have been comforted by the irrelevance of my preachments to anything that had passed between us, anything to do with him at all, God bless the poor devil. The fact was, standing there, I wished there were grounds for my old dread. That amazed me. I felt as if I'd have bequeathed him wife and child if I could to supply the loss of his own.

I woke up this morning thinking this town might as well be standing on the absolute floor of hell for all the truth there is in it, and the fault is mine as much as anyone's. I was thinking about the things that had happened here just in my lifetime— the droughts and the influenza and the Depression and three terrible wars. It seems to me now we never looked up from the trouble we had just getting by to put the obvious question, that is, to ask what it was the Lord was trying to make us understand. The word "preacher" comes from an old French word, *prédicateur*, which means prophet. And what is the purpose of a prophet except to find meaning in trouble?

Well, we didn't ask the question, so the question was just taken away from us. We became like the people without the Law, people who didn't know their right hand from their left. Just stranded here. A stranger might ask why there is a town here at all. Our own children might ask. And who could answer them? It was just a dogged little outpost in the sand hills, within striking distance of Kansas. That's really all it was meant to be. It was a place John Brown and Jim Lane could fall back on when they needed to heal and rest. There must have been a hundred little towns like it, set up in the heat of an old urgency that is all forgotten now, and their littleness and their shabbiness, which was the measure of the courage and passion that went into the making of them, now just look awkward and provincial and ridiculous, even to the people who have lived here long enough to know better. It looks ridiculous to me. I truly suspect I never left because I was afraid I would not come back.

I have mentioned that my father and my mother left here. Well, they certainly did. Edward bought a piece of land down on the Gulf Coast and built a cottage for his own family and for them. He did it mainly to get my mother away from this ferocious climate, and that was kind of him, because her rheumatism became severe as she got older. The idea was that they would spend a year down there getting settled in, and then they would come back again to Gilead and only go south for the worst of the winter until my father retired. So I took his pulpit for that first year. And then they never did come back, except twice to visit, the first time when I lost Louisa and the second time to talk me into leaving with them. That second time I asked my father to preach, and he shook his head and said, "I just can't do it anymore."

He told me that it had not been his intention to leave me stranded here. In fact, it was his hope that I would seek out a larger life than this. He and Edward both felt strongly what excellent use I could make of a broader experience. He told me that looking back on Gilead from any distance made it seem a relic, an archaism. When I mentioned the history we had here, he laughed and said, "Old, unhappy far-off things and battles long ago." And that irritated me. He said, "Just look at this place. Every time a tree gets to a decent size, the wind comes along and breaks it." He was expounding the wonders of the larger world, and I was resolving in my heart never to risk the experience of them. He said, "I have become aware that we here lived within the limits of notions that were very old and even very local. I want you to understand that you do not have to be loyal to them."

He thought he could excuse me from my loyalty, as if it were loyalty to him, as if it were just some well-intended mistake he could correct for me, as if it were not loyalty to myself at the very least, putting the Lord to one side, so to speak, since I knew perfectly well at that time, as I had for years and years, that the Lord absolutely transcends any understanding I have of Him, which makes loyalty to Him a different thing from loyalty to whatever customs and doctrines and memories I happen to associate with Him. I know that, and I knew it then. How ignorant did he think I was? I had read Owen and James and Huxley and Swedenborg and, for heaven's sake, Blavatsky, as he well knew, since he had virtually read them over my shoulder. I subscribed to *The Nation*. I was never Edward, but I was no fool either, and I almost said as much.

I don't recall that I actually said anything, taken aback as I was. Well, all he accomplished was to make me homesick for a place I never left. I couldn't believe he would speak to me as if I were not competent to invest my loyalties as I saw fit. How could I accept the advice of someone who had such a low estimation of me? Those were my thoughts at the time. What a day that was. Then in a week or so I got that letter from him. I have mentioned loneliness to you, and darkness, and I thought then I already knew what they were, but that day it was as if a great cold wind swept over me the like of which I had never felt before, and that wind blew for years and years. My father threw me back on myself, and on the Lord. That's a fact, so I find little to regret. It cost me a good deal of sorrow, but I learned from it.

Why is this on my mind, anyway? I was thinking about the frustrations and the disappointments of life, of which there are a very great many. I haven't been entirely honest with you about that.

This morning I went over to the bank and cashed a check, thinking to help Jack out a little. I thought he probably needed to go to Memphis, not right away necessarily, but at some time. I went over to Boughton's and waited around, talking about nothing, wasting time I couldn't spare, till I had a chance to speak to him in private. I offered him the money and he laughed and put it in my jacket pocket and said, "What are you doing, Papa? You don't *have* any money." And then his eyes chilled over the way they do and he said, "I'm leaving. Don't worry." I took your money, your mother's money, of which there is a truly pitiful amount, and tried to give it away, and that is how it was received.

I said, "Are you going to Memphis, then?"

And he said, "Anywhere else." He smiled and cleared his throat and said, "I got that letter I've been waiting for."

My heart was very heavy. There was Boughton sitting in his Morris chair staring at nothing. Glory told me the only words he had said all day were "Jesus never had to be old!" Glory is upset and Jack is wretched and they were making polite talk with me about nothing, probably wondering why I didn't leave, and I was wishing to goodness I could just go home. Then the moment came when I could do Jack the little kindness I had come for, and all I did was offend him.

Then I came home and your mother made me lie down and sent you off with Tobias. She lowered the shades. She knelt beside me and stroked my hair for a while. And after a little rest I got up and wrote this, which I have now read over.

Jack is leaving. Glory was so upset with him that she came to talk to me about it. She has sent out the alarm to the brothers and sisters, that they must all desist from their humanitarian labors and come home. She believes old Boughton can't be long for this world. "How could he possibly leave now!" she says. That's a fair question, I suppose, but I think I know the answer to it. The house will fill up with those estimable people and their husbands and wives and their pretty children. How could he be there in the midst of it all with that sad and splendid treasure in his heart?—I also have a wife and a child.

I can tell you this, that if I'd married some rosy dame and she had given me ten children and they had each given me ten grandchildren, I'd leave them all, on Christmas Eve, on the coldest night of the world, and walk a thousand miles just for the sight of your face, your mother's face. And if I never found you, my comfort would be in that hope, my lonely and singular hope, which could not exist in the whole of Creation except in my heart and in the heart of the Lord. That is just a way of saying I could never thank God sufficiently for the splendor He has hidden from the world—your mother excepted, of course—and revealed to me in your sweetly ordinary face. Those kind Boughton brothers and sisters would be ashamed of the wealth of their lives beside the seeming poverty of Jack's life, and he would utterly and bitterly prefer what he had lost to everything they had. That is not a tolerable state of mind to be in, as I am well aware.

And old Boughton, if he could stand up out of his chair, out of his decrepitude and crankiness and sorrow and limitation, would abandon all those handsome children of his, mild and confident as they are, and follow after that one son whom he has never known, whom he has favored as one does a wound, and he would protect him as a father cannot, defend him with a strength he does not have, sustain him with a bounty beyond any resource he could ever dream of having. If Boughton could be himself, he would utterly pardon every transgression, past, present, and to come, whether or not it was a transgression in fact or his to pardon. He would be that extravagant. That is a thing I would love to see.

As I have told you, I myself was the good son, so to speak, the one who never left his father's house—even when his father did, a fact which surely puts my credentials beyond all challenge. I am one of those righteous for whom the rejoicing in heaven will be comparatively restrained. And that's all right. There is no justice in love, no proportion in it, and there need not be, because in any specific instance it is only a glimpse or parable of an embracing, incomprehensible reality. It makes no sense at all because it is the eternal breaking in on the temporal. So how could it subordinate itself to cause or consequence?

It is worth living long enough to outlast whatever sense of grievance you may acquire. Another reason why you must be careful of your health.

I think I'll put an end to all this writing. I've read it over, more or less, and I've found some things of interest in it, mainly the way I have been drawn back into this world in the course of it.

The expectation of death I began with reads like a kind of youthfulness, it seems to me now. The novelty of it interested me a good deal, clearly.

This morning I saw Jack Boughton walking up toward the bus stop, looking too thin for his clothes, carrying a suitcase that seemed to weigh almost nothing. Looking a good deal past his youth. Looking like someone you wouldn't much want your daughter to marry. Looking somehow elegant and brave.

I called to him and he stopped and waited for me, and I walked with him up to the bus stop. I brought along *The Essence of Christianity*, which I had set on the table by the door, hoping I might have a chance to give it to him. He turned it over in his hands, laughing a little at how beat up it is. He said, "I remember this from—forever!" Maybe he was thinking it looked like the kind of thing he used to pocket in the old days. That thought crossed my mind, and it made me feel as though the book did actually belong to him. I believe he was pleased with it. I dog-eared page 20—"Only that which is apart from my own being is capable of being doubted by me. How then can I doubt of God, who is my being? To doubt of God is to doubt of myself." And so on. I memorized that and a good bit more, so I could talk to Edward about it, but I didn't want to ruin the good time we'd had that one day playing catch, and the occasion really never arose again.

There were two further points I felt I should have made in our earlier conversations, one of them being that doctrine is not belief, it is only one way of talking about belief, and the other being that the Greek word *sozo*, which is usually translated "saved," can also mean healed, restored, that sort of thing. So the conventional translation narrows the meaning of the word in a way that can create false expectations. I thought he should be aware that grace is not so poor a thing that it cannot present itself in any number of ways. Well, I was also making conversation. I knew he must have heard more or less the same things from his father any number of times. My first thought was that nobody ought to be as lonely as he looked to me walking along by himself. And I believe he was glad of the company. He nodded from time to time, and his expression was very polite.

As we walked he glanced around at the things you never really look at when you live in a town—the fretting on a gable, the path worn across an empty lot, a hammock slung between a cottonwood and a clothesline pole. We passed the church. He said, "I'll never see this place again," and there was a kind of sad wonder in his voice that I recognized. It gave me a turn. So I said, "You take care of yourself. They could need you sometime." After a minute he nodded, conceding the possibility.

Then he stopped and looked at me and said, "You know, I'm doing the worst possible thing again. Leaving now. Glory will never forgive me. She says, 'This is it. This is your masterpiece.' " He was smiling, but there was actual fear in his eyes, a kind of amazement, and there might well have been. It was truly a dreadful thing he was doing, leaving his father to die without him. It was the kind of thing only his father would forgive him for.

So I said, "Glory talked to me about all that. I told her not to judge, that there might be more to the situation."

"Thank you."

"I understand why you have to leave, I really do." That was as true a thing as I have ever said. And I will tell you, remarkable as it seemed to me, at that moment I felt grateful for all my old bitterness of heart.

He cleared his throat. "Then you wouldn't mind saying goodbye to my father for me?"

"I will do that. Certainly I will."

I didn't know how to continue the conversation beyond that point, but I didn't want to leave him, and in any case, I had to sit down on the bench beside him on account of my heart. So there we were. I said, "If you would accept a few dollars of that money of mine, you'd be doing me a kindness."

He laughed and said, "I suppose I could see my way clear."

So I gave him forty dollars and he kept twenty and gave twenty back. We sat there for a while.

Then I said, "The thing I would like, actually, is to bless you."

He shrugged. "What would that involve?"

"Well, as I envisage it, it would involve my placing my hand on your brow and asking the protection of God for you. But if it would be embarrassing—" There were a few people on the street.

"No, no," he said. "That doesn't matter." And he took his hat off and set it on his knee and closed his eyes and lowered his head, almost rested it against my hand, and I did bless him to the limit of my powers, whatever they are, repeating the benediction from Numbers, of course—"The Lord make His face to shine upon thee and be gracious unto thee: The Lord lift up His countenance upon thee, and give thee peace." Nothing could be more beautiful that that, or more expressive of my feelings, certainly, or more sufficient, for that matter. Then, when he didn't open his eyes or lift up his head, I said, "Lord, bless John Ames Boughton, this beloved son and brother and husband and father." Then he sat back and looked at me as if he were waking out of a dream.

"Thank you, Reverend," he said, and his tone made me think that to him it might have seemed I had named everything I thought he no longer was, when that was absolutely the furthest thing from my meaning, the exact opposite of my meaning. Well, anyway, I told him it was an honor to bless him. And that was also absolutely true. In fact I'd have gone through seminary and ordination and all the years intervening for that one moment. He just studied me, in that way he has. Then the bus came. I said, "We all love you, you know," and he laughed and said, "You're all saints." He stopped in the door and lifted his hat, and then he was gone, God bless him.

I made it as far as the church, and went inside and rested there for a long time. I believe I saw in young Boughton's face, as we walked along, a sense of irony at having invested hope in this sad old place, and also the cost to him of relinquishing it. And I knew what hope it was. It was just that kind the place was meant to encourage, that a harmless life could be lived here unmolested. "There shall yet old men and old women dwell in the streets of Jerusalem, and every man with his staff in his hand for very age. And the streets of the city shall be full of boys and girls playing in the streets thereof." That is prophecy, a vision of the prophet Zechariah. He says it will be marvelous in the eyes of the people, and so it might well be to people almost anywhere in this sad world. To play catch of an evening, to smell the river, to hear the train pass. These little towns were once the bold ramparts meant to shelter just such peace.

Your mother seems to want every supper to be my favorite supper. There is often meat loaf, and always dessert. She puts candles on the table, since dark is coming early now. I suspect she has brought them from the church, and that's all right. Often she wears her blue dress. You have outgrown your red shirt. Old Boughton's family have gathered, except the one his heart yearns for. They pay their respects and invite us for dinner, but these days we three love to be at home. You come in reeking of evening air, with your eyes bright and your cheeks and fingers pink and cold, too beautiful in the candlelight for my old eyes. The cold has silenced all the insects. The dark seems to make us speak softly, like gentle conspirators. Your mother says the grace and butters your bread. I do wish Boughton could have seen how his boy received his benediction, how he bowed his head. If I told him, if he understood, he would have been jealous to have seen it, jealous to have been the one who bestowed the blessing. It is almost as if I felt his hand on my hand. Well, I can imagine him beyond the world, looking back at me with an amazement of realization—"This is why we have lived this life!" There are a thousand thousand reasons to live this life, every one of them sufficient.

I promised young Boughton that I would say goodbye to his father for him, so I strolled over there after dinner when I knew the old fellow would be asleep, and when the room was empty I whispered a few words. My good friend is so nearly gone from the world that the clouds have settled over his mortal understanding. And his hearing has been doubtful for years. I knew if I spoke that name to him while he was awake he would struggle to gather himself, he would be avid to understand, and I'd have created an eagerness in him that I could not then, could never in my life, by any means placate. As if anything I could say could resolve any part of his great mystery for him. He would be alone in the confusions of his grief, and I just did not have the strength to witness that.

I thought how good it would be if he could be like ancient Jacob, the cherished son who had been lost to him bringing for his blessing the splendid young Robert Boughton Miles—"I had not thought to see thy face, and, lo, God hath let me see thy seed also!" There was a joy in the thought of how beautiful that would have been, beautiful as any vision of angels. It seems to me that when something really ought to be true then it has a very powerful truth, which starts me thinking again about heaven. Well, I do that much of the time, as you know.

Poor Glory put a chair for me beside Boughton's bed and I sat with him a good while. I used to crawl in through the window of that room in the dark of the morning to wake him up so we could go fishing. His mother would get cross if we woke her, too, so we were very stealthy. Sometimes he would just not want to quit sleeping, and I'd pull on his hair and tug on his ear and whisper to him, and if I thought of something ridiculous to say sometimes he'd wake up laughing. That was so long ago. There he was yesterday evening, sleeping on his right side as he always did, in the embrace of the Lord, I have no doubt, though I knew if I woke him up he'd be back in Gethsemane. So I said to him in his sleep, I blessed that boy of yours for you. I still feel the weight of his brow on my hand. I said, I love him as much as you meant me to. So certain of your prayers are finally answered, old fellow. And mine too, mine too. We had to wait a long time, didn't we?

When I left I saw Glory standing in the hallway, looking in on all the quiet talk there was in the parlor, her brothers and sisters and their wives and husbands and their children, grown and half grown. Trading news and talking politics and playing hearts. There were more of them in the kitchen and more upstairs. As I was leaving I met five or six who had been out for a walk. It shames me that I had not thought till then how hard it must have been for her to have Jack gone, and to have been left alone in that orderly turbulence of fruitfulness and contentment, left alone to tolerate all that tactful and heartfelt kindness, with no one there even to smile with her at the sheer endlessness of it. And no one there for her to defend—which is the worst kind of abandonment. Only the Lord Himself can comfort that.

It has seemed to me sometimes as though the Lord breathes on this poor gray ember of Creation and it turns to radiance—for a moment or a year or the span of a life. And then it sinks back into itself again, and to look at it no one would know it had anything to do with fire, or light. That is what I said in the Pentecost sermon. I have reflected on that sermon, and there is some truth in it. But the Lord is more constant and far more extravagant than it seems to imply. Wherever you turn your eyes the world can shine like transfiguration. You don't have to bring a thing to it except a little willingness to see. Only, who could have the courage to see it?

I'll just ask your mother to have those old sermons of mine burned. The deacons could arrange it. There are enough to make a good fire. I'm thinking here of hot dogs and marsh-mallows, something to celebrate the first snow. Of course she can set by any of them she might want to keep, but I don't want her to waste much effort on them. They mattered or they didn't and that's the end of it.

There are two occasions when the sacred beauty of Creation becomes dazzlingly apparent, and they occur together. One is when we feel our mortal insufficiency to the world, and the other is when we feel the world's mortal insufficiency to us. Augustine says the Lord loves each of us as an only child, and that has to be true. "He will wipe the tears from all faces." It takes nothing from the loveliness of the verse to say that is exactly what will be required.

Theologians talk about a prevenient grace that precedes grace itself and allows us to accept it. I think there must also be a prevenient courage that allows us to be brave—that is, to acknowledge that there is more beauty than our eyes can bear, that precious things have been put into our hands and to do nothing to honor them is to do great harm. And therefore, this courage allows us, as the old men said, to make ourselves useful. It allows us to be generous, which is another way of saying exactly the same thing. But that is the pulpit speaking. What have I to leave you but the ruins of old courage, and the lore of old gallantry and hope? Well, as I have said, it is all an ember now, and the good Lord will surely someday breathe it into flame again.

I love the prairie! So often I have seen the dawn come and the light flood over the land and everything turn radiant at once, that word "good" so profoundly affirmed in my soul that I am amazed I should be allowed to witness such a thing. There may have been a more wonderful first moment "when the morning stars sang together and all the sons of God shouted for joy," but for all I know to the contrary, they still do sing and shout, and they certainly might well. Here on the prairie there is nothing to distract attention from the evening and the morning, nothing on the horizon to abbreviate or to delay. Mountains would seem an impertinence from that point of view.

To me it seems rather Christlike to be as unadorned as this place is, as little regarded. I can't help imagining that you will leave sooner or later, and it's fine if you have done that, or you mean to do it. This whole town does look like whatever hope becomes after it begins to weary a little, then weary a little more. But hope deferred is still hope. I love this town. I think sometimes of going into the ground here as a last wild gesture of love—I too will smolder away the time until the great and general incandescence.

I'll pray that you grow up a brave man in a brave country. I will pray you find a way to be useful.

I'll pray, and then I'll sleep.